Murder in the Pacific Northwest

When young Seattle attorney Annie MacPherson
boards the ferry for the San Juan Islands, she has no
idea that she's embarking on a sea of troubles. Her
investigation at a luxury resort soon broadens from
real estate legalities to kidnapping and murder.
Whether to unravel the past's tangled secrets, or to
sport with kayaks and killer whales in the deadly
straits, that is the question. But it's in suffering
love's slings and arrows that Annie ultimately
discovers her outrageous fortune.

Sea of Troubles

Sea of Troubles

by Janet L. Smith

A mystery from Perseverance Press
Menlo Park, California

Art direction by Gary Page/Merit Media
Photography by Al Fabrizio/Fabrizio Camera Graphics
Typography by Jim Cook/Book Design & Typography

Copyright ©1990 by Janet L. Smith

Published by
  Perseverance Press
  P.O. Box 384
  Menlo Park, California 94026

Manufactured in the United States of America.

This book is printed on acid-free paper.

2   3   —   92   91   90

Library of Congress Catalog Card Number 89-63605

ISBN 0-9602676-9-7

This novel is a work of fiction. Any resemblance to real situations or to actual people, living or dead, is completely coincidental.

In memory of my grandfather,
Geoffrey Moore,
who always loved a good story.

Prologue

A PALE, SLENDER HAND reached out and switched on the portable tape player. The tape crackled, silent for 30 seconds except for some distant traffic noise.

"Nicholas, darling, it's me, Marguerite. Don't worry, I'm all right." The voice was slow, heavy, possibly drugged. "I guess you know by now that I've been kidnapped. They are telling me what to say, and I'm supposed to tell you that I'm all right, and that I'll be safe so long as you do what they say. That's very important, Nicholas, you must believe them."

The woman's voice was deep, with a vaguely discernible foreign accent. There was another crackly pause. The tape was of poor quality, possibly recorded on a hand-held microphone. The volume wavered as if the person holding the microphone had been moving around.

"Don't try to look for me. They say you won't be able to find me. If you disobey their instructions, they'll kill me." The young woman's voice had grown softer, and she had started to cry. For a full minute there was nothing on the tape but the woman's barely audible sobs.

"They want one million dollars, Nicholas, American currency, unmarked bills. . . . You . . . you're supposed to start gathering the money now. You have two days. That's all the time they will give you." Another pause. Only a slight hissing sound indicated that the tape was still running. "Instructions about what to do with the

will come later. Don't call the police, Nicholas. Please, these
/ serious men. . . . Goodbye, Nicholas, I love you so much."
At first it sounded like the tape was finished, but then the
woman's voice cut through the silence like a sharp knife, crying out,
"Nicholas!"

The hysterical scream was cut short by a slap, a muffled "Shut
up!" A chair fell over, a body hit the floor. The tape was dead.

Chapter 1

THE SAME PALE, feminine hand switched off the machine. Marc Jarrell looked at the blonde woman expectantly. She broke into a smile. "It's perfect. Especially that scream at the end. This definitely calls for more champagne."

"You got it." Marc jumped up to get the bottle out of the silver bucket. He took a swig before refilling Daisy's glass. "I can't believe we're finally going to pull this off. Are you really sure Forrestor's going to fall for it—and believe his lover's been kidnapped?"

"He'll fall for it. Nicholas Forrestor is a fool. Believe me—I ought to know by now. Just stop worrying about it. I'll take care of all the details."

He took the crystal glass from her hand and set it on the table.

"Come here, you," he said, pulling her up into his arms. The top of her head barely came up to his chest. He picked her up like a child until she begged him, giggling, to put her down.

"Stop it! Come on, you've got to get out of here before the old man gets home. Are you sure you remember everything? Once we get to the resort we won't be able to communicate."

Marc smoothed down his thick black hair.

"Tomorrow I'll fly to Seattle, pick up the rental car and drive north to Anacortes. Catch the San Juan Island ferry to Orcas Island.

Everything I need is in the black carry-on bag. I won't check any luggage."

"Do you have the chart that David Courtney drew?"

He nodded. "I've got everything—the fake ID and credit cards for 'Mark Jones', and all the gear on Courtney's list."

"Okay, now here's the schedule again. Listen carefully. Nicholas Forrestor and, uh, 'Marguerite Boulanger' will be arriving on Wednesday, with plans to stay until Monday morning. All you have to do is keep a low profile the whole time. Then unless you get a message from me that the plan is aborted, we'll pull it off on Sunday night, actually Monday morning, at 1 A.M." She laughed as she mimicked the voice on the ransom tape. "A million dollars, American currency, unmarked bills!" She kissed him quickly, ushering him to the door. "It's going to work!"

Alone in the luxurious apartment Daisy Baker felt the thrill of anticipation. She always felt this way before she pulled off a job. She looked out the window of the highrise to the noisy streets of New York below, sweltering in the July heat. Only a few more days. The adrenaline was already pumping.

All her life she'd been pulling off con jobs. She was good at it, a natural actress. She thought back with pride to her first success, that lawsuit when she was seventeen. It had been so easy to convince the jury that she hadn't been drinking, that the fatal accident really hadn't been her fault. Looking at the jury with her big brown eyes she had explained how an animal must have dashed in front of the car, the road was so icy. It all happened so fast. Poor little Daisy was just an innocent victim of circumstances.

It had all been a lie, of course, but the jury bought it. What a surge of power she had felt. She learned on that day ten years ago that she had an uncanny ability to make people believe her. At seventeen, Daisy Baker had found her true career. Now, at twenty-seven, she was about to pull off her biggest job yet.

Chapter 2

THURSDAY AFTERNOON, JULY 19

A FERRY WORKER IN AN orange vest directed Annie MacPherson to pull her aging Fiat convertible onto the lower car deck of the Washington State ferry to the San Juan Islands. She got out of the car and climbed the clanging metal stairs to the passengers' lounge, taking her place in line for a cup of coffee she knew in advance would be wretched. She found an empty seat and spread her belongings out on the green vinyl bench. The ferry pulled away from the dock only a few minutes behind schedule.

The large green and white vessel moved surprisingly fast given its size, plowing ahead forcefully between the heavily forested islands. Annie watched a sea gull bob up and down in the air current created by the moving ferry. She stretched her legs out in front of her, welcoming the first opportunity she'd had in months to get out of Seattle. After almost three years of struggling to make ends meet, Annie's private law practice with her partner, Joel Feinstein, was finally getting off the ground. Now they were so busy, Joel accused her of taking files home and putting them under her pillow, so she could work on them in her sleep. A moment of panic crossed Annie's mind as she pictured the state of her in-basket, overflowing with unread mail and unanswered briefs. She sighed. Nothing she could do about it from here.

The call had come at about 6:30 Tuesday night from a lawyer in Friday Harbor, the county seat of the San Juan Islands. She was, as usual, working late.

"Ms. MacPherson, I'm glad I was able to reach you. I'm calling regarding one of your clients. A Mrs. Dorothy Lymon. The nursing home said I should contact you."

"Is she all right?"

"Oh yes, she's fine. But I'm afraid her husband Curtis has passed away."

"Her husband?" Annie racked her brain. She'd known Dorothy Lymon since law school, when she'd rented the basement apartment in the older woman's house. Despite the difference in ages they had become good friends. They'd shared many cups of tea over the next few years, but the subject of husbands had never come up. Then Annie remembered. "Oh, you must mean Dorothy's ex-husband." Annie had only met him once. He had stopped by the house for some reason once when Dorothy wasn't home. All she could conjure up was the acrid smell of cigar smoke and a shiny bald head. When Dorothy heard about the visit she had just smiled and shook her head, as if amused by something a small child had done.

"You're still Dorothy Lymon's guardian, I take it?"

"Yes, I have full power of attorney over all her affairs." Dorothy had no children or other close relatives. Soon after her Alzheimer's disease was diagnosed Annie had taken over responsibility for the woman's financial affairs. Curtis Lymon had been out of the picture for years.

The lawyer from Friday Harbor went on to explain the provisions of the will. Despite the fact that Curtis Lymon had been divorced from his ex-wife for over fifteen years, he apparently retained some feelings for her. He had left her his only piece of property, the Windsor Resort on Orcas Island.

"Before you get too excited, I have to tell you the place is heavily mortgaged, and a fairly risky venture. Your client's ex-husband was a gambler—he enjoyed the risk. If you feel it would be in Mrs. Lymon's best interest, I think a sale could be arranged which would result in a slight profit."

"Do I need to do anything at this point to protect Mrs. Lymon's interests?"

"As I'm sure you know, the wheels of probate can turn slowly. In the meantime, the will provides that the general manager, a fellow named Russell Perkins, will run the business as usual until the transfer of ownership is finalized. He's a good man—young, but he's got an MBA from Harvard and some good solid business experience. Real intense worker, you know the type? Now, I do have a message here in my file from Perkins that he wants you to call him as soon as possible. Something about a meeting with a potential buyer. I'm not sure what that entails, but feel free to call me if you need any assistance. I'll be handling the probate of the estate."

It was nearly seven, but she tried Perkins' number anyway, and was put through immediately.

"Ms. MacPherson, thanks so much for calling," Perkins said breathlessly. "I know this is terribly short notice, but this meeting has been set up for months. Nicholas Forrestor is a very interested potential buyer, and if the meeting doesn't go ahead as planned, the entire deal could fall through. I understand there are all sorts of problems as far as probating the will, but as a show of good faith, I'm afraid you'd have to be here."

"This Friday? Three days from now?"

"Yes. Does that present a problem?"

Annie sighed. Nothing that her extraordinarily competent secretary couldn't handle. When she finished talking to Russell Perkins she began madly scribbling notes to Val to reschedule all of her appointments onto her partner's calendar, adding a few extra days for a well-deserved vacation. She chuckled. Feinstein was going to kill her for this.

Annie sipped her bitter, lukewarm coffee and turned her gaze back to the scenery out the ferry window. It was a radiantly clear summer day, probably not over 75 degrees. A gentle breeze was making patterns in the billowing white clouds overhead. Parallel to the ferry's course a sailboat was trying to get the most out of the light wind with a rainbow-colored spinnaker. She hoped that this Forrestor character who wanted to buy the resort would be easy to deal with. Life as a trial attorney was stressful enough, even when the parties were polite to each other.

It had been years since Annie had visited the San Juan Islands, a shame since they were so accessible to Seattle—just an hour-and-a-half's drive north, then an hour or so on the ferry. It really felt like a getaway to be surrounded by water, close enough to see the lights of Canada on a clear night. It took Annie back to her days growing up when she spent so much time around boats and water.

She walked out onto the passenger deck, oblivious to the chill wind to watch as the ferry passed through a narrow channel between two islands. The deep opaque blue of the water contrasted sharply with the red bark of the madrona trees and dense evergreens which covered the islands. The land jutted sharply out of the water with trees reaching right to the water's edge, between and around huge gray rocks. It was enough to take Annie's breath away.

The ferry reached Orcas Island more or less on time. Annie followed the road signs for Westsound, and after a couple of wrong turns, finally pulled up her red Fiat Spider in front of the Windsor Resort about four. A cool breeze blew salt air in from the bay.

She had barely turned off the engine when a valet in a neat gray jacket opened her car door. Annie was embarrassed for him to park the battered vehicle, but the valet didn't seem to mind. She cringed as the Spider's engine sputtered and whined before he sped off to the other end of the parking lot.

She started to carry her own bag, but a doorman jumped to take it from her. Another held open the heavy wooden door. While it wasn't exactly what Annie was used to, she decided that she could get used to it pretty quickly.

On the ferry, Annie had taken the opportunity to read through some materials Russell Perkins had faxed to her. She learned that the resort had been built around the turn of the century by Jeremiah Windsor, one of the area's early shipping barons, and the estate originally encompassed over 1,000 acres. The expansive home was nestled in the small sheltered inlet called Westsound. It had become a resort in 1934, and had made a reputation of quietly catering to the very rich, offering privacy, solitude, and a very good glass of sherry. It had expanded over the years, but retained the style and elegance of the original buildings.

Inside the lobby, Annie removed her dark glasses and let her eyes readjust from the brightness outdoors. To her left was a medium-sized sitting room decorated with Victorian-era furniture. A fireplace with a pink marble mantelpiece stood at the far end of the room, with a fire carefully laid for that evening. The furniture was arranged in small, intimate groupings on an oriental rug, in a way that invited use. To the right, a broad carpeted stairway curved up to the second floor. Straight ahead was the reception desk, an expanse of dark mahogany that glistened from polishing.

The doorman carried Annie's bag to the reception desk, where the clerk, a young Japanese-American wearing crisp white shorts and a blue Windsor Resort polo shirt, had his head buried in a physiology textbook. Annie cleared her throat loudly. He jumped.

"Oh, I'm sorry. I was just so caught up . . . reservation please?"

"Annie MacPherson."

"Oh, Ms. MacPherson, hold on a sec. Mr. Perkins wanted to know the minute you got in." He picked up a red house phone. "Russ? Yes, she's here. At the front desk."

Within moments the manager appeared, a tall, slender man with prematurely gray hair and intense green eyes. Annie picked up hints of workaholism: overly fast speech, a tic in his jaw muscle, skin just a little too pale. Worried about becoming a workaholic herself, she knew the symptoms well. He pumped her hand firmly.

"Ms. MacPherson—may I call you Annie?—please, call me Russ—so glad you could make it on such short notice. Nathan, please have Ms. MacPherson's bags sent up to room two-oh-one. Annie, I hate to spring this on you, but Nicholas Forrestor is extremely anxious to meet you. Can you come this way? We're having drinks in the solarium."

Before Annie had time to object, or even get a word in, Perkins was galloping down the hall. She glanced down at her scruffy jeans and Nikes, clothes fit for ferry riding but not intended for business deals. Her pearl gray linen suit and matching suede pumps were at this moment being whisked up to room 201 by the bellhop. This was not starting off well.

Russ held open the door and Annie walked into the solarium. Three bay windows, complete with cushioned window seats, looked out onto Westsound. Seated rather incongruously on a white wicker loveseat surrounded by potted palms were a man and a woman, both silently sipping drinks. The man looked to be in his mid-to-late 60s, with neatly combed steel-gray hair and a thin mustache. His stark black suit and monochrome tie might have looked appropriate in a Wall Street board room, but were distinctly out of place in the greenery of the sun room. The only spot of color was a red silk handkerchief neatly folded in his breast pocket. At first, Annie thought the tiny woman with him was a child, her skin and features were so delicate. On second glance, Annie saw she was an extremely beautiful adult. Short, fashionably cut blonde hair framed a round face dominated by large brown eyes. She had kicked off her shoes and sat with her feet tucked under her. Wide gold bracelets clinked against each other on her wrists.

When the man stood, Annie could see he was no taller than her own five feet six inches. She could feel his gray eyes appraising her casual attire, registering instant disapproval.

"Nicholas Forrestor, I'd like you to meet Annie MacPherson. Annie, this is Nicholas Forrestor and his friend, Marguerite Boulanger." She held out her hand which the man reluctantly shook. The woman on the love seat merely looked up briefly, then resumed staring out the window at the water.

"Hmph. What's the deal here, Perkins? I thought you said a 'lawyer' would be here on behalf of Mrs. Lymon." He said the word in a most unpleasant tone.

Russ Perkins looked uncomfortable. Annie jumped in. "I am an attorney, Mr. Forrestor. Please excuse my attire. I just now arrived." And a pleasure to meet you too, she thought.

Forrestor resumed his seat with a grunt. "So, just out of school are you? Too young to be a lawyer."

Annie wasn't overly upset by his manner. She was accustomed to having to prove herself to older men. She did it successfully in court every day. Besides, she knew she looked younger than her 33 years.

"No, in fact, I've been practicing for some time. I spent five years in the prosecutor's office in the felony division, and I've had my own practice in Seattle for the past three years." She felt like throwing in her Magna Cum Laude and Phi Beta Kappa, but didn't want to overdo it. Besides, it might make future negotiations easier if Forrestor underestimated her.

A waitress appeared at the door and took Annie's drink order. "How are you doing, Mr. Forrestor? Another martini?" Russ asked. "Ms. Boulanger, another glass of champagne?" Instead of replying, the woman merely looked expectantly at Forrestor. "Yes," he replied for both of them, "I think we have time for another."

"What? What is it?" Forrestor asked with irritation when the woman laid her hand on his arm. She spoke for the first time.

"Please, Nicholas, darling, may I wait in my room? I am so very tired." Her voice was deeper than Annie had expected, with a luxuriant hoarseness to it.

"No. I told you. I want you here with me. So be still and finish your drink."

Annie felt her muscles grow tense. "Tell me, Mr. Forrestor. How did you come to be interested in the Windsor Resort?"

"Perkins, here, set it up. Made it sound like a good deal. In fact, it was practically a done deal until you came along. I hope this isn't going to cause all sorts of delays. I'm a busy man, I don't have time for delays."

Annie hardly felt like apologizing for Curtis Lymon's untimely death. She was starting to get the idea that this was not going to be an easy week.

"I'm sorry for any inconvenience, but I was under the impression that this was just a preliminary meeting. And of course I will have to be brought up to speed before anything can be finalized. Russ, I was hoping we could meet tomorrow morning?"

"Of course. It's all planned. I'll give you a full tour, show you the books, and all that. Then we'll all meet after lunch to talk details. How's that sound?"

Another grunt from Forrestor. "As long as everything's wrapped up by this weekend. We have a flight to catch back to New York on Monday." He glared at Annie. "I don't like people who waste my time."

"Nor do I." Annie took a deep breath, pushing her irritation to the back corner of her mind. The next few days were going to be very challenging.

The awkward meeting finally over, Annie returned to the front desk to pick up her key. The desk clerk—Nathan Komatsu according to his name tag—was occupied with checking in a guest, so Annie took a seat in a brocade wing chair and amused herself with her favorite game of people watching. Perhaps it came from reading too many Sherlock Holmes stories, but she loved to look for clues and speculate what total strangers did for a living.

The woman checking in was quite a subject for scrutiny. Striking was the adjective most people would use, the type whose appearance demanded attention. She was close to six feet tall, a good half foot taller than the desk clerk. Her shoulder-length hair, lacquered into fullness, was a rich shade of chestnut. Perfectly shaped burgundy nails tapped impatiently on the mahogany desk. Her dove gray leather ensemble—a tight fitting skirt that stopped a few inches above the knee and blouson jacket—were straight out of this season's *Milan Vogue*. As she leaned towards the clerk, Annie could see that where the jacket dipped to a V-closure, there was nothing but a suntan underneath. Annie thought women only dressed like that on the cover of *Cosmopolitan*. A model? No, too voluptuous for that. Show business? Real estate? Cosmetics sales? Annie impertinently eavesdropped, hearing the woman give her name as Lisa Hargraves, in a way that implied she expected recognition.

"What do you mean," the woman asked, sounding appalled, "this is as hot as it's going to get? This is an *island* for God's sake, isn't it?" The desk clerk remained polite. Where Annie might have caustically reminded the out-of-towner that Greenland was an island, the clerk merely informed the woman that this was typical weather for July in the San Juans, but that she might enjoy the saunas and tanning booths in the health spa downstairs. The tall woman heaved an exasperated sigh, disgusted with the resort's failure to supply sweltering summer heat. She next asked, in a pointedly bored voice, for directions to the pool and tennis courts. Nathan Komatsu got out a map of the resort grounds, glad to be of assistance. He didn't appear anxious to get back to his textbook.

The clerk looked up for a moment while the woman studied the map, and hailed a man coming out of the gift shop carrying a *Sports Illustrated*.

"Oh, Mr. Jones, I have a message for you." The large man with thick black hair didn't appear to hear. Nathan called his name again. "Excuse me, sir, aren't you Mark Jones?" The woman at the desk glanced over her shoulder, and the pen dropped out of her hand.

"Marc?" she asked incredulously. "What on earth are you doing here?"

The man, looking baffled, met her eyes for a moment, but said nothing. He rushed over, grabbed the pink message slip from the desk clerk, and hurried out the front door.

"Look like someone you know?" Nathan Komatsu asked. "I do that all the time, you know, go up to someone I think I recognize, and then it turns out to be someone else. Isn't that embarrassing?"

"Yes, it is," the woman said softly. She wasn't laughing.

FRIDAY MORNING, JULY 20

Annie picked up a paper at the front desk on her way to the crowded dining room for breakfast. She had just enough time to eat before her meeting with Russ. Her table looked out past the terrace to a small marina. There was no wind, and the water was glassy. A bustling movement on a few of the boats moored in front indicated that their owners were rigging sails and securing lines in preparation for Sunday outings.

The waitress came with hot coffee and directed Annie to the buffet table, laid out with a bountiful array of fresh fruit, freshly baked muffins and croissants, a variety of breakfast meats and egg dishes. Annie had trouble selecting.

"I recommend the eggs Florentine and the fresh fruit salad," she heard from behind her.

"Russ, good morning. I thought our meeting wasn't until nine o'clock."

"Don't worry, I'll give you time to eat. There's just so much we had to cover, I thought we'd better get started."

He ushered Annie back to her table and beckoned the waitress to bring him some coffee.

"I, uh, got the impression that you didn't much care for Nicholas Forrestor."

"The feeling was mutual, I'm sure."

"I wouldn't take it personally."

"I don't intend to. But tell me, Russ, why was it so important that we go ahead with the meeting this week? I really feel at a disadvantage knowing nothing about the resort. And until probate is complete, I'm not sure what authority I have. Was Forrestor really that insistent that we go ahead this week?"

Annie noticed the tic in Perkins' jaw. "No," he said hurriedly, "it was my idea. I felt that, well, Forrestor is so unpredictable. I, uh, wanted him to see the place during the peak tourist season, before he had a chance to change his mind."

Annie was puzzled. For a business manager with an MBA from Harvard, Perkins should have known that she'd need more time. She let it drop.

"Do I even want to recommend that Mrs. Lymon sell? It looks like business is booming. Isn't the resort turning a profit?"

"It is," Russ replied, "but there's the question of capital improvements. The place is mortgaged to the hilt right now, and a lot of the old buildings are desperately in need of repair. For someone who has the money to put into the place, it could be a darned good investment. But Curtis Lymon was having cash flow problems and saw difficulties ahead, and decided it was time to get out. It was the right choice for him, and probably for her, too, unless she has access to large sums of money. And, of course, Forrestor is the optimal choice for a buyer," he added quickly.

Why? Annie wondered. The gruff man hadn't seemed particularly interested in the charming old buildings. There was some reason Perkins was pushing for Forrestor, and Annie was determined to find it.

When Annie was finished with her breakfast they rose to stroll around the resort. The main building, usually referred to simply as "the House," was the building constructed in 1907 as Jeremiah Windsor's island hideaway. The character of the period had been faithfully maintained throughout, recreating as closely as possible the elegance and style that would have been present when the Windsors were in residence.

The House was built on a slope, with the main entrance at street level in front, and the dining room and bar at the back of the main level raised one floor off the ground on stilts. Large picture windows looked out over the marina.

Russ's office, located right off the main dining room, had originally been Jeremiah Windsor's private study. "One of the perks of the job," Russ said proudly, showing Annie the comfortable looking office, filled with books and leather furniture, the walls crammed with family photos.

"Are these your family?"

"Yes, when my sister and I were growing up. They're all gone now—my father just passed away last Christmas—so I enjoy having the pictures there for the memories." Annie scanned the pictures on the wall, stopping in front of one showing a seven-year-old boy in overalls and his toddler sister pretending to drive a tractor while their father looked on. "That's me and my sister, Cordelia, on the farm where we grew up."

"I can see the family resemblance. I bet she grew up to be a real beauty."

"She did." Russ suddenly looked as if he were miles away, perhaps back on the family farm on a sunny afternoon. "I miss her so much," he said softly.

Annie studied the rest of the old photographs. "I wouldn't have pegged you as a country boy."

"I left Kansas ten years ago when I got out of college and haven't looked back."

"Only ten years? Are you that young?"

"Just turned thirty-one. It's the gray hair that fools people."

"Think if I dye my hair gray Nicholas Forrestor will take me seriously?"

"I wouldn't count on it."

Outside, running the entire length of the building, was a wide wooden terrace. White wrought iron tables and chairs were scattered about. It was still chilly, and the terrace was empty but for a teenage girl sipping a Coke.

To the right of the marina was a small stretch of pebbled beach. To increase the resort's capacity, cottages with kitchenettes had been added, some quite remote from the main building. The farthest were almost a mile down the beach, hidden from Annie's view near the front entrance, each with its own access to the pebbly beach.

They concluded the tour in the "library" bar. The leatherbound books lining the walls and comfortable overstuffed arm chairs made Annie want to curl up for the afternoon with a pot of coffee and a good mystery novel. There was even a brass library ladder. She found herself automatically perusing the bookshelves, the way she did whenever she entered someone's home for the first time.

"Go ahead, feel free to browse. The books are genuine," Russ explained. "It's not Jeremiah Windsor's library, of course. His books are locked in glass display cabinets in the music room. These are all books we've picked up at estate sales, mostly Pacific Northwest history and Victorian novels. Anyone who's interested can check them out, just like a library. But most people prefer to sit and read them here. We usually have some Mozart or Vivaldi playing softly in the background, and the old timers know that the Windsor still serves an excellent glass of sherry."

Annie had stepped up on the ladder, reading titles on the top shelf, when she heard someone enter the bar.

"Russ, there you are. I've been looking all over. Listen, one of the outboards needs some parts and I'm going to have to go into Anacortes today. Will it be okay if I show that lawyer gal around some other time?"

"Gal?" thought Annie. She hadn't heard that one in a long time. She turned around to see a broad-shouldered man, about forty, with a bushy blond beard that compensated for a receding hairline. He was wearing a long-sleeved blue T-shirt with a Northwest Indian design of a leaping whale on the front. His faded khaki shorts with bulging pockets looked like something from the Australian outback.

"Annie," Russ called her over. "I'd like you to meet David Courtney. Resident marine biologist, natural historian, astronomer, sailing and kayaking instructor . . . "

"Don't forget boat mechanic," David added with a smile.

"David, this is Annie MacPherson, she's here on behalf of the Windsor's new owner."

"Annie, pleased to meet you," David said. He sheepishly wiped his hand on his shorts before offering it to her to shake. "Sorry, a little grimy." Annie saw that his twinkling eyes were the same deep blue as his shirt.

"We were just on our way down to the dock," said Russ, looking distressed. "You're sure you don't have time today, David? We're meeting with Forrestor this afternoon."

"I'm really sorry, Russ. If I don't go today, that outboard will be out of commission for a week. But I'll be back in the morning for my classes." David looked at Annie and she could almost swear he winked. "How about taking my beginning kayak class?" he asked.

"I'll see if I can squeeze it in."

"Great. I'll look forward to it."

Interesting, thought Annie. Different, but very interesting.

"Hey, Russ. Can I take the speedboat? It'll save me a lot of time."

"Sure, no problem." Russ fished a key out of his pocket and handed it to David.

They watched him go. "David's one of the reasons for the resort's success. One of the main attractions of the San Juan Islands is outdoor recreation, but the seas around here are a lot more dangerous than they look. I wanted the best instructor I could find, and he's it." Russ's cautious tone seemed out of place on such a calm and sunny day.

Annie looked out towards the peaceful sound. "Certainly there can't be that much risk, can there?" she asked.

"The waters around here are deceptive, Annie. You look on a chart, and it looks like the San Juans are in a protected inland waterway. Not so. David can explain it better, but because of the huge volumes of water that are being forced with each tide through narrow passages, the currents are powerful and tricky, sometimes treacherous, and the water's extremely cold." He looked strangely serious. "I don't know of a single year where there hasn't been at least one fatality."

Chapter 3

LATE FRIDAY NIGHT

THE TINY BEACH cottage was hardly big enough for Marc Jarrell to work out in. The message from Daisy had said she'd arrived, and the plan would go ahead as scheduled. Now he was so keyed up he could hardly stand it, and needed to work off some of his pent-up energy. By pushing aside some of the furniture he made a space on the floor large enough to do sit-ups. He turned the TV to rock videos, cranked up the sound, and started to go to it.

He had worked up a good sweat when he heard the knock. Without stopping to think, he jumped up and pulled open the door. The tall woman pushed past him into the beach cottage.

"I'm not going to wait for you to invite me in, because it's just too chilly outside. I swear, here it is the middle of July and I bet it's not even sixty degrees. Do you have anything to drink around here?"

"Lisa! How did you—?"

"Oh, don't be cute, Marc. I saw you in the lobby. Did you honestly think I couldn't find what room you were in? Give me some credit." Lisa Hargraves picked up the remote control and flicked off the TV on her way to the tiny kitchenette. She found a glass and helped herself to a hefty measure of Scotch from the bottle on the counter. "Black Label? Since when did you start drinking Scotch? I hardly recognized you without a can of Budweiser in your oversized fist. And good Scotch at that. Oh, I know. It must be Daisy's. She picked that habit up from me, you know. One of the many things she picked up from me. So, you two are still together, are you?" Lisa opened the freezer door and dropped two cubes into the tumbler.

This can't be happening, thought Marc. Everything was going so perfectly, and now this. He followed her, grabbing the bottle away, slamming it down hard on the counter. "Look, I don't know why you're here, or what you want, but you've got to get out. Now. I mean it." He wanted to grab her and throw her out, but for some reason he couldn't. He stepped aside so she could walk past him out of the kitchen. But instead of heading for the door, she perched on the arm of the sofa, sipping her drink. She was dressed in a broad-shouldered, tight-skirted denim mini-dress, zippered up the front. The double ended zipper was provocatively unzipped a few inches at the hem and more than a few inches at the neckline, revealing her ample cleavage. Lisa paused and ran her eyes up and down Marc's muscular body. "I must admit, hon, you're looking *very* good. She must be treating you well."

Marc was wearing nothing but skimpy nylon running shorts. He picked up a towel off the back of a chair and started to wipe his forehead.

"Oh, don't do that, I've never minded a little sweat."

"Lisa, come on. Please. You've got to do what I say." Marc was angry at himself as he heard the pleading tone creep into his voice. He really ought to just throw her out.

It made it worse when she laughed. "Do what you say? I never did before, why should I start now? Oh, that's a good one." She came up to him and ran a talon-like fingernail through the curly hair on his chest. He stood rigidly, wishing he could strike her. "So you're calling yourself 'Mark Jones' these days, are you? How *very* original." In her high heeled sandals she could almost look him straight in the eye. "You know, there's something I've been waiting a long time to do," she murmured, sensuously caressing his hip with her left hand.

"What's that?"

"This." With her right hand, she slapped him as hard as she could across the face.

Quickly recovering from his initial shock, Marc managed to get both of Lisa's wrists grasped tightly in one hand. With his free hand he rubbed his stinging cheek. He was holding her so tightly that she winced. "Down, boy, you can let go now. I've done my bit. The rest I'll save for the little blonde bitch."

He threw down her hands, turning away so she couldn't see his burning face. This was bad, but he didn't even want to think about what Daisy was going to do to him when she found out.

Lisa massaged her wrists until the blood flowed back into her hands. "Where is she now, by the way? I don't see her dozen suitcases, so obviously she's not here. What, is she planning another one of her hare-brained schemes and roped you into it this time?"

"That's it. You're out of here." Marc grabbed her by the shoulders and shoved her towards the door.

"Wait a second. I haven't told you the real reason I'm here. You're curious, aren't you?" She shrugged off his grasp. "Now where did I set my drink? Are you sure you won't have one? You look like you need it. Come on, I'll get you one." She slid past him back into the small kitchen.

"Here you go." Lisa returned to the living room and handed Marc a tumbler full of Scotch, neat. "You never were a big talker, darling, but tonight you're particularly silent." She lowered herself sensuously onto the suede sofa and fished a red leather cigarette case out of her purse. "You still don't smoke, do you? So virtuous of you. Well, I've never pretended to be virtuous, as you well know." Lisa lit a thin brown cigarette and blew the smoke slowly towards the ceiling, then glanced around for an ashtray. She set her gold lighter on the end table, stood up and opened the desk drawer.

"Stop it!" Marc practically jumped across the room and slammed the drawer shut. "I'll get you your fucking ashtray." He moved towards the kitchen.

"Well, well, well. We're hiding something, aren't we? This is turning into such an interesting evening. I had no idea we'd have so much fun!"

Marc broke into a sweat. This time it wasn't from exercise.

"Don't you want to chat, catch up on old times? What's it been since New York, two years? God, doesn't time just fly?"

"What do you want? Just tell me what the fuck you want!" Marc downed the rest of his Scotch, and stood, tensed, in the middle of the room as if ready to fend off an attack.

"Feisty tonight, aren't we?" Lisa stubbed out her cigarette, blowing the remaining smoke in his direction. She stood and moved to the center of the room to where he was standing and draped her arms around his waist. "You can't still be wondering why I'm here, can you? Are you really that stupid?"

As she spoke Lisa edged close to him, reaching her hands inside down the back of his nylon shorts. She pulled him close, until his body was pressed up against her. He was tense, yet she nevertheless felt him responding as she tightened her hold. "That's right, you might as well enjoy it. You always did as I recall. Because I'm not leaving. Not yet anyway." She ran a hand up and down his back, gently scratching him with her long nails.

"You see, hon, I haven't had anyone to play with since you left."

She reached up and slowly lowered the zipper at her neckline. "So, before I leave . . . ," she brought her face close to his, "I'm going to get my big, beautiful boy to give me a really good time, and then . . . ," she pressed him to her tightly and whispered, "I'm going to get back every damned cent the two of you stole from me."

SATURDAY MORNING, JULY 21

Saturday morning was ordinarily a time dedicated to sleeping in, but for some reason Annie found it easy to drag herself out of bed. Certainly being away from the city and not having to make a weekend trek to the office made a difference. But in the back of her mind she wondered if her scheduled meeting with David Courtney had anything to do with her mood.

After dressing casually in jeans and a cotton sweater, Annie still had enough time for a caffeine fix in the dining room. Ordering the continental breakfast, she expected a microwaved danish and black coffee, but was surprised to be presented with a real French *petit dejeuner*—a basket of warm croissants, orange marmalade, real butter, and two small pitchers of steaming hot liquid for *café au lait*. Into the large, bowl-shaped cup she poured the thick black coffee, topped it off with foamy steamed milk, stirred in a half-teaspoon of sugar and practically purred as she tasted it.

The idea of another cup was tempting, but she decided to forego. David was expecting her, and it would be an interesting experiment to arrive someplace on time for a change.

As she neared the boat dock, she saw David engaged in conversation with two young women. His back was to Annie so that he didn't see her arrive, and she hung back a few paces, not wanting to interrupt. They were talking about David's sea kayaking class, looking down at an odd-looking yellow boat, about 18 feet long with a single opening in the center.

"I just don't think I can do it. I'm so afraid of flipping over," said the shorter one, a cheerleader-type whose Hard Rock Cafe T-shirt barely contained her rounded bustline. She twirled a strand of chocolate brown hair around her finger. "What if I can't get back up?"

Annie cringed. She had never understood why some men were attracted to that particular brand of helpless "femininity." She noted with some degree of pleasure that the fragile little girl act didn't seem to be having much of an effect on David Courtney.

"That's a common fear, Marcie," David said in a reassuring tone, "but you'll be glad to know that you won't be required to learn how to roll over. That's an advanced technique." The Shirley Temple pout turned into a smile. As she fluttered her mascara-laden eyelashes, Annie couldn't help envisioning streaks of makeup running down her cherubic face once she got wet. The lanky friend looked embarrassed.

"Then what do we do if we fall over? Get out and swim to shore?" the friend asked. Her tone of voice implied she was the intelligent, no-nonsense type. No streaks of makeup would be running down this serious face. The cheerleader, not wanting to relinquish control of the conversation, quickly interjected, "I can't swim very far." Annie tried to form a mental image of the busty girl having trouble floating, and stifled a smile.

"Don't worry. I'll be going over rescue techniques in class. Getting back in the boat is not as hard as you'd think, provided, of course, there's another boat or two around to help you. Now, I've got work to do, so I'll see you gals in class." The tall one nodded, while the cheerleader waved a giggly farewell.

David knelt down to pick up the boat, hoisting it up to balance on one shoulder. As he turned, he caught sight of Annie and broke into a lopsided grin.

"Annie, there you are. Right on time. Come on, I'll show you around." He was wearing the same Australian shorts as the day before, a red bandana hanging out of a pocket laden with tools, and a T-shirt from the Port Townsend Wooden Boat Festival.

"Isn't that heavy? Do you want help?"

"Nah, just a little awkward." He carried the kayak about twenty feet to a wooden rack holding some other boats. With his craggy features and thinning hair, David wasn't exactly good-looking, she concluded. But there was something about him, a certain easy-going self-confidence she found very appealing.

"So, how did the negotiations go yesterday?"

"Terrible," Annie replied. "To be blunt, Nicholas Forrestor is one of the most bullheaded, overbearing characters I've ever had to deal with. He's definitely not going to be happy unless everything goes his way. No doubt he's off somewhere saying similarly nice things about me. Needless to say, we didn't finish, and I'll be back at it tooth and nail this afternoon. I am not excited."

"Whoa, turn down the thermostat, lady, I can see the steam coming out of your ears from here."

"Sorry, some people just push the wrong buttons, and Forrestor happens to be one of them. I didn't mean to burden you with this."

"No problem. That's what the teacher's for, isn't it?" He gave her shoulders an encouraging squeeze. Annie found his touch not at all unpleasant.

"So anyway," she continued, "it looks like I won't be able to take your kayak class this afternoon."

"No problem. I've got another beginners' class tomorrow. You won't get out of it that easily."

Annie paid close attention as David led her proudly around the boat dock, showing off the small fleet of rental boats. In addition to runabouts for fishing there were all sizes of sailboats, brightly colored sail boards, and finally the sea kayaks. They were different from the whitewater kayaks Annie had seen once shooting the rapids of the Colorado River; these looked much more stable, and were almost as long as canoes. Annie was intrigued.

"Is it a very dangerous sport?" she asked, remembering what Russ Perkins had said about the treacherous waters. Her experience in sailboats seemed vastly different from that of encountering the ocean in such a tiny craft, so close to the water. Even so, as she looked out over the glassy calm of Westsound, dappled with sunshine, it was hard to imagine any danger.

"The ocean can always be dangerous, Annie. It's important to remember that, and learn to read the water and the weather indicators. These are awfully small boats in a large sea. But with a good helping of common sense and the mastery of some basic techniques, the risk can be minimized. That's what the class is for. In the beginners' session, I concentrate on rescue techniques. You'll learn how to get out of the boat safely after a capsize, bail out the water, then climb back in."

"Climb back in from the water? You're kidding, right?"

"No, afraid not. It's an essential skill if you want to avoid hypothermia."

"Hypothermia? I've heard the term, but I can't recall exactly what that is."

"That's the condition where your core body temperature decreases to a dangerous level. After a certain point, the body gets so chilled it can't recover without being rewarmed by an external heat source."

"But wouldn't the temperature have to be almost freezing for that to happen?

He shook his head. "Cold water conducts heat away from the body very rapidly. The water around here is about fifty degrees all year long. An average person will start to get hypothermic in about twenty minutes. First your muscles get rigid, then comes violent shivering, and then you lose your sense of judgment and coordination. Very few adults actually drown in water accidents—usually it's hypothermia that's fatal."

Annie shivered just thinking about it. David noticed her concern. "Enough of that—didn't I tell you it's not dangerous if you use common sense? I'll teach you the fun parts of kayaking, too. Then if you enjoy it, I'll take you to my own secret spot to see some sea lions. Is it a deal?"

Once David broke into his crooked grin again, Annie couldn't refuse.

Chapter 4

LATE SUNDAY NIGHT, JULY 22

STANDING ON THE pebbly beach outside his cottage, Marc glanced up at the nearly full moon, not sure whether it was a blessing or a curse. It would help them to accomplish their plan, but it would also make them visible. He hadn't had a chance to tell Daisy about Lisa Hargraves showing up. But he'd had such a good time with her, Lisa didn't seem like that much of a threat any more. Maybe he wouldn't even tell Daisy. She had enough to worry about already.

The black wetsuit felt clammy and tight as he stretched it on over his huge frame. Marc wondered if the jitters he was feeling were excitement or just fear. Getting all the camping supplies, the food, stashing the stuff in the boat down where no one would see it—that had all been a breeze. He'd even had fun poring over David Courtney's chart, figuring out where they were going, looking at the spot they had to land. But now, for the first time it was starting to dawn on him that they could get themselves killed with this crazy scheme. And it wasn't just the water he was scared of—no telling what Forrestor would do when he found out his precious little Marguerite Boulanger was gone. Marc had a strong temptation just to take the boat back to the mainland and disappear. No, then he'd have Daisy looking for him instead of Forrestor. Of the two, she was undoubtedly the more dangerous.

Marc got out the black grease paint and started applying it to his face, the only part of his skin that would show in the wetsuit. It was almost time. The security guard, consistent in making his rounds, had checked out the boat dock at the same times each night, once at 1:00, then not again till daylight. That gave them plenty of time to get the boat out and back without being seen. He looked at the diving watch on his wrist. 1:10 A.M. This was it.

Marc had always been a good swimmer, but the tension in his body made him cold and stiff. Luckily it was only about 500 yards from the beach in front of his cottage to the boat dock. He turned off all the lights in the cottage and waited five minutes. Seeing no one outside, he walked quietly down to the water, lowering himself in until only his head was above the surface. He moved slowly, trying not to cause any ripples or splashes.

After swimming about fifty yards offshore, he turned in the direction of the boat dock. That far out with his face blackened, even if someone saw him they would take him for a seal. If he saw anyone on shore, all he had to do was duck under water and come up somewhere else, mimicking a seal's behavior.

From out in the water Marc was able to see the guard's high powered flashlight. It looked like he had just finished his inspection of the boat dock and was starting off in the other direction.

Marc headed towards the dock, then suddenly stopped. Movement. He wasn't quite sure what he had seen. There, someone walking from the resort down towards the dock. Marc lowered himself underwater, trying not to splash, hoping that whoever it was wouldn't hang around too long. He didn't think he'd been seen.

With his breath about to burst, he came up, forcing himself not to gasp as he broke the surface. What the . . . ? Sure enough, there was someone standing on the boat dock, looking out over the water. It was definitely a different silhouette from the beer-bellied security guard. Back under water he went, cursing the cold.

Daisy Baker lay alone in her room, staring at the ceiling. From the adjacent room in the suite she could hear the grunting snores of Nicholas Forrestor. It was a good thing the old goat had always insisted on separate bedrooms. It was bad enough putting up with his fumbling, pawing lovemaking, without having to sleep in the same bed with him. Even with a wall between them his snoring was hideous. She smiled. Not much longer.

She ran over the plan again in her mind. It played so perfectly on Nicholas's warped personality, it had to work. Not only would she finally get away from the old man's insufferable possessiveness, she would be rich as well. The paltry amounts she'd managed to embezzle from the gullible old bastard over the past six months were nothing compared to what she'd be walking away with from this scam.

Daisy normally didn't drink coffee, so the caffeine pills were having an irritating effect. Her fingers twitched, as if small electric currents were being transmitted down her arms and legs. She shouldn't have worried about staying awake. There was no way she could have slept tonight. She'd been waiting far too long for this moment.

She listened intently as the hoarse breathing in the next room grew more rhythmic, indicating deeper sleep. She glanced at the clock. 12:30. Another half hour and Marc would be on his way. The waiting was the worst part.

"Marguerite Boulanger"—she thought about the name she had chosen for herself a little over six months ago. Pretty clever, how the French translation of her real name, Daisy Baker, could sound so classy. "Marguerite" had definitely been one of her better roles. It was a pity she'd have to cast it off and choose a new persona once they got to South America. Of one thing she was positive. She'd never play "Daisy Baker, Small Town Hick" again. *Never.*

She looked at the clock again. It was finally time, the plan was in motion. She rose and walked to the door which joined her room with Nicholas's. The grunting and wheezing was heavy now. She hadn't been sure how much of the tranquilizer to put in his coffee. She'd wanted it to be effective, but was afraid that he'd notice the taste. If he had, he'd not mentioned it. Daisy made the bed, tightly, as the maids would have done. It wasn't hard to remember how. Being a hotel maid was one of the many jobs she'd been forced to endure while trying to make a living in New York.

The next part would be more difficult. She had to get away from the building and down to the water without even the slightest chance of being seen. Leaving on her skimpy nightgown, she pulled on the black clothes she had bought and hidden in the bottom of her suitcase. Then she sat down at her makeup table and set to work.

His lungs nearly bursting, Marc surfaced for air a second time. He scanned the dock. He saw no movement, but there were so many dark shapes. Could one of them be a person? Probably just his imagination running wild. There was no way to be a hundred percent sure.

Slowly, he made his way to where the skiff was moored. This part would take concentration. For days he had been practicing untying knots with the bulky diving gloves on. It was a lot harder in the water in the dark.

Marc had to get the boat away from the dock, in full moonlight, without anyone noticing. He'd tied the Boston Whaler at the very end of the dock, loosely, so that he could untie it easily from the water. He didn't have far to go to get it around the point, to the beach where Daisy would be waiting. It would have to look like the boat was drifting if anyone spotted it. With more difficulty than he had anticipated, he finally got the line untied. Once the boat was free, Marc attached the extra line he'd brought to the boat's bow— 50 yards worth. Leaving the boat where it was, he smoothly sidestroked out to sea, barely rippling the water.

The boat was beginning to drift now, carried by the outgoing tide. He tried to ignore the cold creeping into his muscles. Marc put enough distance between himself and the boat that when he began pulling it, his head wouldn't be visible anywhere near it. Damn, this was slow going. All these crazy details had seemed so logical when Daisy dreamed them up, but now, they seemed like nothing more than a stupid waste of time. Marc was sure he could've come up with a better, more streamlined plan. And he was going to tell her so, too.

He strained to see the deserted beach around the point where they'd agreed to meet. *All right!* Marc saw Daisy's seated figure on a driftwood log. *Wait. It wasn't her!* The seated figure rose and walked toward the water, but not looking in his direction. He saw a flash, a cigarette being lit. In the glow, he saw that it was just some punk teenager with spiky fluorescent hair. Shit—the guy was sure to see Daisy arrive and blow the whole plan!

Marc stayed about fifty yards offshore, watching the teenager pace up and down the beach. The kid looked like he was angry about something, or maybe just stoned. Marc continued to watch in amazement as the kid glanced back toward the road, then walked straight into the water and began swimming towards the boat. Marc froze with terror.

"Marc, you idiot!" The swimmer whispered hoarsely, reaching up to grab the boat's gunwales. "Why didn't you come onto the beach to get me like you were supposed to? Were you expecting a formal invitation?"

"Daisy?! Is that . . . where'd you get those clothes?"

"You didn't expect me to just saunter down here wearing a nametag, did you? When I'm supposed to have been abducted? For

Christ's sake, 'Einstein,' help me get in the boat before I freeze my ass off. And help me get this orange goo out of my hair."

The crouching man on the boat dock rose and watched the Boston Whaler slowly move away from the beach. Everything had been going too well. This was certainly an unpleasant complication. What were they up to? It would be too obvious to follow them at this hour, with no other boats around. Besides, the speedboat would make too much noise. He'd just have to wait until they returned. He sat down with his back against a crate, staring out at the water. It was going to be a long, cold night.

The cold sliced through to Marc's bones, despite the wetsuit. He shivered the entire three miles to Traxler Island while Daisy pored over the chart drawn by David Courtney. When they reached the tiny island, they circled around to the northwest side, straining their eyes looking for the crescent cove. They pulled in where it was supposed to be, trying to avoid the jagged rocks sticking up out of the murky water which were almost impossible to see in the dark. When they got close to the steep cliff wall, Marc shone the small beam of his flashlight towards the shore looking for the beach that was supposed to be there. Nothing.

"Shit, Daisy, this must be the wrong place. There's no beach here, all I can see is a cliff." They both gazed up at the smooth wall of rock rising vertically out of the water, illuminated by the light of the full moon.

"I'm sure this is it. It has to be." She grabbed the flashlight from his hand and shone it on the chart. "He said there was only one cove on the whole island. Come on, this has to be the cove." Daisy's voice was quivering slightly from fear. "We'll just have to go in and get a closer look."

They turned off the outboard and lifted it out of the water to keep it from getting tangled in the huge fronds of red kelp that clogged the entrance to the cove. Marc took out the canoe paddle and began awkwardly pulling the boat forward. The last ten or twelve feet were impossible to paddle, the flat-bottomed boat was so mired in kelp. Marc had to get into the water and pull the boat through himself, untangling the slimy fronds as he went.

When they got close to the cliff wall, there was still no beach. Marc found himself standing in about three feet of water holding on to the boat, staring up at the immense gray rock.

Daisy threw down the chart in disgust. "Damn it, Marc, it's high tide! That's why there's no beach. We didn't even think of that."

"Think we should forget it and go back?" Marc asked hopefully, imagining himself pouring a glass of Scotch, then sinking into a warm bed.

"Are you out of your mind? We're not turning back now. Here." Daisy handed Marc a bundle of rope. "I'll hold the flashlight for you."

"What d'you mean?"

"Up, dummy! Climb the cliff."

"Climb the cliff? What the fuck do I know about rock climbing, you want me to break my neck?" Even in the dark Marc could see Daisy's features harden.

"Do it," she said icily.

Christ! Marc thought, doesn't this woman ever quit? He was starting to get serious second thoughts about this whole deal. The more he thought about it, the more he became convinced that Forrestor would catch on. He was no dummy. The problem was Daisy. Once she had her mind made up, there was no changing it, even if it got them both killed. He'd have to think of a way out of this.

He slung the rope over his shoulder and started up. He was scared shitless, there was no other way to describe it. It seemed like anywhere he stepped his foot would slip on the moss-covered rock.

At last Marc threw himself over the top. He glanced around and saw that he was on a small ledge. By climbing another ten feet on boulders he could make it to a grassy bluff, about twenty yards square, sheltered on three sides with more high cliffs, just the way Courtney had described it. This *was* the place after all.

"Come on, Marc, throw down the rope. We don't have that much time. Get moving!"

He threw down one end of the rope, muttering under his breath, envisioning the thugs Forrestor would send after them once he found out he'd been conned. She fastened her duffel bag to the end and he hauled it up, then threw the rope back down for her to use. It took Daisy, with her bad knee, twice as long to scale the cliff. Finally, panting with exhaustion, they both scrambled up to the grassy bluff. Once again, Daisy took command.

"All right. We need to set up the tent over here, facing this way, back towards the water so I can see if anyone's coming. Put the pile of firewood there, next to that rock."

Marc's black eyes glared. God, how he hated her.

The man on the dock was cold and stiff when a rosy light began to appear on the horizon. Mesmerized by staring out at the black water, his mind had begun to play tricks on him in the early hours of the morning. Fantasies of what he would do when she was standing in front of him, alone and vulnerable, danced in his imagination. Would he play with her emotions, ask her all the questions that had been gnawing away at him for so long? Or would he want to get to the point quickly? He created a dozen versions of their next meeting, then a dozen more.

Above all, he refused to believe she'd gotten away from him. Not when she'd been so close, so real. The boat had to return. But as dawn approached he began to worry.

He heard the distant hum of the outboard before he saw it. Then, breaking through the early morning haze was the outline of the skiff. He looked hard, saw it was the right boat, but that it only had one occupant. What was going on here? No matter. He hadn't come this far with his plan to quit now.

Returning to the cottage, Marc cranked up the thermostat, peeled off the slimy wetsuit and collapsed naked on the suede sofa. He felt hungover, but it was just exhaustion. It was a full ten minutes before he even had the strength to stand up. He lurched into the bedroom, grabbed the comforter off the bed and wrapped it around him like a cocoon. From there he managed to stagger out to the kitchen, down a couple of glugs of Scotch straight from the bottle and grab a handful of stale peanuts from the can.

Marc crashed on the sofa again and pulled the bedspread around his hunched shoulders. His head throbbed, his stomach did somersaults. He felt like he'd been attacked by every variety of flu ever to leave Asia.

He had no idea of the time when he woke up. He must have managed to fall asleep after all. His headache was better, but his stomach was still trying out for the Olympic gymnastic team. All he wanted was more sleep, but there was work to do.

He got the package out of its hiding place, handling it as carefully as he could, wiped off any fingerprints, and slid it into a small manila envelope. Using his left hand he scribbled the name on the front, intentionally misspelling.

NICKLUS FORSTER
THE WINSUR RESORT
FRAGIL!! DO NOT CRUSH!!
VERY IMPORTANT!! DELIVER IMEDIATLY!

Now, a quick scramble to make the drop, and then he could crash for good. He was almost out the door when he heard the telephone.

Chapter 5

MONDAY MORNING, JULY 23

ANNIE SAVORED EVERY sip of her *café au lait*, wondering if life ever got any better than this. After two more long, grueling sessions with Forrestor over the weekend, they had reached an agreement, of sorts. Forrestor was interested in further negotiations on the purchase of the resort, and would have his lawyer prepare an offer. In the meantime, Annie would do more research, have an accountant go over the books, and discuss everything with Joel, who did real estate law. She felt confident she was doing her best for Dorothy Lymon. With any luck, Nicholas Forrestor and his little lady friend had caught their morning flight back to Seattle, and were even now on their way back to New York and Forrestor's busy schedule.

Annie, on the other hand, had nothing to concern herself with but a few days of vacation full of blue skies, cool breezes . . . and a most intriguing kayaking instructor. David had convinced Annie to take his class on Sunday afternoon, and he had paid her just a bit more attention than he had the cheerleader.

Her daydream was abruptly disturbed by the sound of her name. She looked up to see Russ Perkins hurrying across the restaurant to her table.

"Annie, sorry to bother you," he was out of breath, "but I've got to talk to you right away." Dark circles under his eyes betrayed his exhaustion.

"Russ, what is it? You look so serious."

He nodded, "It's had, Annie. I need your help with Forrestor. I think he's gone off the deep end. I need you to help me try to calm him down."

"Forrestor? But I thought he left this morning."

"He was supposed to. He had reservations for the 7 A.M. shuttle back to Sea-Tac. I was up early . . . wanted to see them off . . . was surprised when I didn't see them check out. Then a little while ago, Forrestor came down to my office. Furious, practically in a rage. It appears that his companion, Marguerite Boulanger, is missing."

"Missing?"

"Forrestor is convinced that there's foul play involved, that she's either been kidnapped or killed. He's making noises about it being the resort's fault, for having poor security. He's threatening to sue, of all things."

Annie knew such lawsuits were not unheard of. Joel, her partner, had recently obtained a $500,000 verdict for a woman raped in her own apartment, where the landlord had failed to maintain adequate lighting and locks. Still, Forrestor's anger was premature.

"How long has the woman been gone?"

"Not that long. He says they went to bed around ten or eleven o'clock last night. He fell asleep, says he overslept, and when he woke up she wasn't there. Her bed hadn't been slept in."

"Her bed? I though that . . . "

Russ shook his head. "Forrestor reluctantly told me they, uh, sleep in separate rooms. They're booked into a connecting suite. He says she usually waited till he fell asleep before going to her own room. He went to her room this morning to wake her, but she wasn't there and her bed was undisturbed."

"But it's only eleven A.M. now." Annie said, looking at her watch. "Surely he can't be that concerned. She's probably taking a walk on the beach, or . . ."

"I know this sounds odd, Annie, but he says that she never left the room in the morning without his permission."

"His permission?" Annie was shocked. "You mean she couldn't even go for a swim, or have breakfast?"

"That's what he says, and at least at this point, I have no reason to doubt him. She did seem very submissive the times I met her."

"Russ, maybe I'm reading too much into this," Annie paused to try and comprehend the situation, "but what if she just took off? Maybe she had had as much as she could stand of the way he treated her?"

"Of course that's a possibility, but I think you might be applying your own values to the situation. Forrestor is a wealthy man. He provided well for her. Expensive clothes, jewelry, trips. From what I understand, she was penniless when he met her. That's a lot to give up. And there's no indication that she was dissatisfied with the arrangement."

Annie found it hard to take in.

"Come on, Russ. The separate bedrooms. The difference in their ages. Being treated like a child. Do you really think she was happy with him?"

"You could be absolutely right, but the point is, it just doesn't *look* like she ran off. She had no money of her own. Forrestor says none of his is missing. All of her jewelry, clothes and suitcases are still in the room. The only item missing is the nightgown she was wearing."

"But isn't it possible," Annie interjected, "that she could have hitchhiked to the ferry dock? And since you only pay for a ferry ticket coming the other direction, she could have gotten all the way to Anacortes without money."

"In her nightgown?" Russ asked. "And even if she caught the last ferry at eleven thirty, then what? Would she have hitchiked into Seattle as well? She really couldn't have gotten far without money.

And that would take guts. We're talking about a woman who practically had to ask permission to breathe. And I didn't get the impression that her English was that good. No, Annie, I just don't think your theory fits."

"Have you talked to the staff?"

Russ nodded. "No one saw a thing."

"Have you notified the authorities?" she asked.

"I did," Russ replied, "at Forrestor's insistence. The Sheriff's Department gave me the usual line. A person can't be declared missing for at least twenty-four hours. We have in-house security combing the grounds, and I sent the chauffeur out to check the road from here to the ferry dock. I've done all I can think of. I don't know, Annie," Russ's voice sounded weary and full of dread as he ascended the steps, "I have a strong suspicion that whatever we do won't be enough for Nicholas Forrestor."

Apprehensively, Annie followed Russ into the book-lined office in the main building. The short, stocky man was pacing in front of the picture window. He pivoted on his heel when he heard them enter the room. His face was bright red, his steel gray eyes flashing with anger.

"Perkins, where the hell have you been—the moon and back? How dare you leave me alone like that, wasting precious time. Did you call the police yet? The FBI?"

"Now Mr. Forrestor, please, have a seat."

Russ was speaking slowly, in a low, soothing tone. It reminded Annie of the way one might speak to a raging animal to calm it down.

Annie walked across the room and extended her hand. Forrestor ignored the gesture and sat down in one of the leather arm chairs with a grunt.

There was a tentative knock on the door, and Russ's secretary entered with a tray containing hot coffee and cups. She was about to offer some friendly small talk when she saw Forrestor glowering at her. Instead she set down the tray and beat a hasty retreat, as Russ tried to telegraph an apologetic look in her direction.

The silence in the air was thick. Russ handed Annie a cup of coffee, after Forrestor declined. He rose from the chair and placed his body between Russ and Annie, his back towards her.

"You still didn't answer my question, Perkins. Did you call the police?"

Russ looked uncomfortable. "Mr. Forrestor, you have to understand what this looks like . . . your friend has only been missing a few hours . . . "

"Her bed wasn't slept in!"

"All right. Possibly she's been gone all night. There's really nothing to indicate that any harm has come to her. But in the meantime, I want you to know that we will do everything in our power to help you regarding Ms. Boulanger's disappearance . . . "

Forrestor interrupted with a vengeance. "Disappearance? That's a hell of a polite word for it, Perkins. Let's not mince words—she was either kidnapped or murdered and you know it as well as I do!

"You pretend to call this place a resort. Hmph! Where were the security guards, will you tell me that? This wouldn't have happened if there had been any competent personnel around. I've been to resorts all over the world—some of them run-down hell holes—but all of them had better security than this rat-trap." Forrestor stepped forward and grabbed Russ's arm. "Could we please continue this in private?"

Annie had had just about enough. "Mr. Forrestor, I can understand how upset you are, but please let me assure you we will do everything in our power to help you. Even though I'm here on Mrs. Lymon's behalf, I also have quite a bit of experience dealing with criminal matters. When I was with the prosecutor's office my specialty was homicide, but I also handled cases involving rape, kidnapping, arson and conspiracy. Believe me, sir, I know what I'm doing when it comes to criminal investigations. You've also made some rather serious allegations about the way the resort is run. I suggest we put personality conflicts aside and get down to business. Now, what we have here is a missing person, and you believe there may have been foul play. I think I can be of assistance, if you let me. Please, what exactly are your concerns?"

Forrestor seethed, struggling to come up with a suitable reply. "Well, for one thing, you've got windows onto the balcony, easily accessible, no bolts whatsoever. What's the good of having dead bolts on the doors, for Christ's sake, if you can't bolt the windows?

And were the grounds enclosed? No. Available for anyone, anyone at all to come right on the grounds. Disgraceful. Absolutely disgraceful. I'm telling you right now, Miss MacPherson, I'm holding your Mrs. Lymon and her goddamned resort one hundred percent responsible for what happened. One hundred percent! I suggest you contact your insurance company immediately."

On and on, the tirade continued, as if resorts were supposed to be fitted out like high-security prisons. Annie wondered what the man's home looked like.

It kept turning into an awkward three-cornered conversation. Forrestor, the type of man who wasn't comfortable dealing with a woman as an equal, addressed all of his comments to Russ, and Annie answered.

Forrestor glowered at Russ. "Am I wasting my breath? Are you going to do something or aren't you?"

Russ bobbed his head nervously. "I . . . I do have a telephone call I have to make. No, you stay here, I'll go in the next room." As he left, Forrestor turned to stare out the window again, as if he were alone in the room.

"Mr. Forrestor," Annie said softly. "I have to broach a difficult subject. Is it possible that Miss Boulanger left of her own accord?"

His head whipped around. "Absolutely impossible! Nonsense!" He rammed his fist onto the rosewood desk. "She was nothing. Stupid, unrefined. I picked her out of the gutter. She was garbage. I gave her everything. She was a cipher before I found her, don't you understand? I *created* her. She couldn't leave, she wouldn't know how. She wouldn't dare."

Quietly, Annie said, "Perhaps she was more resourceful than you think, Mr. Forrestor."

"Out of the question." In profile, Annie could see Forrestor's mouth silently form the word "bitch," almost in a snarl. Was his comment directed to her, or to the absent Marguerite?

Annie could see they were going to get nowhere on this tack, so she tried a different approach. "Mr. Forrestor, the important thing right now is to concentrate on *finding* Ms. Boulanger, don't you agree? It would help if we knew more about her. Could you tell me about her background? Where you met her?" She took a pen and yellow legal pad from Russ's desk to take notes. This seemed to mollify Forrestor, as if it proved she was finally taking his allegations seriously. He began to calm down, and answered her questions.

"I found her in New York, literally scrounging for a dollar. She was, uh, working at a party I was attending." Forrestor sat in the leather chair with his back to Annie, addressing his comments to the window.

"Working. Was she . . . providing the entertainment?" Annie asked cautiously, not wanting to stoke the flames of his wrath again.

"No!" He whirled around, facing her directly for the first time and continuing in a rapid staccato. "She was in the kitchen, preparing the food. She was just a waif. A gamine. Only a few words of English. Grubby, uncouth. But, Miss MacPherson, she was not, as you imply, a whore!"

Annie was taken aback. She hadn't meant to imply it, far from it. She found it significant that Forrestor had assumed she had.

"She's French, I take it?"

"Obviously." Annie could tell that Forrestor didn't place her level of intelligence much above his opinion of Marguerite's. Annie was relieved, however, that he appeared to be running out of steam.

"I was attracted to her looks," he explained. "I saw tremendous potential in her, took her home with me that evening. I bought her all new clothes, taught her how to eat, how to speak, how to move. I made her into a new person."

Shades of *Pygmalion*, although Forrestor made Henry Higgins sound like Mother Teresa. The steel-haired man had yet to speak of the missing woman as a person, and Annie doubted that he saw her that way. To him she was just his creation, his possession.

Russ quietly re-entered the room. He gave no explanation as to whom he had telephoned.

"Do you have any photographs? They could help us to locate her," Annie asked, subtly trying to steer Forrestor's attention away from the Windsor's liability, and towards finding Marguerite. That should be what Forrestor wanted, after all.

"Of course. Several. I was training her to be a model. She had tremendous talent. I have an entire portfolio in my suite. You can send someone up for it." He brushed an invisible fleck of lint from his trousers.

Russ went to the door and stuck his head out. "Marla, could you come in here a second?" Russ's secretary came to the door. Russ opened the top drawer of his desk and took out a master key on a bright red key chain bearing the Windsor logo. He handed Marla the key and asked her to go up to Forrestor's suite. Forrestor told her to look for a black leather folder on top of the dresser.

Annie was suddenly struck by the extraordinary neatness of Forrestor's attire. The charcoal gray suit was impeccably pressed, the tie perfectly knotted, the red silk handkerchief in his pocket neatly folded. Was his outrage all an act? "How long have you known her?" she asked. Forrestor was getting fidgety under Annie's questioning. She could tell he wouldn't put up with much more.

"Six months was all. Her progress was extraordinary. Her English had improved to the point that it was practically flawless. Except for the accent, you would never have known she was a foreigner. The photographs are most impressive, as you'll see. She would have been an extremely successful model. We were ready to launch her career. Her first shooting for *Vogue* was to have been the first of the month, as soon as we returned from this vacation. But now this. A tragedy!"

Annie noted his words carefully. Nicholas Forrestor was speaking of Marguerite in the past tense, even though she'd only been missing since eleven o'clock the night before. Very odd.

Nicholas's story, if it were true, was inconsistent with Annie's theory that the young woman had run off voluntarily. Why would this "waif" have gone with Nicholas, put up with him for six months of being groomed to be a model, then run out on him at the moment she was about to become successful? Another month or two and she would have been on the cover of *Vogue*, and able to do as she pleased.

"Did she know anyone on the west coast, anyone she could have gone to?"

Forrestor jumped from his seat and glared at Annie. "I *told* you she did not leave of her own accord. She would not!" He was breathing heavily, and his face was beet red.

"Why, Mr. Forrestor?" She had to push. "Why are you so certain of that?"

"Because," he spoke slowly, deliberately, his eyes narrowing to mere slits, "she knew I would not allow it."

Marla returned at that moment with the portfolio. She handed Russ the red key chain and was about to leave when Forrestor barked, "You, go to the bar and get me a Bloody Mary, double Stolychnaya." Marla straightened her shoulders and glared at Russ. She had never in her career as an executive secretary been asked to fetch drinks. Russ nodded at her apologetically.

He slipped the key into his pocket and laid the large leather case on the desk. Annie moved next to him where she could see. Forrestor lowered himself into a chair, drumming his fingers impatiently as he waited for his drink. Russ unzipped the case and carefully withdrew the professional photographs of Marguerite Boulanger.

Even having met the woman, Annie was taken aback. The photos were truly exquisite. In a way, she did look like a "waif," barely older than a child, although Forrestor said she was twenty-seven. Her range was incredible. In some poses she looked hungry, afraid, her large doe eyes welling with emotion. In others, she was the precocious child, looking smug at having gotten away with some unknown mischief. In one of the most striking pictures, with a T-shirt slung off one shoulder and her blonde hair cut short, Marguerite had the look of a wide-eyed adolescent boy. Different makeup and lighting turned her into a sophisticated jet-setter, looking older than her true age. Yet another series of pictures was avant garde, with blue lips and sculpted hair, in which she looked both evil and innocent at the same time.

Marla returned with Forrestor's drink. He rose and took it from her without a word of thanks. Annie was afraid he would reach into his pocket and tip the executive secretary. He didn't.

Of one thing there was no doubt—Marguerite was tremendously photogenic. She either had an amazing natural talent, or a lot more modeling experience than Forrestor gave her credit for. Through it all, Annie's gut reaction remained unchanged. Especially after meeting Forrestor face to face, she believed that Marguerite had "escaped" of her own free will. The photographs showed a woman of depth and character, surely someone who could elude her tyrannical lover if she wanted.

Russ flipped through the photographs a second time. "I'm truly amazed, Mr. Forrestor. I don't know much about fashion photographs, but these pictures look incredible to me. It's hard to believe they're all the same person."

"Did you see the last photo? The proof of my success?" Forrestor interjected, in an almost pleasant tone, for the first time since they began examining the photographs.

"The proof?" Annie asked. "What do you mean?"

"It shows just how far she progressed," Forrestor announced proudly. He strode to the desk and lifted the stack of photographs. Underneath was a Polaroid snapshot, yellowed with age. It showed a young girl leaning on the back of a car on the side of a highway, a wheatfield in the background, her straggly white-blonde hair reaching to her waist. The girl was dressed in faded Levis and an oversized white sweatshirt. Annie carried the snapshot to the window for better light. It was unmistakably a picture of a young Marguerite.

"She gave me that picture before our first photo session," Nicholas explained. His erratic anger was slowly dissipating, overcome by his possessiveness and pride. "It was taken many years earlier, of course, but it captures perfectly what she looked like when I found her. Her hair was long and straight, and whenever she could she would dress in those dungarees and a stretched-out white shirt. Hideous. I kept the picture to show the miraculous transformation I was able to achieve."

Annie was impressed. If Nicholas really had transformed the young French waif into a high fashion model in a mere six months, he had worked magic. She paused, lingering over the photo. Something about Forrestor's story didn't fit with this snapshot, but Annie couldn't place what it was. Russ had picked up the snapshot again, his gaze intently focussed, as if it somewhere in that wheatfield was the answer to their problem.

"Mr. Forrestor, if we could make copies of one of these photographs, for identification purposes, it might help us locate Ms. Boulanger." Nicholas waved his hand, a sign Annie took to mean consent. She flipped through the pictures again, finally selecting the one that most closely resembled Marguerite Boulanger in real life. It might have been an ad for jewelry or expensive perfume. Her hair was relatively short, but styled conservatively. She was wearing a black silk suit, a long rope of pearls, and spiked high heels. The expression was haughty. It wasn't a perfect resemblance, but someone looking at the photo could easily have recognized her as the woman Annie had met in the solarium that first day.

Forrestor stood rigidly at the window, staring out over the water. "Don't misunderstand me, Miss MacPherson." His voice was subdued, the anger completely gone. It seemed hard for him to find the right words. "I just want her found. That's the only thing that matters."

Powerful emotion shook his voice, but Annie was unable to discern its source. Fear, greed, possessiveness? Or did he really care for Marguerite? Suddenly the man speaking to her was one who desperately wanted his companion back. Annie wasn't quite sure why.

"I guess I love her, you see," he said softly, in a tone Annie had not heard before.

"I don't know if she loved me. Women pretend. You're such practiced deceivers, all of you. I don't know how to discern if a woman's telling the truth. I've never been any good at that." He paused, his voice barely audible. "But I need her, that's all I know. Please God, bring her back!"

Annie didn't know what to say, and the heavy silence in the small office was uncomfortable. Forrestor's mood swings were frightening. One moment he was furious, the next compassionate. How quickly would he turn again? Before she had time to attempt a response to Forrestor's new-found grief, Nathan Komatsu stuck his head in the door. They all turned at the sound of the desk clerk's voice.

"Mr. Forrestor? I hate to disturb you, sir, but I thought you might want to know. There's a very strange package for you. I thought it might be important."

"What? What is it? A package?" Forrestor stammered, mopping his damp brow with a white linen handkerchief.

"Where did it come from?" Russ demanded.

"Chuck brought it in with today's mail delivery. He found it in the mail box out in front of the resort. There was no postage and no return address, but it looked so odd, he thought he'd bring it down and see if someone here could claim it."

"Set it on the desk, gently." Forrestor barked, his mood shifting suddenly back to anger, his face reddening. Nathan complied, slowly placing the bulging five by eight inch manila envelope on Russ's desk. They could barely make out the name and address scribbled on the front in a spiky scrawl.

"I've received bomb threats before," Forrestor explained, still sweating profusely. "In the past, they've all been harmless, but frightening, nevertheless."

"It wasn't very heavy," said Nathan. "It felt like a small box, maybe three by four inches. And it rattled."

"You shook it?" Forrestor shouted in horror. "You idiot!"

Nathan shrugged his shoulders, unruffled by the outburst. "Nothing happened, sir. My first thought was that it was a cassette. You know, a tape. I mail them to my family in Japan all the time. That's what it felt like."

No one said a word. After an uncomfortable pause, Russ said, "I think we should open it." He looked at Forrestor. Forrestor agreed. Secretly, Annie wanted to wait in the next room. No one stepped forward to do the deed.

"I'll do it," Nathan finally volunteered. "After all, I'm the one who thinks it's a cassette, right?" He smiled nervously and pulled a chair up to the desk. He reached for Russ's brass letter opener. Touching only one corner, he slid the manila envelope toward him until it was sitting directly in front of him on the desk. Slowly, as if dissecting a laboratory specimen, Nathan inserted the brass tool under the flap of the envelope, and began to tear the crease. The incision grew until the entire edge was cut.

Holding one side down on the desk, Nathan used the letter opener to lift open the envelope, and placed his head down on the desk to look inside.

"Well, if it is a bomb, they sure did a good job of making it look like a cassette!" Everyone breathed a sigh of relief. Still moving slowly, Nathan slid the tape out of the envelope. A small plastic cassette box contained a recording tape, the type sold in any record store. There were no identifying markings. Nathan picked up the envelope and shook it. Nothing else.

"Perkins—where can I play this thing?" Forrestor barked. "I need a tape recorder, now."

"Here, use the dictaphone," Russ replied, stepping behind the rosewood desk. He inserted the tape in the machine and pushed the start button.

The tape crackled and buzzed.

"Nicholas, darling, it's me, Marguerite. Don't worry, I'm all right. I guess you know by now that I've been kidnapped. They are telling me what to say . . . "

"Oh, my God, my God." Forrestor's face was ashen as he dropped weakly into his chair. His voice was shaky. "It's her. That's Marguerite's voice. Where is she? What have they done to her?" No one else spoke as the tape continued.

"One million dollars . . . American currency, unmarked bills . . . start gathering the money now . . . "

When the message was over, Russ reached to turn off the machine. Annie held up her hand.

"Wait," she said, "let it run to the end." She was baffled by the background noise. She was almost certain she detected traffic in the background, not just a few cars, but heavy city traffic. There wasn't anywhere in the islands that would sound like that.

Then they heard it, at the very end of the tape. "Nicholas!" the accented voice screamed out in pain, accompanied by the sound of a sharp blow, what sounded like a man's shout. Annie glanced at Forrestor. It looked like he himself had been struck.

Annie stared out the window at the calm waters of Westsound as Russ dialed the number for the San Juan County Sheriff's office in Friday Harbor. The morning's events had boggled her mind. She had been so put off by Forrestor's personality that she had been convinced he was just a crackpot, and that his companion had merely run off. She had been unable to comprehend how any woman in her right mind could have tolerated his company even for a day. Now she found herself presented with an entirely different scenario. Could it be that Marguerite Boulanger had really been kidnapped? Why was she still not convinced?

"Well, when will he be back? Yes, this is an emergency!" Russ was practically yelling into the phone. Forrestor was silently glaring. "Yes, I'll hold."

Annie suddenly needed air, feeling claustrophobic in the small confines of Russ's office. She motioned that she'd be out on the terrace.

Outside, a cool breeze was blowing, causing the resort's red and white ensign to flutter gently. A boy in bright shorts was trying without much luck to stay upright on a sailboard. Laughing, he fell again and again into the water. The scene looked so peaceful, so far removed from the present crisis.

In a few moments Russ joined Annie on the terrace. They moved to a table at the end, out of earshot of the other guests enjoying the sun.

"What's going on? Where's Forrestor?" Annie asked.

"He went up to his room to rest," Russ replied. "The man looked absolutely shattered."

"What did the Sheriff's office say?"

"All the detectives are tied up this morning on a major drug bust— a big smuggling operation, I think—they'll send someone over as soon as they can, they're not even sure when, for crying out loud. In the meantime, we're just supposed to stay calm, not tell anyone about the kidnapping, of course, and call them immediately if there's another contact. I don't know, I'm still not sure that they're taking this seriously yet."

"What do you mean? Didn't you tell them about the tape?"

"I did, but I think the deputy I was talking to thought it was some kind of joke. This is a pretty quiet place, I think he just didn't believe that a kidnapping could happen here. A joke! I can't believe it." Russ closed his eyes. He looked ready to faint from exhaustion. Annie felt sorry for him—he seemed to be taking the whole incident so personally. She watched as he nervously fidgeted with the master key chain, flipping it from hand to hand.

"Russ, I'm really bothered by that tape . . . "

"So am I, believe me."

"No, I mean it doesn't add up. It's not logical."

"You lawyers and your logical minds."

"Hear me out. I finally figured out what's wrong with that tape. Marguerite disappeared sometime between eleven P.M. last night and ten A.M. this morning. According to the tape, she's been abducted, but it gave no clues as to when she was kidnapped, or where she was being held. The tape was found in the mail box a short while ago. With heavy traffic noise in the background, Russ. City noise. She's been gone at most twelve hours. Is that enough time for the kidnappers to take Marguerite to a city with heavy traffic, make the tape, and then hand carry it back to Orcas Island? Doesn't that seem odd to you?"

"I see your point, " Russ agreed.

Annie continued. "How long would it take a boat to get to Seattle or Vancouver, B.C.?"

"I'm not really sure. Two, three hours, probably. A small plane would be faster, though I doubt you could get off the island in the middle of the night without somebody knowing it, because of the noise. But either way, you certainly could do it round trip in twelve hours, if you wanted to."

"If you wanted to. That's what's bothering me. Why would the kidnappers want to? If they took Marguerite to Seattle or Vancouver, why go through all the rigamarole of making a tape, bringing it back to the resort, and dropping it in a mailbox. What if the kidnapper were seen dropping the tape? Why not a phone call? It just seems so preposterous."

Annie found herself craving more facts. Would the sheriff remember to take prints from the cassette? Have the lab analyze the background noise? Research where the tape might have been purchased, where the envelope might have come from? She was thinking as if she were still a prosecutor, running the endless frustrating details through her mind, waiting for a pattern to emerge. But no pattern was forthcoming. Annie had to keep reminding herself that she wasn't heading up this investigation.

Russ looked at his watch. "It's almost one o'clock. I've, uh, got an appointment. Despite all of this, I've still got a resort to manage. I've got to make sure everything's organized for this evening."

"This evening? What's happening?"

"Didn't I tell you about it? Mondays are 'Guest Appreciation Night.' It's sort of an elaborate happy hour we do every week during the summer, so the guests can get to know each other. No-host bar, complimentary hors d'oeuvres. We always draw a big crowd. You should come, it might take your mind off of all this."

"Maybe I will." Annie replied. "Who knows? Maybe I'll meet a kidnapper."

Chapter 6

MONDAY EVENING

ANNIE SCANNED THE crowded room. The quiet ambience of the library bar had been replaced by the noise and laughter of a mingling throng, spilling out onto the terrace.

She wasn't quite sure why she'd come. The day's events had left her drained. Was there really a kidnapper at large, or was the tape just a hoax, as the San Juan County Sheriff's Office seemed to think? Nicholas Forrestor had seemed almost more concerned with bringing a lawsuit than with finding his companion. He was not a man to be trusted.

After leaving Russ's office, Annie had gone to her room to rest, but found it was impossible. The man's voice on the tape—that was the problem. If the tape was a hoax, who was the man? Could the voice have been Nicholas Forrestor? The more she thought about that tape, the more convinced she was that it wasn't a hoax. And if it was for real, and there really had been a kidnapping, her intuition told her that at least one of the people responsible for the tape had to be nearby. She couldn't shake the idea that a kidnapper was wandering among, them, observing, watching, waiting for something. Annie couldn't stay away. She had to see who was at the resort, and why.

She pushed her way over to the crowded bar. The bartender had just handed her a glass of chardonnay when she felt a hand on her shoulder.

"Annie MacPherson, isn't it?" Annie turned around to respond to the voice and saw a slender, mustached man who looked vaguely familiar. His pleated cotton slacks looked freshly ironed. With a blue and white cotton sweater casually draped over a polo shirt, he was perfectly color coordinated except for the red Vuarnet case clipped to his shirt pocket. His curly dark hair was short and neatly groomed.

"Yes," she replied, quickly trying to place him. He saw the "where do I know you from?" look on her face, smiled and said, "Philip Spaulding, I used to be with the King County Public Defender's office."

"Of course. I knew you looked familiar."

"We had several cases together before I came to my senses and changed jobs. You beat me on all of them as I recall."

"All of them? How rude of me."

"Not at all. My clients were all quite guilty."

"Oh well, then, I guess that's all right. I hope my crushing victories weren't the reason for the career change?"

"Hardly!" He smiled. "I found I didn't enjoy spending all my energy trying to put criminals back on the streets. I'm involved in managing political campaigns now."

"Putting politicians in office. That's not so very different from keeping criminals on the street, is it?"

"No," he chuckled, "but at least I'm more successful at it."

He explained that he was currently working as the state campaign manager for the soon-to-be-announced Democratic presidential candidate. "It's a lot of work, of course, and the stress—more than I'd ever imagined. But I have to admit that I love it. You see, it's a way for me to put my energy behind the causes I believe in. Last year, for example, I managed Hugh Steed's First District congressional campaign. It was a close race, but we were able to beat the Republican incumbent, a man who was one of the strongest advocates in the House for military aid to the Nicaraguan Contras, and an anti-abortionist as well. I really felt like I'd accomplished something."

Philip's enthusiasm appeared to be genuine. Annie wondered if she could cross him off her list of potential kidnappers. No, too early to tell. He had brains and ambition, two good qualities for a kidnapper. She wondered if he also had the guts.

"What about running for office yourself? Is that in the picture?" She surmised that with his rich, broadcaster-like voice and ruggedly handsome appearance he'd have no trouble winning votes.

He smiled. It confirmed her opinion. It was a smile that could kill at fifty paces. Annie had no trouble picturing what it would look like on a campaign poster.

"It's a possibility. To be frank, I think I could do a good job— you know, be a voice for some of the people in this country who currently have no power. But I'm not in a hurry, I'm still young. I've learned from my involvement up to now that it takes a tremendous amount of time and effort, not to mention money, to mount a campaign. I plan to pick a race that I can win. If I do it, I'll accept no less. In the meantime, I'm getting to know the important people in the state's political machine. Without the right support, a candidate doesn't have a prayer. It's a shame, too. I've seen some fine candidates destroyed simply because they didn't know how to play the game."

He flashed that famous smile again. Annie felt that Philip was working hard at exuding an aura of morality and social consciousness. She sensed that underneath all the talk of good causes, Philip had full comprehension of the truth that politics was serious business. Very serious. If I were a candidate, she thought, I'm not sure I'd want Philip Spaulding working for my opponent. Yes, he had the guts.

"What brings you to Orcas Island?" she asked.

"Primarily my nephew, Jimmy. He's staying with me while his parents are in Europe. I lead such an urban lifestyle, I wasn't quite sure what I'd do with him. But he's enjoying it up here."

As they continued to chat, Annie noticed Philip subtly surveying the room behind her. "I don't mean to be rude," he explained, "but there's another guest that I met earlier this week. I was just wondering if I'd see him again. His name's Nicholas Forrestor."

Annie gave a start at the name. Philip Spaulding and Nicholas Forrestor seemed like opposite ends of the spectrum. She couldn't imagine what they possibly could have in common. Phil didn't volunteer that information.

"Actually, Phil, I met Forrestor this morning regarding some business of the resort. I suspect he won't be coming this evening. It seems a bit of an emergency came up."

"He's not ill, is he? Everything seemed fine the last time I spoke with him." Annie was startled by Philip's worried reaction.

"No, I'm sure he's fine." Annie said, leaving it at that. Philip was extremely distracted as they continued to make small talk. After only a few minutes, Philip excused himself and left the bar, leaving Annie very curious. A connection between this almost stereotypical young liberal and the obstinate old conservative Forrestor didn't make sense. Whatever the two men had in common, it was hidden beneath the surface. Annie made a mental note to try to find out.

Again Annie casually surveyed the crowd, half disappointed that David Courtney was nowhere in sight. She wondered if she'd just been imagining that he had paid her an unusual amount of attention in his kayak class on Sunday.

Crushed by the crowd up against the bar, Annie found herself standing next to the two young women who had been flirting with David at the boat dock that morning, and who had both been in the kayaking class. The buxom cheerleader had continued her act throughout the entire class. She was now flirting with a different man, tall, rather greasy, who looked like he might sell time-share condominiums. The lanky friend, pushing her slipping glasses back up on her nose, was casting shy glances in the direction of the boyish bartender, who blushed every time she caught his eye. No criminal minds in that group, Annie decided.

She worked her way towards the buffet table, and soon discovered it was worth the effort. At one end of the long table a server was slicing a juicy steamship round for miniature roast beef sandwiches. Spread along both sides were salmon mousse, crab wrapped in phyllo, bite-size morsels of asparagus quiche, and a heaping dome of cold marinated prawns. No wonder there was such a crowd.

As she was trying to decide what delicacies to enjoy first, a server came out of the kitchen carrying a platter of raw oysters on the half shell imbedded in crushed ice. Annie daubed some cocktail sauce on a silvery gray oyster, popped it in her mouth and let it slither down the back of her throat. For an oyster addict, it was heaven.

"Everything all right?" Russ Perkins had appeared silently at her elbow. "Come on, I'll introduce you to some people." Grabbing her elbow, Russ ushered Annie towards a round table in the corner and stood behind a tiny woman who was excitedly describing the year she ran the Seattle Marathon in a downpour, and won. "I never did know enough to stay out of the rain!" Russ put a hand on her shoulder.

"Ellen, I'd like you to meet Annie MacPherson. Annie, Ellen O'Neill and I go way back. We were at Harvard Business School together."

"Nice to meet you, Annie." The vivacious woman with a mischievous gleam in her eye was probably close to forty, with straight, shoulder-length brown hair. She had the small, tightly-muscled body of a long-distance runner. "I came up here for a week of bicycling, and I know I'm not going to want to leave. This place is fabulous! I told Russ I'd put him up for a week at my 'resort' but for some reason he turned me down."

Russ laughed. "Ellen's a hospital administrator in Seattle," he explained to Annie. "Thanks, but I don't think I'm quite ready for the psychiatric ward."

"Will you two join us for a drink?" Ellen asked.

"I've got a million things to do," said Russ. "Sorry."

"Annie? Have a seat. I'll buy you a beer."

"Thanks, Ellen, I'd love it."

Ellen introduced her around the table. The man she'd been telling about her race was an engineer from Boston. He and Ellen had discovered they'd both run the Boston Marathon the previous year.

"And this is Roger Stokowski, am I pronouncing that correctly? Roger was telling us he owns a chain of women's clothing stores in Chicago. And this is Lisa Hargraves."

Annie recognized the tall brunette she had observed checking in on Thursday. The leather ensemble had been replaced by a clinging purple jersey sheath with a dangerously low neckline. The long talons were varnished an identical shade.

The waiter came for drink orders. Lisa ordered Tanqueray on the rocks, and Roger, seated so close to Lisa it looked like they might be sharing a chair, opted for Chivas, neat. Ellen and the engineer ordered another pint each of Watney's, and Annie got another chardonnay. Ellen was finishing her story about marathons, so

Annie decided to sit back and observe the couple across the table. "Lisa, please don't think I'm being rude," said Roger, addressing his seating companion. "But frankly, you baffle me. What is such an exquisite creature as yourself doing *here*, practically out in the bush?"

Annie imagined that to Roger, a stroll through the Lake Washington arboretum would probably count as a wilderness experience. He had used a touch too much styling gel on his too-long hair, giving him an oily appearance. He leaned over to light Lisa's thin brown cigarette. Her purple tipped fingers closed enticingly over the hand holding the match.

"Roger, dear, I baffle *myself* at times. You would not *believe* what I'm capable of doing in the interest of furthering my career." She took a long, dramatic drag on the cigarette, and blew the smoke towards the ceiling.

Roger lighted a cigarette for himself. "Let me see. My first guess is that you're a fashion model, am I right? And you *must* shop in New York. Your exquisite sense of chic . . . " Annie imagined this was not the first time he had used the same script. He went on to drop the names of the places where his buyers shopped.

Lisa lapped it up. She inched closer. "Oh, you're *so* perceptive, Roger. Yes, I've been working in New York for the past five years. I started out as a model, but moved into acting fairly quickly, so much more *challenge*." She lowered her heavily made-up violet eyelids and whispered conspiratorially, "I've just been offered a spot in a pilot for a series, out in L.A. I'd be a fool not to take it, even though I would just hate leaving New York."

"And where do you fit in—the lead, I'm assuming?" Roger asked, finishing his drink a little too quickly.

Lisa smiled silkily. "It's only a supporting role, but a very juicy one. My character is a beautiful, wealthy, and of course *evil* vixen who gets a lot of bathing suit scenes and sleeps with every man in the cast. My agent thinks I'm absolutely ideal for the part."

Annie stifled a smirk. Lisa ran on, "Bruce, that's my agent, is a genius. If he thinks this series will be the next *Dallas*, who am I to argue? Still, I'm not sure what I'll think of Hollywood."

"Oh, I'm sure you'll fit in just fine," Annie contributed.

"Oh, do you know Hollywood?" Lisa asked, not taking her eyes off Roger.

"I visit my mother and stepfather there."

"Are they in the Business?" Lisa flirtatiously tapped the back of Roger's hand. "I've heard they all say 'the Business' out there a lot. Isn't it cute?"

"As a matter of fact, yes. My stepfather is a producer. Maybe you've heard of him." Annie mentioned the name and Lisa's eyes grew large. Annie neglected to mention that she hadn't spoken to the man for five years and wasn't likely to in the near future. No sense bursting Lisa's bubble.

"Oh, well you'll just have to tell me all about him. I admire his work *sooo* much."

Annie was tiring of this game. "Yes. Maybe we could do lunch sometime."

The smoke and the noise, not to mention Lisa's pretentiousness, were getting to be too much. If there was a kidnapper in the room, Annie decided, this was not the way to find out. She excused herself and pushed her way through the crowd to the terrace. Outside it was crowded as well, but at least she could breathe. She stared, almost mesmerized, out at the calm water and the boats moored in the marina, suddenly realizing how exhausted she was. The sun was getting lower in the sky.

Annie felt a hand on the back of her neck, and she jumped. "Everything okay?" David Courtney asked, casually rubbing the back of her neck. "I thought I might see you down at the boat dock today."

She looked up to see his sparkling blue eyes and lopsided smile. His voice brought a tone of serenity to the confusion in her mind.

"One of the guests has a problem that Russ wanted my help with. I wish I could talk about it, but I can't."

"Under control now?"

"As under control as it can be, I guess. At least for the time being."

He moved behind her and started massaging her neck and shoulders with both of his large, calloused hands. "You're all tense and knotted up. Not good. Let me know if this hurts."

"Oh, no," Annie sighed, "it feels wonderful. Don't stop."

His strong fingers dug deeper into her shoulder muscles.

"There, that's enough for now. I'm afraid it's time to go."

"You have to leave?" Annie asked, hoping the disappointment in her voice wasn't too apparent.

"No, *we* do. We have just enough time to get up to Mount Constitution for the sunset. Sound good?" She glanced at her watch. It was just before eight o'clock. This far north in July, the sun wouldn't begin to sink below the horizon until nine. Annie agreed without stopping to think about it, forgetting how tired she was.

"It'll get chilly. Do you have a sweater?"

"Yes."

"Good. I've got everything else."

David escorted Annie to his vehicle, a battered old VW van with peeling paint and kayak racks on top.

"Don't laugh! This van is tougher than it looks. I drove it all the way to Peru and back one spring. I take the fact that we both got back alive and more or less in one piece to be a lucky omen."

"South America? What were you doing there?"

"Oh, this and that." He didn't elaborate.

Annie could feel her tension dissolving even before they reached the other side of the island. They drove past lush fields full of grazing, black-faced sheep. The tall grass in the pastures, shimmering with moisture, was the brilliant green color of new growth. Along the way, they drove through trees so dense they formed a tunnel of branches over the road.

"Mount Constitution is the highest point in the San Juans," David explained. "It's so clear tonight the view should be spectacular."

The road switch-backed higher and higher till they reached the summit. David was right about the sweater. A cold breeze whistled across the top of the peak. He fetched a knapsack out of the back of the van, and pointed Annie towards a stone lookout tower. From the tower's vantage point they could see in all directions. The deep blue ridges of the islands looked more like a Japanese silkscreen than reality. Annie was entranced.

David could identify all the different ridges, each streak of violet-blue a different island. To the south were Blakely and Lopez. Cypress was southeast. Looking east they could see Lummi Island, with the mainland rising behind it. The tiny islands of Matia and Sucia lay north and northeast, and David said that the lights of Victoria would be visible once it got dark. They descended from the tower and found a spot to sit that was somewhat sheltered from the wind.

"How many islands are there? Annie asked. "Why are you laughing?"

"At high tide or low tide? Do you mean islands with names, or all the chunks of land that stick up out of the water? Depending on what you define as an island, there could be as many as seven hundred and fifty—that's counting all the rocks and reefs. About one hundred and seventy have names, but only a dozen or so are big enough to be worth anything. Have any more difficult questions?"

"Tell me about Orcas Island. It's named after the killer whale, right?"

"Actually, no. It was named for an eighteenth century viceroy of Mexico. Purely a coincidence that the whale frequents these parts. Let's see, this is the largest island, about sixty square miles. Right now we're about a half mile above sea level. This was a favorite spot for bootleggers during Prohibition . . .

"Oh, listen to me prattle on. I can't stop teaching, even when class is over."

"Have you always been a teacher? What did you do before you got this job?"

She saw him stiffen. He said nothing. It was odd—he acted as if he hadn't heard her. She decided to drop the question.

David set his knapsack in front of him and opened the top. "I hope you like Cabernet Sauvignon. This is a 'seventy-eight, I've been saving it for just the right occasion." He pulled more items out of the knapsack one by one. "Glasses, french bread, some gruyere, grapes . . . now all we need for perfection is the sunset."

"You planned all this! What if you hadn't found me? What if I hadn't wanted to come?"

"I figured Russ would have convinced you to come to his little cocktail party, so I was pretty sure I'd find you. I hoped you'd come, but I wasn't sure."

He pulled a Swiss army knife out of his pocket and deftly withdrew the corkscrew. "Cross your fingers," he said as he poured them each a glass. "Rocking around in the hold of a boat isn't the best place to store wine."

"You live on a boat?"

He nodded. "The *Electra*. She's a beauty, too. Built in England in nineteen thirty-eight, all wood. I bought her in San Francisco from a couple that had never even sailed her out of the Bay, can you imagine? She was designed to be an ocean-going vessel. I've been restoring her, and I've finally gotten her ready for the high seas again."

"Where will you sail her?"

"Around the world, I hope. She's fit for it. I just hope I am."

"Will you go by yourself?"

"Probably not. I'm not out to get in any record books or achieve feats of derring-do. I can manage her myself, but I prefer having a hand along. It's easy enough to pick up an able body willing to crew from port to port. I've done it myself more times than I can count."

"When will you be leaving?"

"Soon, if all goes as expected. Only a few more details to take care of, then I'll be ready to get out of here."

Annie felt an unexpected twinge of regret. She hardly knew this man, but already felt she would miss his company.

To change the subject, she told him of her own experience with the ocean. Ever since she was old enough to walk, Annie had spent pleasant summers growing up with her grandfather, Andrew Mac-Pherson, on his sailboat, the *Galloway*. As a young man, Andrew MacPherson had moved from his native Edinburgh to Ventura, California, where he ran a small jewelry and clock shop. But his love was the sea, and each summer he and his freckle-faced grand-daughter would set sail to explore the Channel Islands.

She didn't mention that the reason she was packed off every summer to her grandfather had to do with the bitter power struggle between her divorced parents. She also didn't talk about that painful summer when she was fifteen, and decided to move to

Seattle to live with her father. It was the first summer she hadn't spent with Andrew. He died that June.

As David and Annie feasted on bread and cheese and finished the bottle of wine, she found herself opening up to him, telling him stories from her childhood that she hadn't thought about in years. She described how as a toddler, she learned to walk on sand. As a young tomboy she spent long days fishing, swimming, scrambling over rocks to tide pools. She was soon strong enough to help rig the sails, and they'd take her grandfather's graceful sailboat out to explore, often seeing the fins of sand sharks cutting the water. Her favorite times were when the schools of black and white porpoises would come to play in the bow wake. Her pale freckled skin was always sunburned and peeling, and her curly mane of red hair lightened in the sun to a burnished coppery gold. The more she talked, the more he asked questions, at the same time revealing nothing about himself.

They sat for a few minutes saying nothing, just absorbing the view. Up above their heads cumulus clouds were changing shape in the breeze. They watched, mesmerized for awhile, at the patterns slowly evolving across the sky.

The sun was almost at the horizon, and the blue of the sky was starting to deepen in color. The clouds above and behind them became tipped with pale pink, turning to coral. Gradually they became surrounded in every direction with a dome of rose-colored clouds. The blue had turned to purple, and the sun was half swallowed by the horizon, creating orange streaks on the water. Annie spotted the almost full moon emerging at their backs. The sky was now alive with color in every direction. Just when she thought it was at its peak, more colors would appear. Bright orange and red formed blazing ripples across the sky. The sun itself had turned into a fluorescent disk of bright light, only a sliver on the horizon, slowly sinking. David told her to watch for the flash of green that was supposed to appear right as the sun goes into the water. She couldn't be sure if she saw it, or if the light was merely playing tricks on her eyes.

After the sun had completely disappeared, the purple background continued to deepen. The trees and rocks were losing their color. It was the time of evening that the whole landscape began to make the transition from a world of color to the realm of monochrome shadow. They could see the first evening stars appear. David explained that twilight was long this time of year. And even then, the night sky would be illuminated by the almost full moon.

Neither had any desire to move, but it was getting chillier as a bit of breeze picked up. David put his arm around Annie's shoulder and drew her close. She lifted her face up to his and they kissed, gently at first, then harder. He eased away, then lightly kissed her neck and stroked her hair. She snuggled close to him for warmth.

"Are you cold?" he asked softly.

"Mmm. A little. I don't want to leave."

"I know."

She rested her head on his shoulder. "I'm relaxed now. Freezing to death, but relaxed."

"Freezing to death? That won't do." He tousled her hair. "Come on, before I have a dead body on my hands." He held her hand as they walked back to the van.

They drove back to the resort in comfortable silence, the heater in the van making odd noises but keeping them comfortably toasty. As they were pulling up in front of the Windsor, Annie tried to make up her mind what she wanted from him, whether to ask him in. David decided for her.

"I have to go," he said so abruptly that Annie was startled. "There's something I have to do."

She started to ask what it was, but something in his expression stopped her.

"See you, then," was all he said.

"Thanks for everything . . . " Her voice trailed off. Annie got out of the van, confused by his rapid mood change and walked slowly to the door of the resort. She could hear the raspy engine of the van revving up to drive away.

Chapter 7

HER BODY TENSED, suddenly awake. Daisy strained to listen, unsure whether she'd really been disturbed by a sound, or had only imagined it. It was her first night completely alone on the empty island and she was scared out of her mind. That guy, Courtney, had said it would be safe, but that didn't make the fear go away. She tried consciously to stop her heart from pounding, to think this through rationally. There was no way she could be in danger, she told herself. The island was isolated, accessible only by water. And even then, most boats couldn't make it past the kelp beds and submerged rocks. And who would climb up that damned cliff face? That was the reason they had chosen this place.

The air outside was silent, a striking contrast to the twenty-four-hour city noises she was accustomed to. If there had been a sound it had stopped. Maybe she'd imagined it all along.

How many years had it been since she had slept in a sleeping bag? It brought back memories of being a teenager, sleeping over at Dee's or Stephanie's, giggling in the dark. Daisy shuddered. No, she willed herself not to think about Dee. She could never let herself think about Dee late at night. It always brought back that night ten years ago. But that was in the past, over and done with. Hadn't the jury said that Dee's death wasn't Daisy's fault?

She was just kidding herself. The jury only found in her favor because there hadn't been any *proof* that she'd been drinking that night when she crashed the red convertible. Just because the jury said it was an accident didn't make it true. She felt her knee begin to throb. No matter how hard she tried to forget, the scar was a constant physical reminder of that dreadful night.

Suddenly, as if she were there, she could picture them all sitting in the courtroom. There in the front row were Dee's father and her brother, Bud. Daisy shifted uncomfortably in the sleeping bag, but the pain still stabbed through her leg. Bud, twenty-one, home from college that week. The only person in the world, besides Daisy, who knew the truth. Wasn't he guilty as well? After all, he bought the booze. He had sat and watched her drink the fifth of bourbon practically by herself, then get behind the wheel of his sister's car. But in the courtroom he had seemed so righteous. She could still feel those glassy green eyes of his boring into her, the way they had day after day in the courtroom, registering her lies. Condemning her.

"Stop, stop," she whimpered. All she wanted was a few hours' sleep, but her ghosts wouldn't leave her alone.

Wait, she heard the noise again. Was it a footstep or not? It was so faint. She didn't think she'd been dreaming, didn't think she'd been asleep at all. It was probably just the scrabbling of a small animal. Courtney had warned her to keep her food up high, away from the raccoons. He said there were deer on the island as well, but they were shy, and wouldn't come too close. Those noises she heard must be a raccoon, that had to be it.

She had felt so secure before it got dark. The bluff was high enough that the tent couldn't be observed from the beach below, while she had an unobstructed panoramic view. During the day, she could watch and make sure no one was approaching. And if they did, that's why she had the gun. She'd never shot a gun before, but it couldn't be that hard, right?

The problem was, she'd forgotten all about the gun while Marc helped her set up camp. The damned thing wasn't even loaded, and she wasn't sure where she'd put the bullets. That was assuming she could remember how to load it.

She tried desperately to keep her mind off the night noises. She was starting to believe, with the kind of logic that only applies in the middle of the night, that she was indeed hearing the sound of human footsteps. She could picture someone slowly circling the tent. Try as she might, she couldn't get this vision out of her head.

Suddenly she heard it again, that very faint crackling sound, like twigs breaking. This time she knew she hadn't imagined it. And it was no animal. She held her breath, summoning all her will not to make a sound.

She was immobilized in her sleeping bag, too frightened to decide what to do. She held herself completely rigid, as if pretending not to be there would make a difference. Her vision of a stalking attacker was starting to become gruesome with details. Didn't she recall stories of women campers being attacked, killed in cold blood in their sleep?

But this was all absurd. Her hiding place could only be reached by water, and she hadn't heard a boat. She might have been asleep, of course, but she was always a light sleeper, and especially so tonight. She would certainly have been disturbed by the noise of an outboard, wouldn't she?

No one knew where she was, except Marc. But he wasn't supposed to come back until Wednesday night. It was still only Monday.

She strained to listen. It had to be Marc. She almost called out his name. But if it was Marc, why was he creeping like that? Now she thought she could perceive a shape, large and dark, moving outside the tent. Perhaps if she could find her knife.

She couldn't bear it anymore. Now the silence itself was excruciating. Something, someone was out there, waiting. She wanted to scream, but knew that there was no one within miles to hear. She would never be able to go back to sleep unless she knew for certain she'd been mistaken, that it was nothing. She had to look outside, to find out, but no amount of will could make her reach for her flashlight.

If it was only an animal, a noise or movement would surely startle it. Was that good or bad? She had to bite her tongue to keep from crying out. This time, Daisy needed someone to give her orders for a change, tell her what to do.

The footsteps started again. They had to be footsteps, they couldn't be anything else. By the light of the nearly full moon, she thought she could detect the shape of a person, directly in front of the tent. Suddenly, sharply, slicing through the silence like a meat cleaver, she heard her name.

She froze. The barely detectable shadow outside the tent was motionless as well.

She heard her name again, this time spoken with urgency. "I've got to talk to you, come out here right away," it said.

"Who is it? Who's there? Marc? Is that you?" She slid out of her sleeping bag, shaking with cold and fear as she pulled on her sweatshirt. She found her flashlight, but the beam was dim and flickering. Her hand fell upon the brand new folding knife in the corner of the tent. She fumbled with it, and pulled open the blade.

As she pulled back the flap of the tent and pushed aside the rain fly, a high powered flashlight shone directly in her face, blinding her.

"What's going on? Marc?" She was crying now, almost shrieking. She tripped over the edge of the tent as she tried to stand, shivering, and dropped her flashlight. She had skinned her knee on a rock, but hardly noticed the stinging pain. As she rose, she began flailing wildly with the knife.

The dark form made no reply, but whoever it was kept the light shining directly in her eyes. Blinded by the high-powered beam, she didn't see the gun being raised. Death was instantaneous. She saw and felt nothing as the bullet passed between her tiny breasts, piercing her heart.

Chapter 8

TUESDAY MORNING, JULY 24

ANNIE WAS WRENCHED OUT of a sound sleep by the harsh ringing of the phone. Disoriented in the strange room, she fumbled for the light. The luminous dial of the clock said 6 A.M.

"What?" she groaned into the phone. Anyone who had the nerve to telephone at 6 A.M. didn't deserve the courtesy of a hello.

"Annie, it's Russ. Listen, I'm really sorry to wake you, but it's an emergency. Can you come down to my office right away?"

The tone of his voice brought her instantly awake. She knew this was serious. "What is it? What's wrong?"

Russ was so upset he could hardly speak. "I'll tell you more when you get down here. It's . . . it's bad. A woman on the beach this morning . . . a dead body . . . murdered . . . Please, get down here as soon as you can." He hung up the phone without waiting for a reply.

Annie threw on some clothes. After a whole day had passed with no further contact from any "kidnappers," Annie had started to agree with the Sheriff's office that the whole thing had been some kind of prank. Apparently they had all been dead wrong.

When she got to Russ's office, she found him speaking to a plain-clothes law enforcement officer who looked vaguely familiar. Russ started to introduce homicide detective John Dexter from the San Juan County Sheriff's office.

"Don't bother, Mr. Perkins," the officer said. "We've met. Good to see you again, counselor."

Annie suddenly remembered John Dexter. She'd represented him regarding a shooting when he was on the Seattle police force, getting him cleared of all charges of excessive force. No wonder he remembered her. "Dex. Good to see you again." She looked around. "Where's Forrestor? Hasn't he been told?"

Dexter looked blank. Russ said, "Forrestor? Why should he . . . ? Oh, my God, Annie, did you think it was Marguerite?"

"Will someone tell me what's going on here?" Annie asked, totally confused. "You said a woman on the beach." It was too early in the morning for fragmented conversations.

Russ was barely coherent, he was so shaken up. "No, no. A woman on the beach found the body in one of the cottages," Russ said. "Her dog went to sniff at the door . . . "

"You mean this has nothing to do with Marguerite Boulanger's disappearance?"

"I'm afraid we don't know yet," said Dexter. "All we know at this point is that the homicide victim is a male Caucasian, twenty-five to thirty years old. Approximately six feet, four inches, two hundred thirty pounds, muscular build, black hair. As yet, we haven't established an identity."

"How . . . you said it was homicide . . . are you sure?"

"There's no question. The victim died of a gunshot wound to the brain. There was no gun found at the scene. The bullet entered between and slightly above the eyes, exiting through the back of the skull. No obvious signs of a struggle. We won't know more until the coroner arrives. He's on his way."

"Where did this happen?"

"Cottage Number Five," Russ said. "It's the farthest one from the main building, very isolated. It would be almost impossible for someone to be seen going or coming from there."

"Any sign of a break-in?"

Dexter looked displeased. "We didn't see any signs of forced entry. But Mr. Perkins tells me those cottages are quite old, that it wouldn't be that difficult to force open a window."

"Russ, is this true?" Annie asked, aghast. Nicholas Forrestor's threats to sue on the basis of inadequate security suddenly came to mind. "If the cottages were that easy to break into, and you knew about it, the resort could be in big trouble on this."

"I wish I could deny it, Annie. But I can't. I wrote a memo to Curtis Lymon about the situation just last month."

"Oh, boy. This is all we need right now. Dex, I don't want to ask any special favors, but I'm going to have to be kept apprised of the investigation. We already have one potential lawsuit, and if this death is linked to the resort's negligence, it could mean ruin."

"Hey, I've got no problem with that, as long as you don't impede the investigation. And knowing you, I know that won't be a problem. I think this may be Dr. Patterson now." A small man in corduroy trousers and a red flannel shirt was hurrying down the hall towards the office. He had intense black eyes and a neatly trimmed gray beard that made him resemble pictures of Sigmund Freud.

"Dex, you've done it again. You know you're interrupting my fishing trip, don't you? Well, let's get started before the body gets too cold, shall we?" The sharp black eyes sparkled. Annie suspected that in truth, the coroner enjoyed his job.

"Would it be all right if I come along? I'd like to take a look at the doors and windows," Annie asked.

"I've got no problem with that," Dex replied. "How about you, Doc?"

The coroner shrugged his shoulders. "Well, as long as you don't get in anyone's way, I can't see why not. Now then, let's get on with it."

There were no flashing lights, no bullhorns to control the crowd. There was, in fact, no crowd. Only two sheriff's officers in tan uniforms, one guarding each entrance to the beach cottage.

As they drew closer, Annie wondered if she really wanted to do this. She had never in her life viewed a fresh murder scene. Prosecutors were given photographs, autopsy reports, all after the fact. . . . Her stomach told her she didn't want to go.

She noticed the smell when they were still ten feet from the door. She had always heard that once you had experienced the odor of decaying flesh, you would never forget it. She knew she wouldn't.

Dr. Patterson entered the cottage, followed by Detective Dexter and a uniformed officer with a camera. He left the door open behind him to let in more air. When Annie stepped up to examine the doorframe, she was able to see into the room. Curious, she couldn't help watching.

Dr. Patterson put on surgical gloves. In addition to the full impact of the stench, they were immediately aware of the intense heat in the room. It must have been 85 degrees. The officer located the thermostat. It was turned up to full heat.

"Now what d'ya make of that? In the middle of summer." The officer flashed a picture of the thermostat. "Okay if I turn it down now, Doc?"

"Hold on," he replied. "Don't touch anything yet." He handed Dexter a pair of surgical gloves. "Take care of it will you, Dex? We ought to leave something for the fingerprint boys to do, hm? But we also have to be able to work in here. Let's get these doors and windows open so we can breathe. Get pictures, and make a note before you open them if they were locked."

While the men worked, Annie stood just outside the door and observed, careful to stay out of the way. The sight of the body was less shocking than she would have imagined, once she grew accustomed to the smell. It lay in the middle of the small living room, taking up most of the floor space. The man was lying on his back, wearing gray sweat pants and nothing else. Open, glassy eyes stared up at the ceiling. Annie thought about the old wives' tale that the eyes of a victim retained the mirrored image of the killer. If that were true, there would be no unsolved murders.

Above the staring brown eyes was a neat round hole. Except for a small puddle on the floor underneath the head, there was very little blood. "Take this down, please," Dr. Patterson said. The officer withdrew a pen and notepad. "I am supposing, from the appearance of the wound, that we are dealing with a thirty-eight caliber revolver, possibly a forty-five, quite powerful. The gun was fired from a distance of at least eighteen inches to a maximum of four feet." They moved closer, and looked at the wound through a small magnifying glass. "There does not appear to be any burning around the entrance wound that would indicate a shot fired from closer than eighteen inches. At the same time, there isn't the jaggedness that would indicate farther than four, possibly five feet." He glanced around. "No apparent blood spatter on the walls, but there is a slight amount of blood on the front of his chest. This is consistent with death by head wound."

"Yo, here's the shell, Doc! You're right. It looks like a thirty-eight." Detective Dexter was peering at the wall behind the victim's head. "Right where it ought to be. That's a change." The officer moved in to take pictures.

"Don't get lazy, Dex, I want to know if there was more than one shot fired." Dr. Patterson said over his shoulder as he finished placing bags on the hands. "No grossly apparent gunpowder residue on the hands."

"How long do you think he's been dead, Doc?" Dexter asked.

"Hard to say, given the high heat in the room. That will undoubtedly distort the calculations. My guess at this point, given the state of decomposition, is that he's been dead about a day. Could be less, could be more."

"This could be helpful." Detective Dexter was examining a Windsor Resort notepad on the counter between the kitchen and living room. "The top sheet's torn off, but I think I can see some indentations."

"The lab boys love those," the doctor commented. "They should be able to recreate what the top sheet of paper said."

"Well," said Dex, "it looks like we can rule out burglary."

"How can you tell?" Annie asked.

"The place isn't torn up," Dex explained. "I've been a cop fifteen years, probably seen hundreds of burglaries. In every one, all the drawers were pulled out and tipped over, cupboards were open with stuff pulled onto the floor. Burglars are not neat people."

He stepped outside and looked at the doorframe with her. The wood was old and warped in places. The window frames were the same. "No signs of forced entry. My first guess would be that the victim let the murderer in, or the killer used a key. But Russ is right. A place this old, you probably could force the door or a window without necessarily leaving any evidence."

Annie looked back inside the room. The officer was taking several pictures of an end table, containing an ashtray full of the filter tips of several thin brown cigarettes, and a gold lighter. Dr. Patterson was standing and staring at the corpse. "Doesn't it strike you as odd, Dex, that there's no apparent sign of struggle? I don't see any scratches or bruises, no furniture out of place. Yet this was a big man, a very strong man. Look at those muscles. Would this man have let a stranger or an enemy enter his room, threaten him, and just stand there to be shot? I don't think so, he would have fought back. Was he having a normal conversation with someone, who quite suddenly pulled a gun and fired? Or was he taken completely off guard, taken by surprise? He wasn't ambushed from behind. Ah, such difficult questions, but that is for you to find out, Dex. Me, I am just a simple medical man. With any luck, the victim's body will tell me *how* he was killed, perhaps it will tell me *when*. But what it will not tell me, is *why*."

Annie left the cottage having seen more than enough. Murder is always tragic, but for her own sake, she was worried by the fact that the violent crime had happened in the most isolated, least secure area of the Windsor property. No doubt when Forrestor heard about this incident, he'd somehow manage to use the information in his claim for damages against the resort.

And was there a connection? Crime wasn't unheard of in the islands, but surely two such bizarre events had to be related. Maybe Marguerite Boulanger had been held in the cottage, but somehow managed to get hold of a gun, kill her captor and escape. No, that didn't seem right. Surely she would have shown up by now, or at least sent word to Nicholas. Had Nicholas discovered the kidnapper and taken his revenge? Annie admitted this was all just wild speculation. None of the scenarios seemed to fit. Not content simply to sit back and wait for the sheriff's department to unravel the clues, Annie headed for the main building.

She was pleased to see Nathan Komatsu working the desk, his nose buried in an organic chemistry text book. If anyone could remember specifics about the guests, it was probably Nathan.

"Annie, Russ told me what happened to the guy in Cottage Five. Did you really see the body?"

She nodded. "Not pretty. Listen. I need to know who our man in Number Five was. Do you have his registration card?"

"Sure." He thumbed through a file and pulled out a handwritten index card and a computer-printed invoice for the guest in Cottage Five. "Here you go. His name was Mark Jones, address New York City, Hertz rental car. He checked in on Wednesday, July eighteenth."

That was one day before Annie had arrived. She wrote down the information in a small notebook. "Hand me the phone, will you?"

Annie quickly punched in her long distance credit card number, then dialed the number listed on the registration as Jones's home phone. When a New York pizza parlor answered, she apologized and hung up. She dialed again, this time information for New York. "Yes, the number for Mark Jones, on West Seventy-Sixth, please." She dialed the number that matched the address, and a man who sounded about a hundred answered. She asked for Mark Jones.

"Speaking," the man wheezed.

"Uh, maybe there's been a mistake. Do you have a son named Mark Jones?"

"No, just me and my cat. He's named Alfred, though."

She thanked him and hung up.

The next call she made was to Hertz Rent-a-Car at Sea-Tac airport. Annie used what she hoped was a passable New York accent.

"So sorry to bother you, but my name is Mrs. Mark Jones. My husband and I rented a car from you a while back. Well, it seems my husband has lost his Visa card, and we're trying to figure out when he last had it. Could you possibly check and see if he used his Visa when he picked up the rental car? Yes, that's Mark Jones, from New York." A pause. "No record of it at all? Are you sure? Yes, thank you very much."

Well, she thought, our Mr. Mark Jones wasn't a very truthful individual, registering under a false name and address. She looked at the invoice.

"You don't have a credit card number on here."

"No, see that box there?" Nathan pointed. "He paid cash in advance for a week. We hardly ever see that."

"Nathan, do you recall anything at all about this man? Anything unusual?"

"Let me see," Nathan replied. "I remember him checking in—mainly because of the cash. That was strange. He was real good-looking, a body-builder type. He was by himself, which was also pretty unusual for the beach cottages. They're a favorite with couples. His reservation showed that he'd specifically requested Number Five. He seemed kind of nervous, kept glancing around. Then after I gave him his key, he said, sort of jovially, 'Hope the fishing's good. I'm going to spend all my time fishing.' "

"Hm, nothing strange about that around here."

"It seemed strange for him. He had these fancy clothes on—a white linen jacket, open shirt collar. I pegged him as a real East Coast type. He didn't look like he'd know which was the business end of a fishing pole, if you ask me."

"How many keys did you give him?"

"Just one. The other one should still be right here." He looked on the hooks under the desk. "Yeah, it's here."

"How accessible are these keys?"

"You mean, could someone have taken it, used it, then returned it? I guess it's possible. Not very likely, but it could have been done."

"Is there anything else you can remember about him? Were there any phone calls for him, messages?"

"Yeah, now that you mention it, there was something. He had a phone message. I can't remember what it said, but I recall giving it to him Thursday afternoon."

Suddenly Annie remembered the scene. She was checking in behind Lisa Hargraves when Nathan handed a Mr. Jones his message. The same Mr. Jones she'd just seen lying on the floor of the cottage. Annie thought about the encounter. Lisa had acted like she recognized the man. Annie asked Nathan for Lisa Hargraves' room number.

It was risky going to Lisa's room at ten in the morning. There was a good possibility Lisa might still be in bed, and an even better possibility that she wouldn't be alone. But Annie was spared any unpleasant introductions when she discovered the maid in the process of cleaning Room 204.

"I take it Miss Hargraves isn't in?" Annie stuck her head in the door, taking note of a pair of champagne glasses on the dresser and two empty bottles in the wastebasket. There was a pair of high heeled sandals on top of the television, and next to the bed a bottle of nail polish remover and an assortment of colored varnishes. Black lingerie lay in heaps on the floor. A man's tie was draped over the bathroom doorknob.

The maid, not more than eighteen, had waist length white-blonde hair that she kept pushing behind her ears to keep it out of her face. Still obsessed with visions of Marguerite, Annie couldn't help noticing how much the young girl resembled the earliest photograph, the snapshot of Marguerite leaning on the back of a car. The maid's uniform, navy blue and white polyester, probably the smallest in stock, hung loosely on her tiny frame. The girl jumped when she heard Annie's voice. "Hey, I didn't touch the stuff. Honest. It was like that when I came in here."

"What are you talking about?"

The girl looked around guiltily. "Nothin.' I'm not talkin'. . . . Who are you?"

"My name's Annie MacPherson."

"Oh, I heard of you. You're the lady Mr. Perkins was showing around, huh? Too bad the old guy's dead. I met him once or twice. He was nice to me. Is the new owner gonna sell the place?"

"It's a good possibility. How did you know who I was?"

"Oh, we talk. The staff knows everything around here. None of us are gonna get fired, are we?"

"Not that I'm aware of. Mr. Perkins will be running things as usual. But what did you mean about touching something?"

"Her stash. The lady left her coke out in plain sight, right there on the bathroom counter. Plain as day. But it's all there. I just kinda cleaned around it, you know? I don't wanna get in trouble here."

"That's okay. You're not in any trouble."

"Good, 'cause I sure need this job, such as it is. Can you believe this room? I hate it, let me tell you. It's been like this every day. Clothes strewn all around, empty bottles, dirty glasses. This is better than yesterday, though, when the champagne glasses were *broken*. She didn't even bother to pick up the glass! And will she leave a tip? No. I work my tail off to clean up after 'em and never so much as a thank-you dollar bill." Annie reminded herself to leave the maid a tip, something she usually forgot.

"Tell me, did you see who Miss Hargraves brought to her room?"

"Maybe." She looked Annie up and down. "But I'm pretty busy here. I really should be getting back to work. That's what they pay me for."

"I could pay you for your time. How about ten dollars for ten minutes?" The girl's eyes brightened.

"Well, I don't know that it means much, but I can tell you who she was sleeping with." The girl was direct.

"All right."

The girl nodded Annie inside the room and hung the DO NOT DISTURB sign on the door. "I gotta be quick, or the head housekeeper will have my ass." She glanced around suspiciously. "My name's Sue, by the way. Just in case I get in deep with the housekeeper, maybe you could put in a good word, huh?" Annie agreed.

"Two days in a row, it's been the same guy. The first time, yesterday morning, I, uh, really interrupted something. But they were so hard at it, they didn't even hear me open the door."

Annie didn't press, but she was hoping the girl would reveal that Lisa had been spending time with the dark man from the cottage. She was disappointed.

"The guy was real skinny, not as tan as the lady but pretty tan, and sort of light brown hair. I think he used some kind of goop on it, 'cause there was always junk on the pillow case. It's been the same guy the last two nights, I'm sure, 'cause of the goop on the pillow case every morning. We're usually not supposed to change 'em that often, but I had to. It was gross. Well, anyway, they seemed to be pretty friendly."

Annie filed the information away, but didn't feel it was very useful.

"This morning I saw him leaving the room, all disheveled. Same guy. He was wearing a suit that was really ugly. Flashy, you know? And he forgot his tie." She pointed to a purple monstrosity hanging on the doorknob. Annie knew instantly it had to be Roger, the clothing store king, the one who had been fawning over Lisa in the bar Monday night. That put Lisa and Roger together Sunday and Monday night, with no apparent connection to the man in Cottage Number Five.

Annie felt like she was getting nowhere in a hurry.

She tried one more angle. "Did you ever clean the cottages? I'm particularly interested in Number Five."

"Huh uh. That would've been Renalda. She's here today, I think. Do you want to talk to her? I bet I could fix it."

"Yes, that would be helpful." Annie didn't think the maid had anything else to offer. She pulled a ten dollar bill out of her wallet. "You won't tell anybody we talked, okay?"

"Not a soul. Wow, not bad for my mid-morning break, huh? I'll tell Renalda." She quickly stuffed the bill in the pocket of her oversized uniform. "When do you want to talk to her?"

"Whatever's convenient for her. Have her leave me a note at the front desk if she'll talk to me."

"Hey, you know, if you still wanna talk to that Hargraves lady, you might try either the pool or the hot tub. She was leaving in her bathing suit when I come up here," Sue added.

Annie left the girl to her vacuuming, and headed for the pool. She could smell the coconut oil as she approached. No question about it, Lisa was stunning in a bikini. If that was all it took to be a successful actress, Lisa was well on her way to a brilliant career. Her large silver earrings glistened brightly in the sun. She appeared for all the world to be unconscious. This morning her nails were painted a frosty peach that set off her tan.

"I think you might have better luck indoors in the tanning booth," Annie commented. "It's pretty hard to get a decent tan at this latitude, especially this early in the morning." Annie settled herself on the next chaise lounge, and casually flipped through a magazine.

Lisa lazily opened one eye, and perked up when she saw who it was. "It's Annie, right? Say, you ran off the other night before I had a chance to talk to you about your father, uncle, whoever, that's the producer."

"Stepfather." Annie decided to lie a little. "He was telling me just the other day how he can't seem to find any new talent."

"Oh, he did, did he? Well, now . . . " The glint in Lisa's eye was that of a schemer. She moved her chaise a little closer to Annie's so they could talk.

"Isn't this weather something? They call it 'summer.' What a joke! I'm freezing. L.A. gets hotter than this in January. I'll hit the UVA later, but I've always felt that a natural tan looks so much more, well, natural. Besides, I'm addicted to lying in the sun. My ancestors must have been lizards."

"Not me," Annie replied. "Fifteen minutes without sunscreen and I'm the color of ripe watermelon."

"You're better off in the long run, or so they say. Still, I'm a slave to it. I'll die brown, wrinkled and happy. Hey listen, could you hand me my Perrier?" Annie placed the small green bottle in the oiled hand, and said in an offhand manner, "Say, did you hear about the excitement this morning? That gorgeous hunk in Cottage Five was found murdered."

Lisa choked as she was taking a sip, then quickly tried to regain her cool, like a cat who has just fallen off a table. "Oh, excuse me," she coughed again, "must've gone down the wrong way. I really shouldn't try to drink lying down like that. Did you say something? I don't think I heard."

Lisa's reaction told Annie more than she had been expecting to learn. She repeated the comment, and added innocently, "Did you know him?"

"No. Why do you ask?"

"Oh, no reason in particular. It's just that you looked like you recognized him. You know, in the lobby when he walked past."

"Oh. Uh, he did look like someone I know. Knew. A long time ago. A mistake, that's all."

Annie had never seen the woman so flustered. Lisa rummaged in her bag for a pack of cigarettes, then kept rooting around.

"Damn. You don't have a match, do you?"

An image of an end table in the cottage came to mind. "Why? Lost your lighter?"

Lisa threw down her bag. "What the hell is going on here? Why are you asking me all these questions? I didn't know him, okay? What more do you want? Leave me alone."

Annie realized she'd just about blown her chance to get anything out of Lisa. She decided to play the confidante role.

"Look," she said softly, pulling her chaise a little closer. "I'm not with the police. My interest in this is purely financial. I'm representing the resort's owner. The Windsor may have some major liability problems, and I'm just trying to protect my client's interests. The main thing I need to know is who this guy was. We both know you know something about him."

Lisa was paying close attention, but saying nothing. Annie leaned over and whispered, "I already know that you met him in his cottage." This was a stab in the dark. Annie was inferring a meeting, based on the presence of the gold lighter. It turned out to be a lucky guess. As she said it, Lisa's eyes widened.

"Now, I'm not saying I have any influence over my stepfather, but I'm sure some kind of introduction could be arranged. Very simple. You help me—as a friend. I help you—as a friend." She paused to let her words sink in. "Would you like to have a little talk?"

Lisa took a large breath and let it out slowly. "What the hell. Not here, though."

"Your room?"

Looking around, Lisa said, "No, the sauna's closer, we can go in there." The tall woman picked up her belongings and strode towards the building, without even looking to see if Annie was following.

The Swedish sauna was located just inside the women's changing area off the pool. Annie felt foolish and exposed as she stripped to enter the sauna with Lisa. She modestly grabbed a large white towel and wrapped it around herself to conceal her pale freckled skin. Lisa peeled off her bathing suit and didn't bother with a towel. Annie couldn't help but notice she had no tan lines. Once inside, Lisa extracted a large hairpin from her thick mane of hair and expertly inserted it into the hinge in the door.

"This is how I have private saunas when I travel. Never fails. Now, let's get serious. The man in Cottage Five was my husband."

Chapter 9

Now it was Annie's turn to choke. She certainly hadn't foreseen this.

"You have to believe me—I had nothing whatsoever to do with Marc's death." Lisa's posturing was gone. Perhaps she only put on her act around men. Or maybe she realized the seriousness of the situation.

"He was registered as 'Mark Jones.' Was that his name?" Annie asked.

Lisa shook her head. "No, his name is—was, I should say—Marc Jarrell. Not a very creative alias, was it? At least that was his name when I knew him. God only knows what name he was born with. Marc Jarrell was a stage name—he was an actor—but I seem to remember him telling me he had it legally changed at some point. Same as I did. I was born Mary Margaret Mulligan, if you can believe it." Lisa was nervous, and seemed to be having a tough time keeping her thoughts clear. Annie tried to steer her back to the issue at hand.

"You said 'when you knew him.' How long has it been?"

"Lord, how long? Almost two years ago this month was the last time I laid eyes on him. Until he turned up here, of course. I met him in New York, fell for his looks . . . God, what a hunk," Lisa sighed, a faraway look in her eyes. "No brains, but one hell of a body. And he knew how to use it, too. The boy had talent." Lisa paused, as if it were sinking in for the first time that Marc was dead. Her eyes grew cloudy, and Annie thought the statuesque brunette might cry. But Lisa pulled herself out of it and continued her story.

"My roommate introduced us. We were all in drama school together, working whatever jobs we could get during the day and going to class at night. Hoping for roles." Lisa stretched her long, tan legs out in front of her on the slatted bench. Sweat was starting to glisten on her wrists and forehead.

"Before I knew it, Marc had moved in. What a sucker I was. I just didn't realize the overwhelming appeal of my rent-controlled apartment in Manhattan. Marc was unemployed most of the time, and I supported him. I wasn't getting many roles, either, mind you, but I had a small income from a trust fund. Don't get me wrong, Marc contributed a great deal to the relationship. The sex was dynamite." Lisa stared straight ahead with a glazed look. She was either genuinely surprised and shaken by the news of Marc's death, or she was a much better actress than Annie gave her credit for.

"Please, go on," Annie encouraged.

"After we'd been together about six months, I turned thirty. Listen," she turned to face Annie, "I've never told my age in public. You will keep this confidential, won't you? I can trust you on that?"

Annie nodded silently. Lisa's age was the last thing she was worried about revealing.

"At thirty, I gained access to the principal of my trust fund. The income up to that point had been fairly meager, so Marc really had no idea of the amount. But the total net worth of the trust is about two million."

No doubt the surprise on Annie's face was apparent.

"I know it sounds like a lot, but it's all tied up in long term investments," Lisa explained. "Anyway, when Marc heard about it he went bonkers, constantly asking questions about the money, how *we* were going to spend it. It wasn't long at all before he started pressuring me to marry him."

"Go on."

"I was sure I had explained the provisions of the trust to him, but as it turned out, he hadn't understood. Not surprising, given the fact that Marc had the brain power of a forty watt light bulb. He somehow got the impression that the trust dissolved when I turned thirty. On the contrary, it's still very much in existence. That was just the point where I was allowed limited access to the principal, and freedom to direct the investments. All decisions still had to be approved by the trustee. As it was, I left the vast majority of the investments as they were and merely asked the trustee to increase my living allowance to a modest sixty thousand a year." Annie gulped. "Oh, I know it's not much," Lisa continued, "but I didn't want to be *too* comfortable, or I'd never be motivated to get my career off the ground."

"How did the terms of the trust affect Marc?"

"Very simple. Any man I marry, whether he's a golddigger or a royal prince, has no access to the money. Period. I was so certain Marc understood that."

"So Marc thought that by marrying you, he'd get his hands on the money, but in reality, it stayed the property of the trust?"

"Right. And the trustee retained ultimate control over the funds. The trust was set up by my grandfather. He was born in an era when men believed women couldn't handle money. He felt that the trust would prevent me from squandering it, but also protect me from exactly what happened—someone marrying me for my money. Pretty funny, huh? I guess Grandpa was smarter than I gave him credit for."

Annie tried to formulate another question, but her mind was groggy.

"Are you sweltering, poor thing?" Lisa asked, looking over at Annie's blanched face. "You look like you're about to keel over. We can find somewhere else to talk. Besides I'm dying for a cigarette." Annie had been so intrigued by the tale up to that point, she hadn't even realized how hot the sauna had become. When she stood up her head was spinning. Lisa grabbed her by the elbow to keep her from falling, and Annie was startled by the strength of the grip.

"Don't be embarrassed. I sauna every day." Lisa led Annie out into the chill air outside the sauna. The air felt like an arctic blast. "I forget that it takes a while to build up a tolerance to the heat." They each wrapped themselves in one of the thick white terry cloth robes

stacked in the dressing room for the guests to use, and Lisa grabbed
a foil-covered box of hotel matches from a dish. Annie sank down on
the dressing room bench and could feel her brain begin clear again as
her temperature returned to near normal. Lisa got them each a glass
of water from the water cooler in the corner. Her pompous gestures
and artificial tone were gone now. Annie thought she could even have
liked Lisa, if they'd met under different circumstances.

The dressing room was empty. Lisa sat down facing the closed
door to watch that no one came in. She found her cigarettes, lit the
last one from the pack and took a heavy drag. She automatically
inserted a new pack into the red leather cigarette case, and resumed
speaking in a lowered tone of voice. "This is still confidential, okay.
Besides all this horrible murder stuff, Marc was a negative part of
my past that I'd much rather forget, especially now that I'm starting
to make a name for myself. It's just the kind of story some scandal
rag would love to drag up and libel me with."

Annie was tempted to inform Lisa that a story isn't libelous
unless it's false, but held her tongue.

"Anyway, where was I? Oh, yeah. We got married, fast and
dirty, without a great deal of fuss." Lisa laughed cynically. "I was
such a damn fool. I enjoyed his company, and his sexual ability, and
had the unrealistic notion that we were actually 'in love'. I thought
there was a chance we could make a go of it."

The tall woman stood and began to pace, gesturing with her
cigarette. "I couldn't have been more wrong. It was only a matter of
weeks before Marc realized his mistake. He kept asking me when
we were going to open a joint checking account, things like that. I
finally sat him down with my lawyer and they had a nice little chat.
It took a while to penetrate his thick skull, but eventually he
understood." Lisa looked around for an ashtray to put out her
cigarette. Finding none, she walked over and threw it in the john,
flushing with her foot.

She continued. "As blindly in love (or lust) as I was, I didn't see
what was coming. The very next day, he was gone. So was a thousand in cash, my jewelry, my sable, my stereo equipment, and my
favorite cashmere sweater."

"A sweater?" Annie asked incredulously.

"It was for the little bitch he took with him. If she'd been my size, I'm sure he would have cleaned out my wardrobe completely. And after all we'd been through together . . . " Lisa laughed dryly. "That was the last I saw of my dear husband until he showed up here."

"Did you file charges, try to find him?"

"I wanted to, of course, I was absolutely livid. But the fact was, we were legally married. The police said that a husband taking personal effects from a shared residence technically wasn't theft. Besides, I hadn't a clue where to look for him."

"Lisa, I have to be frank with you, this doesn't sound good. You have to admit, to outside ears, it sounds like you had a pretty hefty motive for murder."

"Murder. Do you think I actually could've killed him, the big, sweet lug? For what? Making me feel like a fool? That's all it was really. The theft didn't matter. He didn't take any heirlooms or sentimental pieces, unless I were to get all weepy over the diamond wedding ring I gave him when I thought he actually cared for me. I had to face it—I was conned. Granted, it made me angry for awhile, but what could I do? My lawyer got me a quiet annulment and that was that. I just kept working, and now my career's finally going places. Marc is history. That sounds terrible, now that he's dead, but I mean it. I was over him. Hell, if being made to feel embarrassed were a motive for murder, we'd all be serving life sentences."

"Is that the *whole* story?" Annie asked pointedly. Lisa had been convincing, but something seemed to be missing. Annie felt as if the story she'd just heard was probably the truth, but not the entire truth.

"Honestly, that's all there is. Except of course, the Windsor Resort epilogue."

"What did you do after you saw Marc in the lobby?"

"I knew instantly it was him, that I hadn't made a mistake. I figured that overly perfect desk clerk wouldn't give me his room number, so I cornered a bellman and let him see a little cleavage. Works every time."

"So you went down to the cottage?"

"Late Friday night. Very late. And it was just the one time, I

swear it." Her eyes were large and brimming. Annie was sure it was
an actress' trick, but that didn't necessarily mean Lisa was lying.

Annie ran her mind back over the events of the past few days.
Marguerite had disappeared Sunday night. Marc had probably been
dead about a day when his body was found on Tuesday morning. If
Lisa had killed Marc, she probably hadn't done it on her Friday
night visit.

"Was he surprised to see you? Afraid, upset?"

"At first he was furious, but he calmed down after he found out I
wasn't going to blow his cover. I went in, we talked, had a drink.
We ended up making love. For old times' sake, I guess. One thing
just led to another."

"Did you stay the night?"

"No. After it was all over, we both just sort of laughed, admitted
we were fools, with nothing in common but great sex. I'd say I
wasn't there much more than an hour or two. I kissed him on the
cheek and left with the understanding that we'd amiably go our
separate ways. I didn't even give him another thought until you told
me he was dead."

There was a pause.

"I . . . I know it looks bad, but I didn't kill him. You do believe
me, don't you?"

Annie couldn't answer that question.

Having showered and changed in a hurry, Annie was still feeling
a bit drained by the sauna. Or maybe she was overwhelmed by the
incredible tale she had just been told. Lisa had seemed so sincere
while telling it, so upset by the news of Marc's death, that Annie
hadn't felt a glimmer of doubt at the time. But thinking back, she
wasn't sure. How much was Lisa acting? And there were fragments
of the conversation that were nagging her, some minute details that
was out of place. It was like one of those pictures in children's
magazines—"what's wrong with this picture?"

As Annie passed the front desk, Nathan handed her a folded piece
of paper with her name printed in large letters on the outside. Inside
was a short message written in a big, looping hand.

Dear Miss MacPherson—My name is Renalda Maria
Ruiz. My Friend Sue said you wanted to talk to me.
Sue said you were a nice Lady so it's O.K. to talk to
you so I will. I finish my work at four o'clock. Is that
fine to talk then because I can not miss work? If that is
O.K. you can find me in the laundry. P.S. Even tho Sue
told me about the tip you gave her, I am not intrested
in the money.

> *Your Friend,*
> *Renalda Maria Ruiz*

Anxious to talk to the girl, Annie glanced at her watch and saw that it was only two-thirty. An hour and a half until Renalda got off work. Just then her stomach emitted a petulant growl. No breakfast, no lunch, barely enough coffee to keep her mind functioning—this was not an intelligent way to operate.

In addition, Annie was feeling claustrophobic. She decided to get completely away from the Windsor to sit down, let her mind clear, and start sorting through the information she had gathered thus far. She stuck Renalda's note in her purse and headed for the parking lot.

There were several tiny communities scattered across Orcas Island, consisting of a hotel or restaurant, a store or two. All were linked, however, to the main community of Eastsound, located at the northern edge of the large bay which divided the island. Annie decided to see what the village had to offer in terms of lunch.

With a commercial district about four blocks square, it was far from a bustling metropolis. Entering town, Annie spotted two great blue herons lifting off from a gravelly beach near the side of the road. By standing on a single corner she could look around and see all of the major necessities—grocery store, bank, church, and marine hardware.

She parked the Fiat near a restaurant overlooking the water. A sign in the window advertised the world's best clam chowder. It probably wasn't true but it was worth a try. Annie entered and stood waiting to be seated. This late in the day there were several window tables available, a perfect place to let her mind wander.

But as her eyes finished roaming the room, Annie made a quick change of plans. Seated in a corner away from the window were Philip Spaulding, the political campaign manager, and Nicholas Forrestor, their heads bent together in a lively conversation. At one point Nicholas made a comment that caused Philip to chuckle. Nicholas smiled cynically and nodded.

Annie was able to beat a quick retreat before the hostess approached. She didn't want to join the two men, and doubted they would have wanted her to, but her appearance would have made the situation awkward. And sitting within earshot at a separate table wouldn't have been much better. She got back in the Fiat and headed out of town on the main road going east, not sure where she'd end up.

The route was the same one she and David had taken to Mount Constitution. The road hugged the curve of the water, intense blue on the right, tall virgin growth cedar on the left. Annie followed a sign to Olga, figuring if the place had a name, it must have food.

Annie parked the little red convertible in front of a rough-hewn log building. A sign in front had a painting of a leaping whale and indicated that the building housed a cafe and artists' co-op. Stepping inside the wooden building Annie was assaulted with the vibrant colors of hand-knitted sheep's wool garments displayed on the walls, and the warm aroma of fresh baked goods. A tape of dulcimer music played softly in the background. A woodstove in the middle of the large room divided the artists' display area from the cozy cafe. Hammered gold and silver jewelry glinted in a display case. Ceramics and charming hand-carved wooden toys graced a central table. Remembering that her law partner's son had a birthday coming up, she purchased a tiny carved wooden ferry boat. When an espresso machine near the kitchen caught Annie's eye, she knew she'd found the right place.

After ordering a cappucino and a veggie sandwich on nine-grain bread, she eyed the tempting pastry display, but decided to forego the ginger-brandy cheesecake. As she ate her sandwich, Annie tried to get her mind away from the confusing events of the last few days. It didn't work. Bits and pieces of information kept swirling in her head demanding attention.

"That sandwich looks fabulous—can I join you?"

"Ellen! Hi, please do." Annie looked up to see Russ's old schoolmate Ellen O'Neill taking off her bicycle helmet. The waitress came to take her order.

"Yeah, let's see. I'll start with a bowl of the clam chowder, then the veggie sandwich with extra cream cheese and avocado, and finish off with the blackberry pie a la mode for dessert."

"I'm jealous. Where do you put it all?" Annie laughed, looking at the marathon runner's wiry body.

"Running ten to fifteen miles a day—or riding fifty—uses up a helluva lot of calories! That's one reason I love exercising so much. I love to eat! Isn't this a fabulous place? I discovered it yesterday and had to come back."

Ellen's enthusiasm was contagious. Annie was in a better mood already. "Do you always have this much energy? Maybe I really should start jogging."

"You do look kind of tired. You must be pretty upset about that guy getting killed. Heavy stuff."

"News travels fast, doesn't it?"

"Oh, you can't keep something like this quiet. It's all over the resort."

"I'm really starting to feel it. You know, this is the first time in days I've let myself relax." She laughed. "You're the first person I've talked to recently that I wasn't suspicious of."

"I feel honored."

"Say, let me ask you. What can you tell me about this old classmate of yours?"

"Russ Perkins? Not a lot. He introduced himself when he saw my name on the guest register, and asked if I was the Ellen O'Neill from his class at Harvard Business School. His face was a little familiar. I'm sure we had one or two classes together, I think he was pretty quiet, but his name just doesn't ring a bell. I wanted to call him Bob, Bill . . . ? Heck, Bozo for all I know. Russell just didn't sound right."

"But you did go to school with him?"

"Yeah, I'm sure of that." Ellen set aside her empty sandwich plate and started in on her dessert. "Wait, now. I remember something. Maybe this was why he was so quiet. Right before he

started business school there'd been a death in his family. Or
someone close to him, I can't remember. But I know people said he
was really shaken up by it, maybe even suicidal. We kind of kept an
eye on him, because of that. Hmm. I guess he got over it. He looks
like he's doing fine now. Do they know who the guy was or why he
was murdered?"

"I've been able to find out who he was, but not much more than
that."

"Do they think it could have been random violence?"

"That would be the worst possible solution, from the resort's
point of view. It implies that the grounds and buildings weren't
secure. But my intuition tells me that's not the case. It looked too
much like a, well, an execution."

Ellen shuddered. "Well, the whole thing's pretty frightening, the
idea of a killer on the loose out there somewhere. But at the same
time, I find it morbidly fascinating, you know? I'm totally addicted
to those true crime books about psychopathic murderers—I've read
them all. In fact, I've just finished this one. Have you read it?" She
pulled a book out of her fanny pack.

"Oh, is that the new book about Timothy Baron?" Baron, a
medical student at the University of Washington, had been front
page news when he was convicted of murdering nine nurses. His
friends and family had been shocked to find out the truth about the
good-looking and studious "boy-next-door."

"It was really great, if you want to borrow it. Here." She forced
Annie to take it. "The amazing thing was that no one suspected. He
seemed so, so *normal*."

"I guess a lot of murderers do," Annie replied thoughtfully.

"Hey, this is the laundry room, no guests allowed in here, Miss,
you can send down laundry in a bag if you want."

A large woman in a white uniform was waddling toward the
swinging double doors with the protectiveness of a mother hen.

"It's okay, Consuela. This is the lady I told you might come. She
talked to Sue this morning. Are you Miss MacPherson?"

The younger woman was small and dark. She looked vulnerable
and frightened.

"Yes, I'm Annie MacPherson. Are you Renalda?" The girl indicated that she was. "Is there somewhere quiet we can talk? Just you and me?" The girl looked to Consuela as if for permission. The older woman seemed to understand. She showed them into a supply closet the size of a small room, lined with boxes and smelling strongly of detergent. Renalda looked worried, but the large woman smiled and gave her a motherly nudge. "You don't worry, *poquita*, no one comes in Consuela's laundry room. You talk."

"I was glad when Sue told me you wanted to talk." The girl spoke softly. Her voice was heavily accented, but her English was good. As she spoke, she nervously twisted the ring on her left hand. She appeared to be afraid, but not of Annie. "I heard about the man in the cottage, that he was dead."

"Where did you hear this?" Annie asked.

She shrugged. "I heard from Consuela, but everyone knows. It was the driver, Dan, who got the Sheriff's men to say why they were here. Dan told Ruby, who is the head housekeeper, and Ruby told Consuela. It is not a secret."

Annie wouldn't be surprised if all of the guests knew by now as well.

"I have been waiting for someone to come. I clean the cottage and I see things. I know they will want to talk to me, but I am frightened. My papers, I have only been in this country one year. I don't want them to send me back."

"But you have papers?" Annie asked. "You are here legally?"

The girl nodded. "Consuela is my aunt. She help me get a job here."

"Don't worry. They won't send you back. But it's very important that you tell the truth," Annie said. "Everything you can remember about the man or his cottage, even if you don't think it's important."

"But I *do* think it's important, what I saw."

"What was that?"

"The man in Cottage Five, I think I saw who killed him."

"What did the man in Cottage Number Five look like?" Before she started, Annie wanted to make sure that the maid wasn't confusing the murder victim with someone else.

"He was very large, a big strong man, with black hair that fell in his eyes. Big brown eyes, like an animal. I thought he looked very handsome, but also cruel. That is all I remember, the black hair and that he was so big."

"Do you think you would recognize a photograph of the man?"

"Oh, yes. I got a good look at him." Annie thought the girl was blushing. "I remember him very much."

"Go on. Start by telling me everything you did that day."

Renalda told Annie that she started work at 7 A.M. Monday morning, cleaning rooms in the main building. She believed that she got to the beach cottages around eleven, maybe a little later.

"I always go to the farthest one, Number Five, first. I remember that I knocked on the door and said 'maid service,' but got no answer. The head housekeeper, Ruby, always tells me I have to be louder. The guests, they do not always hear me because I am quiet."

"Had you ever seen the man in Cottage Number Five before yesterday morning? Did you clean it Saturday or Sunday?"

"No, last weekend I traded with another girl. I had to stay home because my little boy was sick." Annie's heart went out to the girl. She looked like a child herself, hardly old enough to have children of her own.

"What happened after you knocked on the door?"

"I knocked and called again, but I don't think he hear me. I use my key and go in, and he is standing at the telephone, writing on a piece of paper. I remember it very well because," Renalda paused, embarrassed, "he didn't have no clothes on." She looked down at her lap. "I try not to look at him, but it was difficult. I make myself look up at his face. He yelled at me, very loudly and used many bad words. I was afraid, and I stood there longer than I should have. He was very angry that I had walked in and told me to go away and not to come back. He told me not to return to clean the room at all. He was very angry, and looked like he might hit me, so then I left very quickly."

"Did you hear any of the phone conversation?"

"No," Renalda replied. "He did not say anything after I walked in, except to yell at me."

"What did you do then?"

"I went to the next cottage, Number Four, but it had a 'Do Not

Disturb' sign, so I passed it by and went to clean the others. Finally, I am at the very end of my rooms to clean. I am not certain of the time, but I see some people going to the restaurant for lunch. On Mondays I leave at two o'clock, so I know it was before two.

"I had to go back to Cottage Number Four to clean it, since that was the one that I skipped. I see that the 'Do Not Disturb' sign is gone. I am standing at the door of Number Four, about to knock, when I hear the door of Number Five opening. I am afraid that the man with black hair will yell at me again if he sees me, or strike me, so I am very silly, and get down behind my cart."

"And did the man come out?"

"No. I look up to see when the man has gone, but I see it was not him. It was another man, also tall, but not so wide, you know, he din't have big shoulders, and his hair was not black and straight. I was very glad to see it was not him, so I stood up and went quickly into the Number Four Cottage."

"Did you ever go back to Number Five?"

"Oh no, because he had told me not to. Since the man with black hair had not come out, I thought he would still be inside and would not want to see me. So I finished Number Four and then I left."

"The person you saw leaving the cottage, are you sure it was a man? Could it have been a tall woman?"

Renalda looked puzzled. "I was sure, although now you ask me, I have to say that I did not get a very good look. The person was wearing trousers, so that is why I think it was a man. I guess it could have been a tall lady in trousers. I just looked very quickly and saw that it was not the big man from Number Five. That is all I am sure of. No, wait. One other thing. Red."

"What?"

"The person leaving the cottage was carrying something red."

"Large? Small? Square?"

The girl shook her head apologetically. "I don't know."

She was starting to shiver, so Annie put a protective arm around her shoulder. "When we started to talk, you told me you saw the man's killer. Why did you say that?" Annie asked.

Renalda paused, again looking befuddled. "Because that was what I think, after, when I hear that the man was dead, and they thought he had been dead for a day. I say to myself that I saw someone coming from his room, it must be the killer. Do you mean it might not have been?"

"There's no way to know, Renalda. The medical examiner will not be able to pinpoint exactly when the man was killed. All you saw was someone leaving the cottage. It may have had nothing to do with the murder."

This seemed to make her feel better.

"Did the person leaving the cottage see you at all?" Annie asked. She was nevertheless concerned about the girl's safety. It was still possible that she had seen more than she should have.

"I don't think so," Renalda answered. "He was quite far away when I stood up, and I went inside very quickly. If he had turned around after I stopped looking at him, I probably would have been inside the other cottage."

"Can you remember anything else about the man, his clothing, how tall he was?"

"No, nothing more."

"How did the man walk. Quickly, slowly?"

"He walked quickly, but he did not run."

"Have you told anyone else about this?"

"Not at the time it happened. I did not think it was anything important. It was afterwards, when Consuela told me that the man in Number Five had been killed, I get frightened. I think then that the man I saw must have been the killer. I told Consuela what I saw, but no one else until now and I tell you. But Consuela has not told anyone."

"That's good. If Detective Dexter comes to talk to you, ask him to show you his badge, then you can talk to him. But don't talk to *anyone* else about this. And I'll tell Consuela that she shouldn't tell anyone. That's very important, Renalda, for your safety."

"Yes, I understand that. Consuela told me the same thing."

Chapter 10

TUESDAY EVENING, JULY 24

ANNIE STEPPED OUT OF the shower and wrapped herself in a huge Windsor Resort towel. Even if this hadn't turned into the relaxing vacation she had expected, the subtle touches of luxury were enjoyable. She thought about Lisa and her trust fund, and wondered what it would be like to be wealthy.

She was concentrating too hard on this case. It was time to force herself to relax a little. It was a good thing she had passed the front desk on the way back to her room and gotten David's message. She glanced at it again.

> *Annie—*
>
> *I know you're busy with your investigation, but I wanted to know if you'd have dinner with me on the boat tonight. I hate to brag, but I am a passable cook. The* Electra's *moored at the marina, white hull with dark green trim. Seven o'clock.*
>
> *I'm fixing the specialty of the house, so I'll be very disappointed if you can't come. I don't have a phone, so you can send one of the bell boys down to the dock with your answer. (Say yes)*
>
> *—David*

At first she had smiled when she read the note. Then she remembered David's abrupt goodbye the other evening after watching the sunset on Mount Constitution. He was certainly a man of changeable moods. Worry about the resort's security had also made her a bit nervous. In all of their conversations to date, David still had told her almost nothing about his past.

She read the note again. This is ridiculous, she thought. He's just inviting me to dinner. Having made up her mind, she found that she was looking forward to seeing his lopsided grin and twinkling eyes.

She rummaged through her disorganized suitcase. None of the various outfits she had brought to Orcas Island seemed right. Her jeans were too scruffy, but the blazer and slacks would be too dressy. She was going to be on a boat, so she had better not wear hard-soled shoes. She finally settled on white slacks and a jade green cotton sweater, an old favorite that she wore whenever her spirits needed boosting. She laughed at her indecision. David was obviously the type of man who didn't place a high priority on outward appearances. But she nevertheless found herself wanting to look attractive for him. He was nothing like the slick professionals she'd dated in the past, but she couldn't deny his appeal.

She glanced at her watch. Running late as usual. There wasn't time to try to do something with her chaotic mass of red hair, which was becoming curlier with every fresh blast of sea mist.

"Ahoy the ship," she called hesitantly from the dock, detecting light and movement on board. She had a lump in her throat, wondering which mood would greet her. Just then David's bearded face appeared from below and he broke into a wide grin, setting her instantly at ease.

"There you are!" he shouted when he saw her. "Come on aboard!" He grabbed her outstretched hand and helped her find a foothold. When she was on deck, he held both of her hands and his eyes reflected how glad he was to see her. "You look great. I'm glad you came—I wasn't sure . . . " his voice trailed off. He dropped her hands and gestured broadly towards the galley, saying, "I'd join you on deck, but we have a crisis in progress, otherwise known as dinner!" He vaulted down the three wooden steps to the cabin below. There wasn't quite enough room for two in the tiny area containing an ice box, a two-burner propane stove, and a small table which served as a work space, so Annie sat at the top of the steps where she could watch.

"Is there anything I can do?"

"Not a thing. I'm sorry to be rude and ignore you, but this is the tricky part, the sauce is just starting to thicken." He was standing in front of the tiny gas stove, stirring a pot of bubbling white liquid.

Watching David maneuver in the small galley, it was obvious he knew what he was doing. Annie was starting to suspect that David's description of himself as a "passable" cook was a bit of an understatement. Her definition of "passable" was someone who, like herself, could interpret the instructions on the back of a frozen dinner or microwave a potato.

She glanced around her. The *Electra* was a charming old wooden sloop. Every piece of brass was polished to a high shine and the wood surfaces glowed from obvious loving care. It wasn't a large boat to live on all the time, but more than adequate for one person.

David continued to stir the creamy mixture methodically and with concentration. A second covered pot simmered on the other burner. "I hope you like seafood curry—you know I didn't think to ask—but it's one of the few shipboard meals I do well. I'm kind of limited down here, with only two burners and no oven. It keeps my culinary repertoire small," he laughed. "If you come back, you get cashew chicken, and the third meal is pasta primavera. Then the choices begin getting repetitive."

"I *love* curry," Annie replied truthfully, "but I've never made it. Can you divulge your recipe?" She was asking only out of politeness, fearing she'd never be able to recreate his masterpiece.

"Sure, it's incredibly easy," David replied. Annie was skeptical. "You just start with a basic white sauce, then add the spices and seasonings and a *lot* of fresh seafood. When I can, I like to use a combination of shrimp, crab and scallops. Just about anything you do with a lot of fresh seafood is going to taste great, so it's sort of hard to go wrong."

Annie didn't want to admit she didn't know how to make a basic white sauce. She found herself thinking that it wouldn't be half bad to have a man around who knew how to cook.

"What are the secret ingredients?"

"I never use a prepared curry powder. I guess I'm kind of a perfectionist when it comes to curry. When I'm in Seattle I stop by the Public Market and buy bulk spices—cumin, coriander, turmeric, a little ginger, some dry mustard, a dash of cayenne—I'm probably boring you."

"Not at all, I'm fascinated." As much as anything, she was

enjoying watching the large man handle himself so skillfully in the kitchen.

"The real clincher—you put this in right at the end—a tablespoon of sherry. It makes all the difference." He suddenly stopped stirring. "Ah ha! Whoa, that's it, it's thickening! God, I'm always surprised when that works. I should have studied physics, maybe I'd know why it does that." David's easy-going mood was contagious, and Annie felt herself relaxing. "Now," he announced, his blue eyes twinkling, "for the good stuff . . . "

Ready at hand were the pre-measured seasonings and a cutting board loaded with fresh seafood. This was no thrown-together-at-the-last-minute meal. As he added the pungent spices, the sauce deepened in color to a rich yellow-gold. "I usually make it pretty hot, is that okay?" he asked.

"Great," Annie answered, anticipating the meal already.

They went on making small talk, and David continued to refuse Annie's help, using the excuse of not enough room. He made sure the heat was still on under both pots, and tore up greens for a salad. He even sliced a fresh pineapple.

David was dressed in faded levis and a white cotton turtleneck with the sleeves pushed up. Compared to his usual shorts and T-shirt, he looked dressed up. But not too much—he was still barefoot.

After a few more minutes of diligent work, he paused and looked around the galley. "All right," he said, heaving a sigh, "now we just wait a bit, till the rice is done, the sauce has to simmer . . . " He was talking to himself, running through a mental checklist to see if he'd forgotten anything. "The salad's under control . . . I guess that's it. We can relax!" He looked up at Annie with a look of delight on his face, as if he were surprised it had all gotten accomplished. "For a few minutes anyway, I can catch my breath and start being a decent host. Can I pour you a glass of wine?"

"By all means." Annie moved out of the gangway and up onto the deck. She expected David to bring the wine up with him out of the galley, but instead he came up on deck and walked over to the far side of the boat, handing her two empty glasses as he passed.

"My extra ice box," he explained, as he pulled a mesh bag

containing two bottles of white wine up out of the water. "It's the perfect temperature." He pulled one bottle out of the bag, then lowered it back into the chilly water. Using the Swiss army knife from his pocket he uncorked a bottle of Château Ste. Michelle Fumé Blanc. He poured a small amount in Annie's glass for her to taste. She played along, swirling the glass, examining the color, breathing in the bouquet. Finally she took a small sip, rolled it around on her palate, and pronounced her verdict. "A fine, dry wine. A touch smoky, but not overbearing. Nutty bouquet . . . somewhat sophisticated in its blend of aromatic textures." He gave a slight bow and they both laughed. Annie counted on her fingers. "Chef, wine steward, boat restorer . . . how many more talents do you have to reveal?" she asked.

"Oh, there are a couple more hidden away." He winked. "I don't want to overwhelm you all at once."

Now that David had come up on deck with Annie she was starting to feel shy and self-conscious again, an odd feeling for someone who was usually so calm and in control. Suddenly she felt like a teenager again.

"So tell me," he said. "You seem much too nice to be a lawyer. What made you do it?"

Annie smiled. It was such a common question she had developed a stock answer. "I got into law very haphazardly," she explained, pausing to take a sip of wine. "I love literature, and spent my college years as one of those English majors who always has her nose in a book."

"Let me guess. You had big round glasses and always a cup of coffee in one hand."

"You've got me figured out, all right. Anyway, I was totally unconcerned about ever having to make a living. I just figured I'd manage when the time came. Graduation loomed, and I put off the inevitable by continuing on with graduate school in Renaissance literature. Friends and family were appalled that I had no plans for what I wanted to do 'when I grew up.' They were positive that I would starve to death in an attic reading Marlowe and Shakespeare."

"Would that have been so bad?"

"I didn't think so, as long as the coffee never ran out. But I eventually caved in to the pressure and decided to pick a career. With no science or business background, law seemed like the logical choice."

"And the end result?"

"I think the choice was a good one. I really love my work. In fact, one of my biggest challenges is to keep myself from working too hard."

David rested his chin on his hand and looked at her intently. "I'm not convinced," he said after a pause. "Don't get me wrong, I believe you like what you're doing now, but maybe you feel like you weren't given a choice."

Annie stared into her wine glass. David's observation disturbed her. He was too perceptive. Annie had told the same lighthearted story about how she accidentally picked law school dozens of times, and he was the first person ever to see through it.

She was saved from answering when a small timer beeped on David's watch, announcing that dinner was ready. He went below and handed up a folding table to set up on deck, silverware, placemats, and candles.

"First," David announced with a flourish, "we'll start with a small Caesar salad." He brought a large teak bowl to the table and started expertly mixing ingredients. He worked without a recipe, and it was clear he had done this before. With his Swiss army knife, he sliced a lemon and mashed a few cloves of garlic. He then added olive oil, romaine, croutons, lemon juice, raw egg. He paused before adding the anchovies.

"What do you think?"

"I really don't care for them," she admitted sheepishly, "but I hate to spoil your attention to detail."

"No problem. Frankly," he confided, "I don't like them either. The small fish are banished."

"Where did you learn to do this?"

"Oh, during one of my past existences." He smiled, taking the time to make sure the salad was properly tossed. Annie waited for him to explain, but he said no more.

David dished up the salad, and it tasted as delicious as it looked.

Next, he brought the steaming curry and rice to the tiny table. He also started bringing up dish after dish of condiments.

"I've been told this is the official Navy way to serve curry," David explained as he set down the variety of dishes. "My great-aunt was married to a rear admiral, and she was the one who actually gave me the recipe. The condiments are called 'sideboys,' let me see if I got them all—raisins, green onions, chopped peanuts, chopped egg, crumbled bacon, coconut, and mango chutney. Good, all here. I know it looks strange, but it's an incredible blend of flavors. You sprinkle them all on top."

Annie followed his lead, topping the mound of rice and pungent sauce with the variety of condiments. He was right, the flavors were exquisite.

As delicious as dinner was, Annie barely noticed what she was eating as the conversation wandered and flowed. It was one of those rare evenings when the topics ranged from pure silliness to high-flung philosophical yearnings. Yet for all their talk, Annie noticed that David expertly avoided talking too much about himself.

The second bottle of wine disappeared with no problem at all. Annie offered to help with the dishes, but David wouldn't hear of it. He carried the remnants of the meal below and out of sight, and returned with a bottle of Grand Marnier and two small glasses.

"I think I'll have to come to this restaurant more often," Annie sighed contentedly. Sometime during the course of the evening she had grown completely relaxed, and just a little tipsy. "The service is excellent—the waiter even knows how to read minds."

David poured them each a glass of the syrupy orange liqueur. He handed Annie hers, then sat next to her on the stern seat, placing his bare feet up on a nearby captain's chair. At first he didn't say a word, then he looked up at the sky and sighed.

"Annie, I've got something terrible to confess."

Taken aback, she gazed at him silently.

"I think I'm falling in love with you." His deep blue eyes looked down at her. "I haven't felt this comfortable with someone for God knows how long."

Annie's own desires were so muddled by the wine and the warm evening that she didn't know what to say. He reached up and brushed a strand of hair away from her face. "I don't ever want to stop feeling the way I feel right now," he said, placing his hand on the back of her neck and gently pulling her face up to meet his. She gave in to the feeling, and found herself reaching her arms up behind his back and leaning in to feel the warmth of his body. It felt wonderful, so natural, as if they'd known each other for years instead of days. All the worries, all the crises of the past week evaporated. She laid her head on his shoulder and returned his warm hug. He held her tightly, for a very long time before letting go.

"Hey, I kind of like this," he whispered softly, gently stroking her hair.

"Mmm," she smiled, and he leaned forward to kiss her again, brushing his lips across her cheek and forehead. "But we really don't know each other," Annie halfheartedly protested, rubbing her cheek against David's bristly beard.

"Yes, we do," he murmured. "We know all the important things." He rose, and taking her by the hand, guided her down the steps to the cabin below.

Chapter 11

WEDNESDAY MORNING, JULY 25

BRIGHT SUNLIGHT STREAMED in through the blue canvas curtains when Annie awoke. She found herself alone in *Electra's* forward V-bunk. Getting dressed, she called for David but got no reply.

On the cabin table was a note scribbled in a broad, slanted scrawl:

> *Good morning, sleepy head! Sorry I had to leave, but I*
> *had an early morning class to teach. Help yourself to*
> *the OJ in the ice box. I'd offer you coffee but I forgot*
> *to show you how to turn on the stove. It's a little*
> *tricky, and I wouldn't want you to blow yourself up.*
> *Want to run away this afternoon? It's going to be a*

gorgeous day, and I want to show you my special place,
Traxler Island, where the sea lions frolic. We can have
a picnic in a perfect spot I know. You did great in the
kayak class, so I'm sure you can handle it. If you're
interested, meet me at the boat dock at noon.
                                                    —Love, David

P.S. Don't say no—I'm terrible at handling rejection.

Annie grinned as she read it. She wanted to go, but knew she'd probably have to decline. Right now, finding Marc Jarrell's killer and the missing Marguerite Boulanger were more important than a summer outing.

Back in her room, Annie found a note from Detective Dexter. He was conducting interviews in the music room and wanted to speak to her. She changed quickly and went downstairs. The music room was located at the north end of the main floor. Like the sitting room off the foyer, it had been decorated with period furniture. Under normal circumstances the guests were free to use the concert grand piano which stood in one corner on an oriental rug. For the time being, however, Russ had made the room available for the Sheriff's Department's exclusive use to carry on its investigation. Annie knocked on the closed door.

"Come on in."

Entering, she saw Nicholas Forrestor seated in a maroon velvet armchair, glaring at Detective Dexter. He momentarily shifted the focus of his angry stare to her, then turned back to the detective. Another man in a dark suit stood next to Dexter.

"If she's going to be here, I ought to be allowed to have my attorney present. I'll be filing a formal complaint against the Windsor as soon as he arrives. He's flying in from New York this afternoon. Can't this wait?"

Dexter smiled at Annie and offered her a seat. "We're just about through, here, Annie. Won't take a second. No need for you to wait outside. Now, then, Mr. Forrestor, just a couple more questions." He handed Forrestor a photograph. "Are you absolutely sure you've never seen this man before?"

The photo, an enlarged driver's license photograph, was a good likeness of Marc Jarrell. Forrestor revealed no sign of recognition. The driver's license was one of two found in the man's belongings, one in the name of "Mark Jones" and the other for "Marc Jarrell." A quick check with the New York DMV had revealed that the license in Jarrell's name was genuine. Forrestor told Detective Dexter he had never heard either name.

Annie took the opportunity to observe the gray-haired businessman. Totally lacking were the emotional outbursts of their prior meeting. He answered the questions dispassionately, his intense gray eyes giving nothing away.

"All right, Mr. Forrestor, thank you for your time. You can go now. But if we turn up anything new, I'm sure we'll be speaking to you again."

"My attorney will be the one to speak to about that, Detective." Forrestor smoothed the wrinkles in his slacks as he stood, and brusquely marched out of the room.

"Annie, I wanted you to meet FBI Agent Marvin Frye. He's here to look into the alleged kidnapping of the Boulanger woman, and possible connection with the Jarrell murder. He'll be working with the Sheriff's Department for a while. Agent Frye, this is Annie MacPherson. She's representing the new owner of the resort."

"How d'ya do, ma'am. Appreciate the cooperation. Uh, there a phone I can use, private?"

"Certainly. Mr. Perkins will be able to help you with whatever you need. His office is right down the hall."

"Thanks, ma'am."

As soon as he was out of earshot, Dex shook his head and fished a pack of cigarettes out of his pocket. "Annie, this guy is going to drive me up a wall. I can't get more than three words out of the guy."

"Oh, he doesn't seem so bad."

"Well, it's still going to be a pain. He doesn't want to be here, either. Thinks this whole 'alleged' kidnapping is some kind of joke. The way he sees it, Marguerite Boulanger just flew the coop. As soon as he can establish that Marc Jarrell's murder is just a plain old homicide, within our jurisdiction, he's out of here."

"You'll still keep me up to date?"

"Yeah, I got no problem with that. In fact, why don't you catch me after lunch, I'll let you know what the lab boys found out. But I'd steer clear of Mr. White Shirt and Tie here. The sooner we get him out of here, the better, as far as I'm concerned."

"Will do. Thanks for the advice."

Annie reached the boat dock a few minutes before noon, but David was nowhere in sight. She regretted having to tell him she wouldn't be able to go kayaking that afternoon, but she was anxious to find out what Dexter had uncovered so far. Suddenly she spotted David coming down the path.

"Hey, there," David smiled at her, "I thought you told me you were chronically late. My watch tells me you're at least thirty seconds early." He put an arm around her shoulders and gave her a hug. It was good seeing him again. No awkwardness or embarrassment. All morning she had been wondering if it had just been a fluke, a one-time thing. But seeing him again in the sunlight, she knew there was more to it than that. Like the night before, she felt she'd known him a long time.

"Are you ready to go to Traxler Island?" he asked expectantly. "I've got the boats ready, and I've thrown a few things together for lunch."

"David, I'm sorry. I just came down to tell you, I won't be able to make it." His face clouded, his disappointment obvious. "It's this damned investigation, I really ought to meet with the detective this afternoon to go over the lab results . . ." Annie didn't sound very convincing, even to herself. The truth was, the Sheriff's Department welcomed her help, but didn't actually need her participation. Detective Dexter was more than competent to handle things on his own.

David looked her in the eye. "If you really need to, I'll understand. You've got your job to do. But this is the only afternoon I have free this week. I was really hoping . . . you just wouldn't believe this spot, Annie. It's incredible. A family of sea lions lives on one side of the island. I've seen them every time I've been out there. But the best part is the island itself. There's this beautiful grassy bluff with a view to the west where I thought we'd have lunch. And the wonderful thing is, I've never seen any evidence of other people there. It's real tricky finding the trail. I think I'm the only one who knows about it."

Annie was wavering. She could probably arrange to have Detective Dexter leave her copies of the reports to review that evening. He didn't really need her assistance, after all. An afternoon of blue sky, a light warm breeze, the gentle sway of the ocean. What difference would one afternoon make?

"All right. You've twisted my arm. What can I say?"

David was unable to hide his pleasure, and gave her a quick embrace. "You'd better bring along a jacket. The wind usually picks up in the afternoon. I've got some extra gloves you can borrow if you need to."

"How far away is this place? Do we have to cross open water?" Despite her lessons in rescue techniques and paddling skills, Annie was hesitant. The ocean seemed like such a big place when she was sitting in such a tiny boat.

"It's not too far. About four miles from here altogether, and the channel we have to cross is about two and a half miles wide. We can do it easily in less than two hours unless it gets too choppy."

"Are you sure? I am pretty new at this, you know. We could find somewhere to go that wouldn't require such a big crossing."

"Don't worry. Look how calm it is today, the water's like glass. You can handle it. Besides, I *really* want you to see this place." His face grew serious. "I can't tell you how much it means to me."

"Well, okay, I guess you've convinced me. I'll just run up and grab a jacket and leave word that I'm not going to be around this afternoon."

Nathan Komatsu had his head buried in an applied statistics textbook, and was taking rapid notes in the margin.

"Nathan, have you seen Detective Dexter?"

"Haven't seen him, Annie. But Russ might know. He's out on the terrace."

The sun-filled terrace was packed. Annie searched for Russ, and finally saw him at the far end reprimanding a waitress. She caught his eye, and he motioned that he'd be a minute.

"Join us for a drink, Annie?"

At the sound of Philip Spaulding's voice, Annie looked down, and realized she was standing over Lisa Hargraves and Philip, relaxing over a lunchtime margarita. Both had apparently been reading. Philip had a treatise on Central American politics and Lisa had the latest Jackie Collins paperback. Annie couldn't help but notice Lisa's hand gently resting on Philip's thigh under the table.

"Lisa, have you met Annie MacPherson?"

"Oh, yes, we're good friends." Lisa had been going out of her way to be chummy since their revealing conversation. "Annie, you know, we still haven't had a chance to talk about your, uh, was it an uncle, who's a producer in Hollywood?" Lisa's voice practically oozed.

"Stepfather. We didn't, did we? Ah, here's Russ now."

"Hi, Annie. What can I do for you?"

"Russ, would you tell Detective Dexter I'm not going to be around this afternoon? I can't locate him."

"Sure, Annie. Where are you off to?"

"David and I are going kayaking this afternoon. To someplace called Traxler Island. I don't think it's far, I should be back by dinner time."

"No problem, I'll tell him."

"Becoming the outdoorswoman, Annie?" Lisa asked. "You'll have to show me how it's done." To Philip, she purred, "I bet you just love athletic women, don't you?" Phil looked embarrassed.

"Did you say Traxler Island?" Phil asked. "That's one I've never heard of. But it should be beautiful out there this afternoon. Have a good time. And don't tip over!"

"Don't worry, Phil. The last place I want to end up is that freezing water!" Annie laughed.

As David and Annie carried the two fiberglass boats down to the water, the afternoon sun felt warm and comforting. David helped Annie into her spray skirt and life jacket, and held her boat steady while she got in. Pushed out into the bay, the narrow boat felt tippy as she struggled to attach the neoprene skirt to the cockpit coaming.

"Hey, you look like a pro," David beamed as he pulled up beside her.

"I don't feel like one! Are you sure I'm ready for this?"

"Absolutely. Especially with perfect weather like this." David instructed Annie to keep her rudder in the water, and above all, to maintain a solid grip on the paddle. He would bring along a spare lashed to the bow of his boat, but it was always a prime concern not to lose that one essential tool. A weak current would be going in their direction, and would make forward propulsion a bit easier.

The first half-mile they stayed close to the shore of Orcas Island. Annie enjoyed the feel of the sun on her face. Looking down at the rocks along the shore she could see bright orange and purple starfish. Occasionally a fish jumped in the water in front of her. Now that she was out on the water Annie was glad David had persuaded her to come. It was a glorious afternoon. It felt good to work her shoulder and back muscles, pushing the craft silently through the deep green water.

After about twenty minutes, they reached the spot where they would begin their crossing to Traxler Island. David had timed their departure perfectly so that when they left Westsound, the current was gently flowing in their direction, helping them along. Now they were approaching slack, the time when the current changed from ebb to flood. By crossing the channel at that time, the current wouldn't carry them too far off course. If they timed their return trip right, they would be able to ride the flood current all the way back to Westsound.

"Explain that one more time, David. Does the 'flood current' mean the tides going in or out?" Annie asked.

"The first thing it's important to get straight is that tides and currents aren't the same thing," David answered. "Tides are the *vertical* movements of water. The rise and fall is measured in feet. A current is the *horizontal* movement of the water. Strong currents, in other words, areas of rapidly moving water, are created when the large amount of tidal water is forced through small passages, such as the channels between islands. You can think of it like a flood gate in a dam. The smaller the passage, the faster the water has to move to get through. Depending on where you are, there can be up to several hours' difference between a tidal change and when the current changes direction. The only way to know what the current is going to be doing at a particular time is to do advance research. A chart will tell you the direction of the current, and a table will tell you when the current will change in relation to the tide. 'Ebb' and 'flood' are the words used to describe the direction of the current. Ebb is current moving toward the ocean, usually associated with the tide going out. Flood is current moving inland from the ocean, usually associated with the tide coming in. But because of the shapes of the islands and channels, ebbs and floods don't always flow in the directions you would expect."

It all sounded pretty confusing. "Does it really make that much difference, waiting for the current?"

"In a kayak, it makes all the difference in the world. It's common to find maximum currents of three to five knots in the San Juans. Even a strong paddler's average cruising speed is only about three knots. You simply can't buck a strong current with your muscles. You won't get anywhere. Today, we'll hardly be able to feel a one-knot current, but it will still increase our hull speed if it's going with us rather than against us."

Next he showed her how to take a range against the point on the island they were heading for, comparing the land in the foreground to the higher blue ridge of another island behind it. By keeping the two points lined up, they would be sure they were traveling a straight course.

They were out in the channel now, about a half mile from shore. Away from the shelter of shore she could feel a slight breeze against her cheek. The gentle wind made tiny ripples on the surface of the water. Rather than frightening, the breeze felt invigorating. Annie began to grow more confident, paddling a little faster.

"There you go—you're catching on. You've got a good stroke, pushing with your shoulder muscles. That's right, just let the lower hand guide the paddle, not pull it. You've got it. I knew you'd be good at this."

David's confidence was infectious. Annie began to feel that she really could handle the tiny craft.

She thought back over the skills they had practiced in class, what to do in the event of a capsize. In class they had put on wetsuits to keep from getting chilled. She'd been able to manage it then, but they had practiced first in the pool, then in the calm water of the bay, with David giving instructions. A capsize in open water would be a different question. And without a wetsuit, the water would be very cold indeed. Despite the practice, she wasn't at all sure she'd be able to reenter her boat in frigid water. Unlike David, she was unable to roll her kayak without falling out.

She also remembered David's lecture on hypothermia. That was the condition in which cold water would make one's body temperature decrease to a point of no return. David had instructed his kayak class that without a wetsuit on, a capsized paddler could last at the most about an hour in the cold water of the strait. Even in summer, the deep water would never get much above fifty degrees. Within minutes the cold would start taking its toll. First would be loss of dexterity, especially in the hands. Cramps in the legs and feet were common. Loss of judgment was a subtle and devastating result, even worse if the capsized victim panicked. Unless one was very close to shore, swimming was out of the question. It would deplete the swimmer's energy far too fast. The only hope in the event of a capsize was to be able to get out of the water, either climbing back in or on top of the kayak. Annie shivered at the thought, and convinced herself to concentrate on the beautiful surroundings instead. There was surely nothing to worry about on such a beautiful day.

David stayed in front as they paddled, frequently looking back over his shoulder to make sure that Annie was keeping up. He smiled at her encouragingly, and gestured that they were about halfway there. He dropped back next to her, close enough to talk.

"Beautiful, isn't it? I just love it when the weather's like this. It's almost hypnotizing, the ocean so large, in such a small boat, perfectly in sync, a slight amount of swell. I feel that my ancestors must have been seafaring folk, going to sea like this to make their living. Or who knows, maybe it was me, in a former life. All I know is it's a part of me. I'm tied to it. I never feel quite as alive as I do on the ocean."

Annie found herself agreeing. It was a new experience, this feeling of being almost one with the ocean. She'd never felt quite like this in a sailboat. It was a different perspective to be so close to the ocean.

So much at its mercy.

They chatted pleasantly to pass the time. Distances were deceiving. Looking forward, Annie thought they were making no progress, whatsoever. But looking behind her, she saw that they'd come quite a distance, and were probably a mile or more from shore.

"What is it? What's that sound?" Annie asked. In the distance they could hear a low, rumbling sound, coming at spaced intervals. It didn't resemble anything Annie had ever heard before. It couldn't be thunder, with no clouds overhead.

"Whales!" shouted David excitedly. "There they are, look!" David pointed off to the right. Rising majestically out of the water were several black and white orcas. The sound they heard was the powerful exhalation of air and water as each whale burst above the surface. There were six or seven in the pod. It was hard to count them as they jumped and dove in a close group. Annie was transfixed. Suddenly they angled the direction of their travel.

"David, they're coming this way. Will they hurt us?"

"No," he replied. "We wouldn't want to interfere with them, but they're not dangerous. I really dislike the term 'killer whale.' The scientists who have studied them have found them to be gentle, sensitive creatures with a highly evolved social structure. Far more peaceful than we are. They're only called killer whales because they eat fish, sometimes seals and sea lions. They don't intentionally bother people, and there's never been a recorded human death from an orca attack. They may be curious and want to take a look at us, though."

The animals were strikingly beautiful—jet black above and white below. The tall triangular dorsal fins were still visible when they were underwater. The sound of their blowing was thunderous. Annie had had no idea whales would be so loud.

"How big are they?" she asked.

"Hard to say. They can get up to twenty-five or thirty feet in length, with dorsal fins six feet tall."

They no longer looked like they were going to investigate the kayakers, but would pass a few hundred yards away.

"I'd love to get closer if we could, without getting in their way," David said. "I've never seen them at such close range before. And so many! This is incredible!"

Annie wasn't sure about the detour. She still felt confident, but didn't want to go so far out of her way.

"Why don't you go. I could sit here and wait for you."

David thought about it, keeping one eye on the approaching whales. He was sorely tempted.

"I really shouldn't leave you—what if something happened?"

"Look how calm it is. What could happen? Really, David, go ahead. I'll be fine." They heard the thunderous noise again of the whales' blowing. David could barely contain his excitement.

"All right. But I won't be gone more than fifteen minutes." They both looked at their watches. "Just keep paddling in the direction of Traxler, try to keep me in sight. I'll keep an eye on you and catch up in a little bit. And here, take this Sky Blazer. It's a flare. If anything happens, you just point it up and pull on the ring." He handed her a small orange cylinder about the size of a cigar. She tucked it inside her life jacket.

"I'll be fine, David. Now, go!"

He returned her smile and sprinted off in the direction of the whales.

Annie kept moving forward at a comfortable pace. She was as excited as David at seeing the creatures. She watched as David paddled off, being careful not to get too close or disturb the whales. She paused for a moment and sat quietly in her boat with her paddle across her lap, content to watch the whales playfully leap in the distance.

Captivated, Annie barely noticed the breeze begin to pick up, turning the bow of her kayak away from Traxler Island. Seeing herself fall off course, she started to paddle again, this time harder, trying to swing the bow back into position. Rather than watch David and the whales, she kept her eyes on her destination, concentrating to keep going forward in a straight line. The breeze stiffened. Annie could feel it buffet the end of her paddle as it was raised out of the water to stroke. Now tiny whitecaps were starting to break the surface.

Suddenly a different sound broke Annie's intense concentration, this one man-made. She turned to look over her left shoulder to see a bright blue ski boat thundering along at full speed. It was rapidly bearing down on her on a dead collision course.

Chapter 12

ANNIE WAS DUMBSTRUCK by the roar of the approaching speed-boat. What was the idiot doing? Was he drunk? Couldn't he see her bright orange life preserver and yellow boat? She frantically waved her arms and yelled, but it didn't seem to do any good. The wind carried her words away.

He was coming straight at her. She picked up her paddle and started pumping frantically, desperately trying to get out of the way. Paddling forward, she was unable to turn and see the boat approach.

Expecting to feel the force of a collision at any second, Annie was astonished when instead, the ski boat veered into a tight slalom turn, missing her by only a few yards. Thank God, she thought, he must have finally seen me.

But the result was almost as devastating as a collision. The massive wake from the speeding boat hit the kayak broadside, flipping her over like a child's toy in a bathtub.

The icy cold of the water went through her like a knife. The shock was immediate and numbing. Stunned, Annie hung upside down underwater for a moment, her legs still in the boat. Desperately needing air, she recovered her senses enough to disengage the elastic of her spray skirt and push herself free. She somersaulted forward under water to extricate her legs from the constricting space and reached the surface, gasping. It was only then that she realized that her paddle had flown from her hands in the capsize.

The speedboat was nowhere in sight. She'd seen only a glimpse of bright blue fiberglass, but had failed to get a look at anyone on board. If the driver had seen her at the last minute, why in God's name hadn't he seen her tip over, and stopped to help?

The kayak was floating upside down, kept from sinking by a sealed cargo compartment at the stern and a plastic flotation bag filled with air in the pointed bow. Annie grabbed on to the kayak, but saw her paddle floating some fifty feet away.

She was disoriented by the fall. From her vantage point in the water, she wasn't sure which direction David had gone. Halfway between the two islands, she couldn't tell which was which. She looked, but could see him nowhere. Calling was next to useless. The wind was blowing even harder than before, swallowing the sound of her voice. She realized with a jolt that she couldn't count on him coming to her aid. If she couldn't see him, he might not be able to see that she was in trouble.

She tried to think rationally. The flare. David had given her a flare. She felt inside her life jacket. Nothing. It must have fallen out when she tipped over. Now what?

She would have to have both boat and paddle to survive, but she knew it would be stupid to let go of the boat to swim for the paddle. She tried a one-armed sidestroke towards the paddle, keeping one hand on the upturned bottom of the boat. It was impossible. She made no progress.

She remembered that the kayak had a line attached to the bow. She reached underwater to feel for it. Already she was having difficulty working her fingers in the frigid water. She had forgotten to borrow the gloves David had offered her. The line should have been easy to unhook, but it was taking precious minutes. The pain in her fingers began to throb. Finally she got the line free, tied it around her waist and began to swim, awkward in the buoyant life jacket, in the direction of the paddle.

Whitecaps were dancing on the surface in the brisk wind, and a slight swell lifted Annie up on the crests of the waves, then dropped her into the troughs. At times the paddle disappeared from sight. Annie had no idea if she was even getting closer to it. The boat, attached by the lifeline to her waist, was drifting away, making the swimming even more difficult.

Annie remembered what David had said about swimming to shore. It was out of the question. It had taken at least half an hour to get from the shore of Orcas Island to the spot where they had sighted the whales. Swimming back would take much longer. Traveling in the boats at two to three knots, that would put them more than a mile offshore, almost exactly halfway between the two islands. She would become exhausted and hypothermic if she even attempted it in either direction.

After swimming after the paddle for about fifteen minutes, Annie realized with a growing sense of panic that she would never reach it. It was being carried by the current much faster than she could swim, even without trying to tow the cumbersome kayak. She would have to come up with a new plan.

She tried to remember the rescue techniques David had demonstrated in class. One method involved two people, with one person in another kayak to steady the capsized boat. She probably could have done it, but she didn't have another person to help. They had also learned how to do a solo rescue, but that involved tying something buoyant to one end of a paddle, and attaching the other end to the boat, to make an outrigger. It would be hard to do without a paddle, she thought grimly. She was starting to get frightened.

And she was damned cold.

Now her feet, as well as her hands, were throbbing from the icy water. Her head felt like it was going to split. She had started to shiver, only slightly at first but now it was becoming uncontrollable. While she was paddling, her windbreaker and cotton sweater had been sufficient protection against the wind. They were doing nothing to warm her in the water. Her only hope was to somehow pull herself out of the water and onto the boat until help could arrive.

If it would arrive.

She examined the smooth hull of the kayak. There was nothing to grasp on the upturned bottom of the boat. Her hands slid off the slippery, rounded fiberglass. She would have to turn the boat right side up.

Positioning herself at the bow, she twisted the boat around until it was upright. But full of water, the cockpit rose only two inches above the waterline. When Annie added her weight, the boat rested slightly below the surface. Useless.

Somehow, she would have to get the water out. There was nothing to bail with. Both the bilge pump and the sponge that had been in the boat had drifted away long ago. She would have to try the method David showed them in class.

Because of the sealed compartment in the stern, all of the water was in the bow and cockpit section. She flipped the boat back over so that the white hull was again showing. She moved to the stern. Careful to avoid the steel rudder, Annie pushed with all her might on the stern of the boat. The pointed bow came up at an angle, and when the edge of the cockpit rose above the surface, water began pouring out of the boat. When all of the water was gone, she quickly twisted the stern so that the boat landed right side up without taking in more water.

Amazingly, it worked.

Now the kayak was righted, and had only two to three inches of water inside. It was resting well above the waterline.

But the difficult part was just beginning. Annie now had to pull herself up onto the boat without flipping it over again. Even that slight amount of water made the boat unstable. She knew that if she tried to climb directly into the cockpit, with no way of steadying the kayak, it would simply roll over again. She was finding it hard to think. Decisions were difficult. She had to act quickly before all of her strength and judgment were gone. There was no question, she would have to pull herself up over the bow or the stern.

In terms of buoyancy, the stern would have been easier. There was a smaller area of flotation to push underwater, and a shorter distance to the cockpit. But the rudder was in the way. She decided to try the bow.

Annie looked at the distance from bow to cockpit. There was nothing on the shiny surface to use as a handhold. She pushed the bow down, and tried to slither up on the boat. With her first thrust up onto the deck the boat flipped again.

Her strength was fading fast, but there was no time to be discouraged. She moved to the stern again, and used the same method for flipping the boat up as she had before. It was easier this time, as the boat hadn't filled with water.

Despite the rudder, Annie would have to try the stern. She made sure the steel blade was in the full down position. She could use elastic shock cords that criss-crossed the rear deck as handholds to pull herself up. She stared at the rudder. She probably couldn't straddle the steel blade without injuring herself. Instead, she pushed down on the stern from the side, as she had done to empty the water from the boat. With the stern pushed underwater, she swung her right leg around and straddled the boat like a horse.

Quickly, before the boat tipped, she laid her chest down on the deck and grabbed the shock cords. Annie held herself steady to make sure the boat wouldn't capsize again, centering her weight on the deck. Slowly, being careful not to tip the boat, Annie slithered forward, an inch at a time. She had to struggle to marshall her last bit of strength. Finally she had pulled herself far enough forward that her entire body was out of the water, except for her legs which were still straddling the back deck. With her hands she reached forward and grasped the coaming of the cockpit for a firm hold. She decided not to go further, for fear of losing her balance.

Her hands and feet were so numb by this time she could barely feel them. Panting with exhaustion, Annie rested her head against the deck. She knew she had to stay conscious to maintain her precarious hold, but she didn't feel capable of it. Images in her head began to spin.

Voices. Movement. Barely conscious, the next thing Annie was aware of was being pulled up into a small boat. Capable hands removed her wet jacket and sweater and wrapped her in heavy wool blankets. Someone pulled a dry wool cap onto her head, and dry socks onto her numbed feet. Thick canvas work gloves were pulled on over her shivering hands. The smell of fish mingled with that of wet wool.

"It's okay, Annie. We'll have you warm and dry in no time." David Courtney wrapped his arms around her shoulders, and gently rocked her back and forth. She was shivering so hard her words were slurred. "David? . . . Where . . ."

"Don't try to talk, yet. Just sit there and shiver. That's a good sign. If you had stopped shivering, then we'd have to worry. Here, have some of this, just a sip." The cocoa from the thermos was tepid and too sweet but felt good going down.

"I think it was about half an hour, maybe forty minutes, that I was gone. It was a good thing you were able to pull yourself up out of the water. If you'd been in the water that long, you'd be in pretty bad shape. I think you're doing okay though. You should be able to warm up with no problem but we're going to get you to the hospital at Friday Harbor just in case."

Annie nodded, still unable to form a reply. The shock of being rescued when she thought all was lost was almost as great as the shock from the cold water.

"Is she gonna be okay, there?" The man asking the question was dressed warmly in a flannel shirt and wool sweater, but minus a wool cap and gloves. He was leaning over the stern rigging a tow line to Annie's yellow kayak floating in the water. David's red boat was already securely attached.

"Just fine, Jake," David replied.

"Do you want some whiskey in that cocoa?"

"No, it wouldn't be good for her. The cocoa's fine." David placed the cup in Annie's still trembling hands. "Just take small sips, don't drink a lot."

"David . . . " There were so many questions she had to ask, but she could hardly control her voice. "What happened? . . . Where were you? . . . It took so long." She was both furious and thrilled at the same time to see him. On the one hand, he had just saved her life. On the other, his paddling out of view might almost have killed her. She wanted answers.

David sensed the anger in her voice. He held her tighter and answered quietly. "It was my fault, Annie. I never should have gone off like that. It was inexcusable. I thought I'd only be gone for a few minutes, that you'd be okay. You were so steady in the kayak, and the water was so calm. I wasn't worried about you. I'm just so glad you're all right." He looked at her, his bright blue eyes clouded with emotion. "Can you ever forgive me for being so stupid?"

She nodded mutely. He seemed so genuinely sorry, she couldn't help but forgive him. But she was still in the dark. "But David, I don't understand why you were gone so long. Didn't you see that I was in trouble?"

"It was a tough judgment call, Annie. Once I got out into the main channel, the current was a lot stronger than I had expected—it was carrying me north pretty fast. I hadn't realized that where I left you, we were still sheltered by the shape of Orcas. So you were staying pretty much in one place, while the current was whisking me away. Then when the wind came up, that's what caused the water to get rough. Remember in class we talked about a 'weather tide'? When the wind blows against the current like that, it causes whitecaps. Are you understanding any of this?"

"I think so, but didn't you see me?"

"It was a while before I looked back and saw you had capsized, maybe ten minutes. I still can't forgive myself. I never should have let us get separated like that. It goes against every safety rule in the book."

"David, it's okay. Just tell me what happened."

"By the time I looked back, we were a lot farther apart than I'd expected, and I would have had to go directly against the current to get back to where I'd left you. But I couldn't see you—all I could see was the upturned white hull in the water. I knew you had capsized, but I wasn't sure you had stayed with your boat."

Annie nodded. "I lost my paddle and was trying to get it back. I had tied myself to the boat, but wasn't right next to it."

"I looked around and saw Jake here fishing, but he was about a quarter mile in the other direction, and probably couldn't see you at all. I had to make a decision whether to go directly to your boat, or to get Jake to help me. If I went towards Jake, the current would be with me and I knew I could make it much faster."

"Don't you be too hard on him, young lady," Jake added, looking back over his shoulder. "Old *Sea Shanty* here can go at a pretty good clip when she has to. I think he did the right thing."

David continued. "I was afraid you had panicked and were trying to swim to shore. Looking for a person in the water from a kayak is almost impossible. I would have been too low in the water to get a good view, and I just wouldn't have been able to cover enough area."

Though her mind still felt muddled, Annie thought she was starting to understand his reasoning.

"Also," said David, "there was the problem of what I would have done if I had found you separated from your boat. There's not much room for a passenger on one of these things. I wasn't sure you'd have the strength to hang on to the deck while I paddled us ashore. And it would be slow going in any event. If you had been swimming, you would have been in a lot worse shape than you are now. You would have used up your reserve of body heat in minutes."

David explained that he felt his only choice was to go towards the fishing boat, and hope that the fisherman had a fast outboard, and possibly a radio to call for more help.

"As it turns out, young lady, I had both," Jake added with pride. "As soon as I got to Jake's boat, we radioed the Coast Guard, who in turn notified all boats in the area to be on the lookout for you. There'll be an ambulance waiting for us at Friday Harbor to get you to a nice warm bed."

"Thank you, David." She leaned into him, comforted by his presence.

"Are you feeling any better yet?"

"Starting to. I can feel my feet again. But I don't think I'm ever going to stop shivering."

He picked up her shaking hands and rubbed them warmly in his own. "I'm just so glad you're all right," he whispered. "Damn it, if I hadn't gone off like that . . . "

"No, I shouldn't have insisted on staying behind. I wasn't that tired."

"Now you two kids just cut it out," Jake interjected. "You're both damned lucky you each had a brain in your head and knew how to use 'em. I swear I've seen such fools out here thinkin' they're better 'n' smarter than this old ocean, and they prove themselves wrong every time. You two'll be just fine. Now, let's get a move on and get this lady warm and dry."

As they pulled into Friday Harbor, Jake spoke into his radio that the immersion victim had arrived. As David had promised, the aid car was waiting at the dock. Even though she was feeling better and warmer by the minute, Annie found when she tried to stand that her legs didn't have enough strength to hold her. David picked her up, still wrapped in two blankets, and lifted her over the side of the boat to a medic waiting with a stretcher.

"Take care of yourself, now," he shouted as she was being loaded into the aid car. "I'll come see you after you've gotten some rest."

THURSDAY MORNING, JULY 26

"Knock knock. You awake?" Ellen O'Neill poked her head into Annie's hospital room. "The fresh clothes brigade has arrived! How's the drowned rat? Are the doctors still willing to release you this morning?"

"Yes, and I'm ready to leave, too. I hate hospitals." The color had returned to Annie's cheeks. "Thanks for coming, Ellen." Annie looked 100 percent better than she had the afternoon before when they had brought her in. "I feel so foolish, having to spend the night in the hospital because I tipped over in a stupid kayak." She took the overnight bag from Ellen and started to get dressed. She threw her jeans and sweater, caked with sea salt, into the bag and zipped it shut.

"Hey, don't knock it. A night of pure relaxation, being waited on hand and foot. Color TV in every room. You wouldn't believe the number of times working at the hospital I've been tempted to check myself in for a little rest!"

"When's the next ferry to Orcas? Do we have time to get out of here and go for a cup of decent coffee?"

"Ah, hospital coffee, I know it well." Ellen pulled the orange and white ferry schedule out of her purse. "We've got till 12:40. Let's grab some breakfast. There's a great country inn right down the street. I'm starving."

"You're always starving."

While Ellen had a three-egg omelet with home fries and fruit, and Annie had coffee, they discussed the accident.

"I called the hospital last night when I found out what happened," said Ellen. "From what I understand, you were in pretty bad shape."

"I guess so, although I was so out of it I really didn't know what was going on. The nurse told me afterwards that my temperature had gotten down to eighty-nine degrees. At eighty-six degrees I would have lost consciousness. I was really lucky David and Jake found me when they did."

"So what did they do at the hospital?"

"Once I got checked in they got me dry and wrapped me up in electric blankets and I just sat and shivered for about an hour and a half. It seemed like forever. The nurses kept bringing me juice to drink and checking my temperature a lot. I guess I didn't really need to spend the night, but by the time I was back to normal it was too late to get a ferry back to Orcas. And I was exhausted."

"Brrr. Better you than me. I'll stick to running marathons—it's so much safer."

"Right." Annie laughed. She gestured to the waitress that she needed a refill.

"The one thing I'm curious about, Annie. I saw you two leaving yesterday, and watched you as you were paddling out. I thought you looked really comfortable in the kayak, just like a pro. Why did you tip over?"

She told Ellen about the speedboat. "It was horrible. I've never been so frightened in my life. I was positive the boat was going to ram right into me."

"You said it was bright blue. Was it that kind of metallic paint, sparkly?"

"I'm pretty sure it was, why?"

"There's a boat like that at the resort. It's moored at the far end of the marina, over by the tennis courts. I noticed it a few days ago, because I like to water ski, and was wondering if I could find someone with a boat."

"Well, that will be number one on my list when I get back—to find out who that boat belongs to. Just thinking about it makes me seethe. Who could do something like that, Ellen? I know the driver of the boat saw me, because he swerved at the last minute. He must have seen me capsize, too. But why didn't he stop to help me? Could anyone really be that callous and unfeeling?"

" 'He?' Are you sure it was a man?"

"No, I have no idea. It could have been a woman, I guess." Ellen looked pensive.

"What is it, El?"

"Annie, I know I read too many mystery novels and they have nothing whatsoever to do with real life, but this is bothering me. You're doing a lot of poking around about that guy's murder, right? And that woman's disappearance? So what if somebody doesn't like you getting nosy? It seems like a pretty strange type of incident to just happen accidentally."

"What? You think someone was trying to capsize me intentionally?"

"Well, I don't know. Maybe just scare you. They did veer off at the last minute. Did you get any kind of a look at the driver's face?"

"No, not at all. I was paddling as hard as I could to get out of the way." Annie thought about it. "No, Ellen, I think that's totally ridiculous. Those types of things happen in books, but we've got to deal with reality here." She glanced at her watch. "We'd better get down to the ferry dock. I'm really anxious to get back and talk to David, thank him for everything he did."

Ellen stopped. "Oh, Annie. I was assuming you knew. I thought you just didn't want to talk about it. You mean no one told you?"

"Told me? Told me what? David—is he all right?"

"He's been arrested."

Chapter 13

ANNIE SAT BACK in her chair, stunned. "I can't believe it, Ellen. I was wondering why he didn't call or come see me like he said. But why? What do they think he's done?"

"It's something to do with the murder of that man in the cottage and the woman's kidnapping. I don't know all the details. Everyone around the resort is just shocked."

"It's got to be a mistake. David would never be involved in a murder." Even as Annie was jumping to David's defense, she thought back to the boating accident. Had David been telling her the truth? Maybe he had gone off and left her alone on purpose. She tried to push the unpleasant thoughts out of her mind, but her doubts lingered. What did she really know about the man? "But how could they arrest him? Do they have any evidence?"

"Apparently they found some papers in the cottage of the man who was murdered, with David's name on them. Maps, or something. The sheriff's department believes the evidence shows that David was somehow involved in the kidnapping scheme."

"And what does David say?"

"He can't explain it. He insists he doesn't know anything about it."

Annie needed answers. "Where are they holding him? I've got to talk to him."

"He's here in Friday Harbor, at the County Jail."

The Sheriff's Department, County Courthouse and Jail were all located in the same square, red brick building near the center of town. It looked more like a utility company than the seat of justice. Not wanting to intrude, Ellen O'Neill left Annie at the courthouse steps and went to catch the ferry back to Orcas. Annie summoned her courage, then went in and asked to see Detective Dexter. He came out to greet her immediately.

"Annie, I heard about your accident. Are you feeling better?" Dex looked like he hadn't slept in days. His clothes were wrinkled and he had dark circles under his eyes.

"I'm fine," she replied coldly. "What's this about placing David Courtney under arrest? There's got to be some mistake. Where is he? I want to see him." She was firing her words at the detective like a machine gun.

"Calm down, Annie. I know you're upset. I'm not too pleased about it myself. But the evidence is pretty bad, I'm afraid. Why don't you come back to my office and we'll talk about this."

"I'd like to speak to David, Detective." She was trying hard to keep her anger under control.

"There's plenty of time for that. I think you ought to see the evidence before you speak to him."

She followed the weary detective back to his tiny cubicle of an office. "By the way," he said over his shoulder, "David is being arraigned at 1:30 this afternoon, if you'd care to stay. There's no reason why he shouldn't be let out on bail." The detective walked around and sat behind his desk, filled two styrofoam cups with coffee and handed her one. He pushed a thick file across to her side of the desk.

"The first section you see there, labeled 'TAPES,' contains transcriptions of five cassette tapes we found in the cottage. They were well hidden, wrapped in plastic bags and stuck inside a cereal box. Marc Jarrell's fingerprints were all over them. As you can see from the typed transcripts, they all deal with the alleged kidnapping of the Boulanger woman, pretty good proof that Jarrell was involved."

Annie remembered the tape she had heard in Russ's office the day Marguerite was discovered missing. Dexter anticipated her thoughts. "We've had the tapes analyzed. The woman's voice on the tapes found in Jarrell's room matches the voice on the tape you heard. Forrestor has identified it as Boulanger's voice. Hers is the only voice on all of them, with the exception of that single outburst on the first tape. We can only assume at this point that was Jarrell. You can read through them later, but in a nutshell, they're all like ransom notes, the woman identifies herself, repeats that she's safe, and gives directions on when and how to drop the money. The tapes all refer to men, plural, implying a gang was involved."

"Do you believe that?"

"I don't know, Annie. It would make one theory fit. If Jarrell was working with a gang, he might have been just a minor player, which would explain why he was supposed to merely deliver the pre recorded tapes, rather than actually give instructions over the phone."

Annie considered this. "It makes some sense. He would have been the most visible member, most likely to be seen. But also dispensable if something went wrong. To cover up mistakes, one of the other kidnappers could have killed Jarrell?"

"It's a possible answer. Maybe he did something wrong. Wouldn't follow instructions, or was trying to act on his own. Maybe someone saw him. But if the other kidnappers did eliminate

Jarrell, then where's Marguerite Boulanger? Still out there somewhere, being held by killers?"

"I'm confused about something," Annie said, looking up from
the pages. "If Jarrell was killed by other members of the kidnap
gang, why would they leave the tapes behind? He's apparently been
dead for awhile, yet no other ransom demand has been communi-
cated to Nicholas. Why not take the tapes and make the ransom
demand themselves?"

"Hmm. I was assuming that it was because the tapes were well
hidden. But now that you mention it, I recall that the cottage
wasn't torn up at all. It didn't look like anyone had searched it.
You'd think they would have looked for the tapes, wouldn't you?
And you're right, there has been time for another ransom demand.
As far as we know, there's been nothing. It doesn't add up, does it?"

Annie looked at Dex. "There's one possible explanation, but I
don't like it."

"What do you mean?" he asked.

"The fact that there hasn't been a ransom demand could imply
that the kidnappers decided to abort the plan completely and get
out, and didn't care about demanding the money."

"But, that would mean . . . ?"

"Exactly. If they've abandoned the plan to that extent, Marguerite could be dead."

Dexter sighed. It was an unpleasant thought, but a possibility
they would have to consider.

"Could I have copies of the transcripts?" Annie asked. "And I'd
also like to listen to the tapes."

"I really shouldn't. This FBI character is a pretty straight
arrow . . . aw, what the hell. I sure don't have any leads. Maybe
you'll find something I missed. Just don't let Frye find out. I've got
an extra copy of the tapes I can loan you."

"Thanks. I'll keep it quiet."

The next document was a mystery. "What's this, Dex?" The
photocopy was hard to read.

"Hard to say. The lab was able to recreate that note from
indentations on the notepad found in Jarrell's room. We think
Jarrell wrote it. We should know for sure after we have our

handwriting expert compare the writing to the signature on his driver's license." She saw some words printed in big letters along with some doodles:

$50,000???   info
DAISY/DAISY/DAISY
1:00 HERE

In the corner were some numbers that could have been a phone number. Annie stared at it long and hard, as if to make a meaning jump out at her from the random scribbling. "Any idea what it means?"

"The phone number was easy. One of the guys recognized it. It's the local charter company that flies shuttles to Sea-Tac. Apparently a guy named 'Johnson' called and made a reservation for one person for Monday afternoon. Never showed up, of course."

"For one, that's interesting. Do you have any idea who, or what, 'DAISY' is?"

"Nope. So far it doesn't mean a thing," Dexter told her. "We're working on it."

"All right, there's no question Jarrell was involved with the Boulanger woman. What about David? Where does he fit into this?" Annie's fury was slowly dissipating while she talked to Dexter, as she realized that the investigation had been carried out strictly by the book.

Dexter rubbed his eyes with a tired hand. "Look in the next section of the file, labeled 'COURTNEY.' Those are photocopies, the originals are locked up."

"Where did you find these?" Annie asked, pulling out the papers.

"They were hidden too, although not as creatively as the tapes in the cereal box. A manila envelope was stuck between the mattress and springs on the bed. Still, we didn't find it until the very end of our search."

There were two sheets of plain white paper, both 8½ x 11 inches. The first page looked like a hand-sketched chart of two islands, with notations regarding compass directions and approximate distances. The larger island, with its distinctive saddle bag shape, was

labeled "Orcas." An "X" at the top of the island was labeled
"Eastsound" and another spot on the western portion of the island
was marked "Windsor." A tiny, round island, labeled simply "TR"
was located to the east of Orcas, with a tiny, crescent shaped
indentation on the northwest shore. An arrow pointing to the
channel between them was labeled "2½ Mi." Asterisks near the
crescent cove were labeled "Rocks/kelp." A note at the bottom of
the chart said "From west side of cove, look for hidden trail to
bluff." The chart was signed, "—Good Luck, David Courtney."

Annie shook her head in amazement. "You know where this is,
don't you?" she asked.

"Traxler Island. I couldn't believe it when I heard that was where
David Courtney was taking you yesterday afternoon. We'll be
heading out there this afternoon to investigate."

Annie could hardly continue. Why had David wanted so badly to
take her to Traxler Island? Thinking back she remembered how
important it had been to him. He wouldn't take no for an answer.
It was all too hard to digest.

The second piece of paper was a typed list of camping gear.
Added to the bottom with a broad, felt-tipped pen were some
additional items: wetsuit, fins, tarpaulin, rope. Annie immediately
recognized the large slanted handwriting. It was David's.

"We're not sure yet what any of it means, Annie. But we felt it
was important to get David into custody, at least until we've had a
chance to check out the island. At this point, he's only going to be
charged with conspiracy to commit kidnapping."

"No murder charge?"

"At this point we can't link Courtney to the crime scene. No
fingerprints, hairs, fibers, nothing to show he'd ever been in Jarrell's
room."

Annie took little comfort in this news, knowing that the lesser
charge was enough to hold David until more evidence could be
gathered. Once the authorities had a suspect in custody, they'd be
doing everything in their power to find enough evidence to get a
conviction.

She took a deep breath, and said quietly. "I'd like to see him now." Detective Dexter got a key out of his desk, and showed her down the hall to an interview room.

"Annie, thank God you're all right! I was worried sick about you, and they wouldn't even let me phone the hospital."

Annie was shocked to see David dressed in the faded red jumpsuit assigned to jail inmates. She involuntarily pulled back as the large man leaned across the table to take her hand. She couldn't help it. The evidence that Detective Dexter had shown her was strong. Unless David could explain that the papers were either stolen from him or faked, it would almost have to mean he was implicated in the Boulanger disappearance, possibly Marc Jarrell's murder as well.

The room into which she'd been ushered was barely large enough to hold the square steel table and two chairs. She'd been in any number of such rooms as a prosecutor, recording confessions, negotiating plea bargains, but never to talk to a friend. She wondered if all those years as a prosecutor had left her too jaded, unable to think in terms of innocent until proven guilty. She was having a lot of trouble with that concept at the moment. Those damning pieces of paper kept intruding into her thoughts. She sat down across from David.

"I'm so sorry about all of this, David." She reached over and laid her hand on his, although it took an effort for her to do so. She couldn't disguise the worry in her voice or the fear in her eyes. He placed his other hand on top of hers and held it firmly, as if to draw strength from it.

"The detectives have been questioning me non-stop. They picked me up at the dock as soon as you were sent to the hospital." His face looked incredibly tired. The twinkle was gone from his eyes, replaced by a somber stare. "They tell me that a couple of hours after you and I left Orcas yesterday, Detective Dexter showed up with a warrant for my arrest. I guess he went crazy when he heard where we'd gone, was going to send out the Coast Guard, but that must've been about the time I reached Jake's boat. We'd already radioed that we were coming into Friday Harbor. They heard the distress call, and were waiting for me at the dock. I was arrested on the spot." David's voice cracked. "They wouldn't even give me the chance to see if you were going to be okay."

"David, are you all right? How have they treated you?"

He shrugged. "Physically, I'm fine. But they've been questioning me solidly since they brought me in. The same questions, over and over and over, even though I can't give them any answers. First, they asked me about the dead man. I swear I've never laid eyes on him in my life. And then they started showing me this glossy photo of some blonde all dressed up in a black suit, they say she's missing and I've got something to do with it. I figured it was the woman whose disappearance you were investigating. I vaguely recall seeing her around the resort this week with an older man, short, sort of mean-looking. But I swear to you, Annie," he looked her directly in the eye, "I just don't know what the hell they're talking about. I never even spoke to her."

He let out a frustrated sigh. "The worst part," David looked down into his lap, "the absolute worst part was they thought I'd hurt *you*. My God, Annie, this is an absolute nightmare. I don't believe any of this, I don't know what they think I've done."

Annie wanted to be reassuring. Instead, a chill ran up her spine. He sounded sincere, but he still hadn't addressed any of her concerns. "David, I want to believe you, honestly I do, but I can't without an explanation." She couldn't block out the questions running through her mind. Why had David wanted to take her to Traxler Island, and why had he been so conveniently absent when she capsized? Not to mention the troubling concerns about the documents in David's writing. "Dex says you don't have an explanation, or won't give one. Do you have a lawyer?"

"Yeah, some guy from Seattle that Russ got hold of. I talked to him on the phone last night. But that's not why I haven't said anything. You've got to believe me, Annie, there simply isn't anything for me to say." He sat before her, clenching and unclenching his fists in frustration. "Damn it, I just don't have an explanation for those things any more than you do! Why can't anyone accept that?"

"I know a handwriting expert in Seattle. He's good, one of the best. If those documents are fakes, he can prove it."

David took a deep breath and closed his eyes. Quietly, he said, "I don't think they're fakes."

"What?"

"I said I don't think they're fakes. It . . . it looks like my writing, okay? And it's *my* island. I don't know anyone else who could have drawn that chart with that kind of detail."

"So it is Traxler Island?"

"Of course it is, and it looks like I drew it." David pushed his chair back and sighed. "But I don't *remember* drawing it, and I don't remember telling anyone else about the location of the beach and the trail to the bluff."

"Do you mean to say you've never told anyone about it?" Annie asked incredulously.

"No, of course not. I've told people about it from time to time. It's hard to explain. I try to protect the privacy of the place, you know? A few years back I took a couple of friends out there they're in Hawaii now. I guess I've been willing to describe it to people I never really thought would go there. But I haven't taken anyone there in the last couple of years, and I can't recall telling anyone about it recently. Certainly not that guy who got killed in the cottage." He raised his voice. "I swear to you I have never seen him before in my life."

"What about the list of gear? Isn't it true, David, that the list is in your handwriting as well?" As she said it, Annie realized that her questions were taking the form of a cross-examination. She wanted to believe in David's innocence, but his answers weren't satisfying her.

"How did you recognize . . . oh, those notes I left for you." He paused and smiled to himself. "It seems like such a long time ago, doesn't it?" He looked away from her, staring at the blank gray wall. "Yes, those are my writing, too. And my standard list of gear. I've used that list for years, as a hand-out in my classes."

She brightened. "So any number of people could have gotten hold of that list?"

"The list, yes. A list with my handwritten additions at the bottom? God only knows."

"David, you mean you have no recollection about writing out that list?"

"No, Annie, goddamn it, I don't." He slammed his hand down and rose explosively from the table. "And it's pretty damned obvious that you don't believe me. Well, that's just fine. That's it, you can get out right now."

"David, I didn't mean . . . " Annie stood up to meet his glare.

"Hey, I'm sorry I yelled, Annie, but I can't take this anymore. Not from them, and especially not from you." There was no room to move in the tiny space. He stepped back one pace into the corner and leveled his icy blue gaze at her. "You haven't believed one word I've said, have you? You don't trust me, Annie."

"No, David, that's not true."

"Don't try that with me. I can read it in your face."

She knew he was right, and looked down to avoid his piercing glare. "If it was just the papers, David. I could deal with that. But yesterday, that trip to the island, what happened. It scared the devil out of me, the fact that you went off and left me like that. I could've died! And even before that. Sometimes, your silences . . . the way you won't talk about yourself . . . I just don't know what to believe." She looked up at his face, pleading. "If you could just give me a logical explanation, David? That's all I'm asking."

His voice was quiet, subdued. She could hear the exhaustion in every word. "Don't you think, Annie, that if I had a 'logical explanation' I would have given it by now?"

There was a heavy silence in the room as neither spoke. "Annie, I want you to leave now. This isn't getting us anywhere."

Angry and confused, she moved to the door and motioned for the deputy.

A low murmur of conversation buzzed in the San Juan County Courthouse at 1:15. Attorneys and their clients filled the first two benches. A mother, there for her son's sentencing, was sitting stone-faced while her husband conferred with the boy's lawyer. Russ Perkins and Annie sat in the middle of the courtroom without speaking. Annie had been surprised to see him there, but after the emotional scene with David at the jail, she was glad to have the moral support.

At 1:20, two deputies led in the criminal defendants, all in faded red jump suits, handcuffed together. Once they were seated in the third row, with a deputy on either end, the handcuffs were removed. Annie had seen similar scenes hundreds of times, but her heart ached to see David being treated like a criminal.

If David had seen Russ and Annie when he entered, he didn't acknowledge it. Annie craned her neck to see if any of the attorneys were speaking to David. She had forgotten to ask Russ whom he had helped David retain, but she hoped it was someone competent. David would need all the help he could get.

Just then she saw a tall, handsome man in a tweed jacket enter through the side door. He exuded self-confidence. He strode over to where the defendants were sitting, and made arrangements with the deputy to confer with his client. He and David moved away from the other defendants, to the far side of the room.

"Russ, that's Harrison King!" Annie whispered, shocked. "That's who you contacted to defend David?"

Russ shrugged his shoulders. "I'd heard he was good."

"Good? He's the best. Didn't you see him on the news last week? He got an acquittal for the Huntington Mall sniper. Can David afford him?"

"I guess so. He told me they'd talked and it was all arranged. David didn't mention any problem with the fee."

Annie was amazed. If the charges against David weren't dismissed and he actually had to stand trial, King's fee could run easily over thirty thousand dollars. The dashing young attorney could pick and choose his clients, but also had a reputation of being in it for the money. He wouldn't have accepted David's case without thoroughly explaining his fee structure, and probably asking for a hefty retainer. Annie had no idea David had that kind of money. There was a lot she didn't know about him.

"Please rise," the bailiff announced. "The Superior Court of the State of Washington in and for San Juan County is now in session, the Honorable Judge Sylvia Hansen-White presiding." The judge was a stern looking woman in her mid-forties. Annie didn't know enough about the reputations of San Juan County's judges to know if she was liberal or conservative in the matter of setting bail.

David's case was called, and the charges against him read. His voice was controlled as he pleaded 'not guilty.'

"Your honor," the Deputy Prosecutor stated, "the State requests that bail be set at two hundred and fifty thousand dollars, given the seriousness of the crime charged. We concede that Mr. Courtney has no prior criminal record, but he also has a history of being transient. He has no permanent residence in the state and no family connections. The state feels that there is a serious risk that Mr. Courtney will flee the jurisdiction."

"Your honor," King was on his feet practically before the deputy prosecutor had finished speaking. "That kind of bail is simply unconscionable in this case. Mr. Courtney is a teacher, and has no access to that kind of funds. He's always been a law-abiding citizen, and, I'd like to point out, the evidence upon which these charges are based is entirely circumstantial and may well be fabricated. We respectfully request that Mr. Courtney be released on his own recognizance. For the court to rule otherwise would be grossly unfair to this honest, trustworthy citizen." Annie admired his style. The attorney evoked sympathy for his client without antagonizing either judge or opposing counsel. She had seen him express moral outrage on behalf of some of the state's most heinous criminals.

"I'm going to compromise, counsel." The judge reviewed the papers in front of her. "In consideration of the defendant's clean record, bail will be set at ten thousand dollars. I have also been informed by the prosecution that the Sheriff intends to investigate an important location this afternoon, and has requested that Mr. Courtney be held in custody until after that investigation has been completed."

"Your honor, that's totally unjustified and I must object on the grounds that . . . " King interjected. The judge cut him off.

"Mr. King, we have a very crowded calendar this afternoon and I don't have time for one of your lengthy harangues. I've made up my mind on this matter and wish to move along to the next case. Mr. Courtney will remain in custody until the site investigation has been completed, and then is free to go upon the posting of bail. Bailiff, call the next case, please."

As the bailiff read the next name, David was escorted by a deputy to the door leading back to the jail. David glanced around the courtroom and his eyes fell upon Annie. He pointedly looked away.

Annie glanced over at Russ. The color had drained from his face. She wondered if he'd ever been in court before. "Come on, let's get some air," she said. Outside, she fished in her purse for the ferry schedule. "We've got about forty minutes before the ferry comes. Let's find a place to sit."

In the cafe overlooking the ferry dock, Russ was still white as a sheet and hadn't said more than three words.

"Russ, is something the matter? More than the trouble with David, I mean." It felt so odd. Clearly, she was the one who ought to be upset about David. Annie couldn't figure it out. The lawsuits wouldn't affect Russ personally, and Annie had assured him from the start that his job wasn't in jeopardy.

"It's hard to explain, Annie. David's a good friend. I just can't stand to see something like this happening to an innocent man. King is good, isn't he? He can get David off?"

"Yes, he's good. Whether he can 'get David off' as you say, that's going to depend on what David comes up with in terms of a defense. Right now, he's not saying anything."

"I just never dreamed . . . at least he won't be in jail too much longer."

"Where did he get the money for bail? Ten thousand dollars is a lot of money."

"Oh, I helped him out with that. Don't worry, not from the Windsor's accounts. I wrote a personal check."

Quite a friend, thought Annie. In all of the time she'd spent with David, she hadn't heard him mention Russ's name once. But then, there was a lot David hadn't talked about.

"How long has David worked for the Windsor?"

"Oh, let's see. He came on this winter. Five, six months, perhaps."

"That's all? Did you know him before that?"

"No. Curtis Lymon hired him. I'm not really sure what his references were."

"So you never saw his resumé?"

"No. But he's certainly well qualified for the job. We've had no complaints."

"Is there anyone around the islands that's known him longer than that? Who could testify as a character witness?"

"Not that I know of. He kept pretty much to himself. Spent just about all his spare time fixing up his boat, as far as I know. Oh, he went off-island every once in a while, but I never knew where he went. It wasn't often. I'll testify for him. There's no doubt in my mind that he's innocent. They can't convict an innocent man of murder, can they?" Russ said emphatically, his jaw twitching. "He's a good man."

Annie didn't say it, but she wished she could be so certain.

Chapter 14

WITH A PHOTOCOPY of the hand-drawn chart to guide them, the Sheriff's Department helicopter piloted by Deputy Neil Crawley, an ex-Navy flyer, and carrying Detective John Dexter and Agent Marvin Frye, lifted off from Friday Harbor and swung northeast towards Traxler Island.

Before they took off, Neil Crawley compared the photocopy of David's drawing to his nautical chart of the San Juans, then passed it to Dex to study. The flight was extremely brief. Looking at the printed chart, Dex never would have thought of the tiny island as a place to land—by air or by water. It was completely round, less that a half mile in diameter, with no visible inlets for shelter. The crescent-shaped indentation, which hardly qualified as a cove, was so slight it wasn't even visible on the printed chart.

The nautical chart was supposed to show the location of sandy beaches, but none was marked on Traxler. Instead, off the northwest shore where David's chart showed an inlet, the chart had small asterisks indicating rocks, a reference to kelp beds, and a warning that the area contained hidden obstructions that would cover and uncover with the tide.

"Hell, no wonder this island of Courtney's is so private," Dexter said. "No navigator in his right mind would go near that shore. You're a boater, aren't you, Neil? Take a look at that."

"It's a sunken disaster area, all right," Crawley replied. "So how'd Courtney find it? A canoe or some damn fool thing like that?"

Dexter nodded. "A kayak, actually."

"They only draw a few inches of water," said the pilot. "I've seen 'em go right through a kelp bed and maneuver around rocks. But hell, it looks like hard work. Give me a six-pack and my Bayliner any day. Right, Dex?"

"I'm with you there, Neil."

"Okay, there's the island up ahead," said Frye stiffly.

Neil banked sharply to the left to come in for a better view. "It sure don't look like much, do it? Tiny li'l thing."

"Head for the northwest shore," said Frye.

"Right. I'll see if I can find that so-called bluff up above the so-called beach."

No beach was visible, probably because the tide was pretty high. Long strands of red-leafed bull kelp were pointing out to sea, indicating that the tide had turned and was now on its way out.

"Anywhere to land?"

"It doesn't look good, sir. That's pretty much just a little mountain top stickin' up outta the water. No beach, no flat areas of land. Wait, look there. That must be the bluff they were talkin' about. Nah, no way I can land there. I'm good, but I'm no miracle worker."

They all turned and saw the small patch of green, surrounded on three sides by steep cliff faces jutting upwards. An eagle, disturbed in its aerie by the noisy machine, screeched angrily at the chopper and spread its long wings in exit. As they approached, they could see that the small grassy plot was occupied by a nylon tent, also green. There was no room for the helicopter to land.

"What d'ya think? Should we just come back in the Zodiac?" Neil asked. "We could probably land one once the tide goes out."

"I don't know," said Dexter wearily. "Wait a sec—take a look! Neil, can you get us in any closer?"

The helicopter nosed in as close to the cliffs as it safely could, and all three men looked down. The green nylon tent was spattered with blood. Protruding from the tent, barely visible from that height, was an object that appeared to be a human foot.

"Looks like what we're here for," said Frye. "Can you get close enough for me to go down on a harness?"

"Yeah, no problem. Let's get 'er set up."

"Dexter, why don't you head back and bring the coroner. Should be able to land a Zodiac down there by that time. I'll start taking pictures while the light's good."

Agent Frye was lowered slowly onto the grass and disengaged himself from the harness. He waved an all-clear sign to the helicopter. Neil Crawley acknowledged the signal, then headed off in the direction of Friday Harbor. Damn, he thought. So the little lady really had been kidnapped, after all.

He circled the small nylon tent, looking at it from all angles. It looked new, as if this were the first time it had ever been used. It was a green Timberline A-frame—a typical two-person back-packer's tent. Frye had bought his son one just like it at REI a few summers back. He didn't expect to have much luck tracing the purchase. It was too common an item in these parts.

He looked at it more closely and saw that it had been set up incorrectly. The rain fly was on upside down and not staked out away from the tent the way it should be. He concluded that whoever set up the tent didn't have the first clue about what they were doing. He examined a hole in the side of the tent and a corresponding tear in the rain fly, the edges singed. They could easily have been made by the path of a bullet. There were bushes a few feet beyond the tent, in the direction the bullet would have traveled. There was a good chance he'd find it in there.

Extending out of the front of the tent was the pale white foot they'd seen from the chopper. There was no need to see if the woman was alive. The body was already starting to decompose. Frye didn't hurry, since he couldn't move anything until the coroner arrived. He got out the 35mm camera, put on the close-up lens, and started taking photographs.

It looked like the body had been moved. An area of grass about two feet in diameter in front of the tent was stained with blood. A lot of blood, which probably meant a chest or neck wound. A red trail led into the tent. Leaning in carefully, Frye pulled aside the tent flap and peered inside, where the woman's body lay in an awkward, crumpled heap. Frye guessed that she had been shot standing in front of the tent, fell to the ground, and lay there for awhile, bleeding heavily. Then whoever killed her must have grabbed her by the shoulders, placed her head inside the tent and shoved her feet and legs in after. Frye lowered the flap and walked away for a moment. He needed some air. No matter how many scenes like this he had seen, it always got to him. He was totally unable to put himself in the killer's place. He couldn't imagine what it would be like to commit such an act of brutality, then calmly manhandle a dead body. It made him sick.

He walked back and resumed taking pictures. A small flashlight lay at the edge of the blood-stained circle. Frye got several shots, and made a note for the lab techs to check out the battery and the on/off switch. It was no doubt burned out by now, but if the flashlight had been on, they could assume the murder had happened after dark.

She was tiny, had short blonde hair, and was wearing nothing but a bulky white sweatshirt. A pair of old jeans and a jacket lay in one corner of the tent. Her right hand was still clenched around a useless-looking little pocket knife. From the physical description, Frye assumed it was the missing woman, Marguerite Boulanger, but she no longer looked like her fashion photographs. It looked like she had been dead a couple of days, at least. In the center of her chest, right between her two tiny breasts was a neat round bullet hole.

What a shame, thought Frye. In her pictures, she looked like a real pretty lady.

Frye paced off the number of feet from the tent to the edge of the bluff. There were no footprints on the grass, but Frye could see that someone scrambling up the slope to the bluff had disturbed the vegetation. That probably wouldn't mean much, though. The woman had gotten up onto the bluff somehow. Maybe she scraped up the vegetation climbing up.

The scene disturbed him. It sure wasn't what you'd expect a kidnapping scene to look like. The victim didn't appear to have been tied up or restrained in any way. Granted, it would have been hard for the woman to escape from the island, but she could have signalled for help from passing boats. There was no evidence that she had even made a campfire. But the really odd part was this crazy camping set-up. A few feet away from the tent a cooking area had been set up—camp stove, aluminum mess kit, a nylon sack of food hung in a tree. A small canvas duffel bag lay nearby.

Frye went back and crouched in front of the tent, holding a handkerchief over his face to keep out the stench.

Only one sleeping bag.

He looked back at the cooking area. A single duffel bag. An aluminum plate with one set of utensils. Not only was there no sign that the woman had been held against her will, there were only camping provisions for one. A kidnap victim without a captor. Would a kidnapper take that great a risk? He walked over and unzipped the duffel bag. Sitting on top in plain view was a brand new Colt revolver and a box of bullets. Now didn't that just beat all?

Nothing about the scene pointed to a kidnapping. Everything indicated a solitary camper. Everything, that is, except the bullet hole in her chest. Frye couldn't ignore that.

If the kidnapper had intended to kill the woman all along, why the damned housekeeping set-up, Frye wondered? Why not just dump the body and take off? Waiting for the others to arrive, Frye cupped his hand against the wind to light a cigarette. He doubted they'd have any better luck than he had sorting this one out.

Annie sat on the gravelly beach near the cottages and stared blankly into space. All afternoon she'd been trying to work, but found herself unable to concentrate. David was still being held while the Sheriff's Department went to investigate Traxler Island. It was driving her crazy wondering if they would find more evidence linking David to the bizarre series of events that had taken place over the past few days. She dug her bare feet into the damp gravel. Even though the sun was warm on her back, she shivered slightly as she thought about the man she had been so attracted to, the man she wanted so badly to trust.

Earlier that afternoon she had tried to go over the material she had obtained from Detective Dexter, copies of the kidnap tapes, the lab results, the list of items found in Marc's cottage. He had even loaned her the entire portfolio of photographs from Forrestor.

The tapes still bothered her. She had played all of them once through on her portable dictaphone with the volume turned up, trying to make sense of the background noise. She was still convinced they had been made in a big city, but she didn't know what to make of it. There were several large cities nearby where Marguerite could have been taken—Seattle, Victoria or Vancouver, B.C.— but something didn't fit.

Annie's mental wanderings were disturbed by the sound of footsteps in the gravel behind her. She turned and saw Jimmy, Philip Spaulding's nephew. He was a miniature version of his good-looking uncle. She had met the 13-year-old in David's kayak class, and found him to be a boisterous, friendly kid. But now he was scuffling along without his usual enthusiastic bounce. "Ms. MacPherson?"

"Hi, Jimmy. What can I do for you?"

"I was just wondering if you had seen my uncle Phil anywhere. I can't find him, and I've looked all over. The guy at the front desk thought maybe he was with you."

"Sorry, I haven't seen him. Were you supposed to meet him somewhere?"

"No, I was just sorta looking for him." Jimmy walked to the edge of the water, slipped off his rubber thongs, and waded in up to his ankles. "He's disappeared a lot this week. It's no big deal." He picked up a flat skipping stone and threw it angrily across the surface of the water.

"How often has this happened?" she asked.

"Oh, I dunno. Pretty much every day." He threw another stone, too hard, and it sank beneath the surface with a plop. "Hours at a time, I haven't been able to find him, then all of a sudden he just shows up." Jimmy kicked at the water, then turned around and sat down on the gravel next to her.

"Does he tell you where he's been?" Annie asked.

"Yeah, sort of. He makes excuses. But he hasn't been telling the truth."

"What makes you say that?"

"Well everyday he's had some story or other, usually having to do with his job, like he had to meet with somebody or drive into town to mail a letter or something. So that's cool. I mean, I know this political stuff he does is important. But that doesn't make it okay to lie to me, like yesterday."

"What happened yesterday?"

"Well, like you know, the same thing happened. I was lookin' all over for him, it must've been a couple hours, you know, and then I finally found him in the lobby. He was all red in the face, and I asked him about it and he said he'd been in the weight room working out."

"That would explain why he was flushed, wouldn't it?"

"No." Jimmy sulked, picking up bits of shell and tossing them into the water. " 'Cause I was in the weight room the whole time. I know he wasn't there." Jimmy looked like he was on the verge of tears. "I guess I'm just a pain to be around."

"Jimmy, don't say that. Of course you aren't."

"Then why is Uncle Phil avoiding me and lying about it? I mean, like, I know I talk to him when he's reading and stuff, but if he just told me to shut up or buzz off for a while, I would. But he never said anything. He just ditched me, you know? Just like my big brother used to do when we were kids." Jimmy sniffed and wiped his nose on his sleeve, as if the battle to fight off the tears was getting harder. He shrugged. "I thought he liked me."

"He does, Jimmy, I swear to you. He even told me so the other day. Philip's crazy about you." She didn't know what else to say. "I'm sure he's got a good reason, Jim. Something that he just can't tell you about."

"Yeah, sure."

"Do you think Philip has a girlfriend that he doesn't want you to know about?" Annie remembered seeing Philip with Lisa, but somehow didn't think that was the explanation. It hadn't looked like the attraction was mutual.

"Nah. I wish you'd be his girlfriend, Annie. He likes you, I think, and I'm pretty sure he doesn't have a steady girlfriend. I don't know why, women are always asking him out, he's so good looking."

"What about evenings, Jim? Has he been spending his evenings with you?"

Jimmy thought about this. "Yeah. Except for one night I went to the movie in town. He dropped me off then picked me up after. Other than that, we've pretty much been together from dinner until about ten, or so. He likes to get up really early so he goes to bed about then. He lets me stay up, so long as I don't get into trouble or go anyplace."

"So you haven't seen him after ten at night?"

"Huh uh. We've just both gone to our rooms."

"You had separate rooms? Did they connect?"

"Nope. I guess there weren't any of those left. The rooms are right next to each other, but separate."

Annie registered the fact that Philip would have no alibi for the night Marguerite disappeared. She also wondered about the day Marc was killed.

"I want you to think hard about something, Jimmy. Did Philip disappear in the middle of the day on Monday, say between ten and two?" Annie had just learned that that was the coroner's best approximation of when Marc had been killed in his cottage.

He screwed up his face in concentration. "Yeah. Now that you mention it, I think so. Phil and I played tennis in the morning after breakfast. We had the court reserved from nine to eleven. Then after that Phil said he wanted to run some errands in town, so I had to eat lunch by myself. I looked for him again before my swimming class started at one-thirty but I couldn't find him. I think that might have been the first day he disappeared like that. Then Tuesday, he did the same thing. He just took off at lunchtime with no explanation."

Tuesday? That was the day Annie had observed Philip eating lunch with Nicholas Forrestor in town. But why would he need to be so secretive about that? She decided it merited checking into.

"Jim, how about if I talk to Phil about it? Would that make you feel better?"

"Uh huh," he said shyly. He reached into his pocket and came up with a few quarters. "Wanna come play Space Invaders? I'll warn ya, I'm pretty good."

"I think I'll pass. Maybe later."

"Okay." Jimmy headed off towards the resort, quarters jingling.

As soon as Jimmy had gone Annie was alone with her thoughts again. It was getting to be late afternoon. She wondered if the search of Traxler Island was over yet. She decided to go back up to the resort and see if Russ had heard anything.

She met him coming down the path looking for her. "Annie, there you are. Detective Dexter is here. He wants to talk to us."

She quickened her pace. She was both afraid and anxious to hear the news. "What did they find?"

"He didn't say. But I don't think it's good. He seemed pretty grim. And he asked Forrestor to be present."

They assembled in the music room, where there were enough chairs for everyone to sit. Nicholas Forrestor looked as calm and unfeeling as ever. Despite the warm afternoon, he was again attired in a business suit and starched white shirt.

They all sat silently while Detective Dexter gave his report. He didn't go into great detail regarding the condition of the body, except to say that Marguerite had died of a gunshot wound to the chest. The medical examiner estimated that she'd been dead two to three days. Her flashlight, which had been switched on, and the way Marguerite had been dressed indicated that she had been killed at night. Combining all of the evidence it looked highly probable that Marguerite had been killed late Monday night or early Tuesday morning, any time between 10:00 P.M. and 3:00 A.M.

Even after all the events of the past few days, the news came as a shock. Annie had been concerned for Marguerite, but hadn't actually expected her death. But she found she was even more surprised by Forrestor's reaction on learning of Marguerite's death.

The man had no reaction whatsoever.

"Is this the point where you ask me what I was doing on Monday at midnight, Detective?" Forrestor asked in a cynical voice, calmly inspecting the back of his well-manicured hand.

Dexter ignored the tone and answered politely. "Any information would be helpful, Mr. Forrestor. However, it's not at all uncommon for someone not to have an alibi for the middle of the night."

"Quite right, Detective. I was sleeping. *Alone.*" It seemed an out of place assertion for someone who had just been informed of his lover's death. "But there was no doubt she was murdered, you say?" Forrestor asked calmly. Much too calmly.

"No question whatsoever. We recovered the bullet, and I'm expecting the ballistics report to show that Ms. Boulanger was shot with the same gun that killed Marc Jarrell, a thirty-eight calibre revolver."

"I see." Forrestor rose and looked at his watch, as if he had a tight business schedule to keep. "I appreciate your taking the time to come over here, Detective. And if you could, I'd like a copy of the death certificate as soon as possible."

"Can I ask why?"

"The insurance company requires it."

"Insurance company?"

"Life insurance, Detective. I may as well tell you the details— you'll undoubtedly ferret them out eventually. Marguerite was very valuable to me. Of course her life was insured. Far below her value, unfortunately. There was, again, I'm sure this will interest you, a double indemnity clause for cases of 'accidental death,' which under the terms of the policy includes death by the hands of another. Murder, in other words. That will bring the total amount up to five hundred thousand dollars. A drop in the bucket of my total worth, if that's of any relevance. If you need any of the details, I can refer you to my insurance agent. Now, if you'll excuse me, gentlemen," as usual he ignored Annie, "I have some business to attend to."

Annie returned to her room to sort out what she'd just heard. It was time she sat down with all the information she'd gathered and tried to make sense of it all. None of the explanations she could come up with were satisfactory. It was going to be a long night.

She called room service to bring up a thermos of extra-strong coffee, pulled out a fresh legal pad, and gathered up her file of material. She had the kidnap tapes with typed transcripts, the portfolio of photographs from Forrestor, the reports from the search of Marc's cottage, and her handwritten notes of Detective Dexter's report of the search of Traxler Island. She located a pen and got ready to start making lists.

On one sheet of paper, she put the names of anyone who had any connection to Marguerite Boulanger or Marc Jarrell. The list was depressingly short—Nicholas Forrestor, Philip Spaulding, Lisa Hargraves, David Courtney. She wondered about putting Russ Perkins on the list, because of his connection with David. Not really much to go on.

The list wasn't exclusive, of course. Anyone on the island could have committed the murders. But why? The bizarre facts surrounding the death of Marguerite indicated this was no random act of violence. There had to be an answer.

Marguerite had probably been killed late Monday night. Where did that leave the various suspects? It couldn't have been Marc, since he was killed sometime during the day on Monday.

Forrestor? He said he'd been sleeping alone that night, so he had no alibi. He certainly had a motive. Five hundred thousand dollars in insurance was no small sum, even to a wealthy man like Forrestor.

Philip's daily disappearances were troublesome. Jimmy had said Philip had "run some errands" on Monday around lunchtime, and that he had never seen Phil after ten o'clock at night. That would leave him with no alibis for the times of the two murders. Philip had been spending a significant amount of time with Forrestor. Could Philip's connection to Forrestor provide him with a motive?

What about Lisa? Annie wondered just how much Marc Jarrell had mattered to the glamorous brunette. Could she have murdered her ex-husband out of revenge? That still wouldn't explain the disappearance and death of Marguerite Boulanger.

And then there was David. She couldn't ignore the evidence against him. Added to the papers found in Marc's cottage, there was now the fact that Marguerite's body had been found on Traxler

Island. David's island. Apparently, David was the only person in the area who knew it was possible to land and camp on Traxler Island. David admitted that he must have drawn the chart found in Marc's cottage. A list of camping gear in David's handwriting was found in the dead man's wallet, and Marguerite, surrounded by all the gear on the list, was found murdered on the secluded island. Yet David denied any knowledge of Marguerite or Marc Jarrell. The information about the island and the gear had to have come from David. There was no other explanation.

On top of all that, on Wednesday David was insistent that Annie accompany him to Traxler Island. Why, Annie asked herself, over and over again. According to the medical examiner, Marguerite would have been dead by that time. Did David know about the murder? Was he perhaps going to destroy evidence? Under the circumstances, Annie just couldn't make herself believe that the trip was purely coincidental. Annie didn't want to think about the possibilities.

The accident with the ski boat had her even more confused. Maybe the accident had in fact been a lucky break, saving her from a far worse fate at the island. Or maybe the speedboat accident itself had been set up, a murder attempt that failed because Jake the fisherman had been on the scene. That reminded her—she still had to find out who the ski boat belonged to. Annie put that on her list of things to do.

Evaluating criminal cases had been her job for five years. A prosecutor's first task was to look at the evidence against a defendant the way a jury would, and decide whether to go to trial, strike a deal, or drop the charges. Although there was no direct evidence linking David to either Marguerite Boulanger's or Marc Jarrell's murder, the circumstantial evidence made him look like an accomplice, and an accomplice could still be charged with first degree murder. Looking at this case as a prosecutor might, Annie had to admit that unless David could come up with a reasonable explanation, the evidence was strong enough to justify going to trial.

The state was only required to prove the elements of the crime, not the motive. It was nevertheless disturbing not to have a reason why David would have been involved. It could be money, of course.

Annie had been surprised to learn that David had enough money to retain a high-priced defense attorney. Had he been paid a hefty sum for his participation?

If the case against David were true, Annie would have been with David within hours of the crimes being committed. It was a terrifying thought. Could he have murdered Marc at noon, then casually instructed a class at 1:30? Worse than that, could he have shared a romantic sunset with Annie on Monday evening, then traveled to Traxler Island to commit yet another brutal murder at midnight? The mere concept made Annie's blood run cold.

It wasn't impossible, of course. She thought back to the book Ellen had loaned her, the one about the psychopathic medical student, Timothy Baron. He had murdered a series of nurses, all petite, wholesome-looking brunettes in their early twenties. After each gruesome murder, he had returned home to his live-in girlfriend and made passionate love to her. The girlfriend had remained convinced of his innocence in the face of damning evidence, and had even testified at his trial. She said that despite the evidence, she could never believe that the man she knew as sensitive and caring could be capable of violence.

Was Annie deluding herself? Was she placing too much emphasis on her feelings for David, and ignoring the facts?

A knock at the door made her jump. Then she remembered she had called room service. She got up and opened the door.

"Annie, we've got to talk."

She took a deep breath. Without a word she let David Courtney into the room and shut the door behind him.

Chapter 15

HE MOVED TO put his arms around her. Her body stiffened, enough for David to notice and back away.

"You really believe I'm guilty, don't you?" he said, shaking his head in disbelief.

"David, I won't lie to you, but I'm confused. I don't know what to believe."

He moved away from her to the far side of the room and looked out the window, avoiding her questioning gaze. "As soon as the Sheriff's Department finished their search of the island, they let me post bail and get out of there. God, I've never been so glad to get out of anywhere in my life." Annie noticed him clenching and unclenching his fists. "The reason I came by was to apologize for getting so angry at you at the jail. I *thought* I was just overreacting. But now," he looked at her face, searching it for answers, "I can see you really don't trust me. I don't know what to say."

She moved a stack of papers and sat down on the bed. "David, I want to trust you . . . "

"That's not the same thing, is it?"

"If there were only some reasonable explanation . . . you know they found Marguerite Boulanger's body on Traxler Island, don't you? Along with all the gear specified on your list?"

He nodded. "I know." David gazed out the window. The peaceful water beyond held no answers. "I'm sure there must be a logical explanation, Annie, it's just that I don't know what it is. I was hoping that you might help me figure it out, but I guess that's out of the question."

"Damn it, David, you're asking for too much. You want me to have blind faith in you, and to ignore all of the evidence that connects you to these crimes. I can't do that. I . . . I don't really know you."

"I thought we'd gotten to know each other pretty well."

"I'm sorry," she whispered, looking away. For a long moment, neither spoke. "But I am trying to find the answers." She gestured to the bed, where the tapes and reports were spread out. "If there's an answer in there, I'll find it. I just need time to sort it all out." She looked up at him. "Can you tell me what you were doing on Monday, between ten A.M. and two P.M.?"

"More questions? Damn it all, I've been answering questions day and night. I though that being let out on bail meant that would stop for awhile."

"I'm sorry, David, but you're asking me to believe in you. I want to, but I can't unless I know the facts."

He sighed. "*Facts.* It's just that the *facts* don't seem to be much help. All right," he sat down in the chair by the window and stared up at the ceiling, "I was down at the workshop near the boat dock doing some repair work. When I finished, around noon I guess, I went back to the *Electra* and grabbed some lunch, and read a book till I had my class at one thirty."

"You were alone the whole time?"

"Yes."

"What about Monday night, after we watched the sunset and you dropped me off?"

"That was the night the woman was killed, wasn't it? I was alone. After our evening together, I was feeling a little overwhelmed. I needed some time by myself to pull my thoughts together. I stayed up for a couple of hours just thinking and watching the stars, then went to sleep. I spend a lot of time alone, Annie. It's the kind of person I am. That doesn't make me a killer."

The next question was harder. Annie had no way of knowing whether she'd get an honest answer. "Why were you so insistent on taking me to Traxler Island?"

"You want logical answers for everything. Is that the way lawyers are, that everything has to have a 'reasonable explanation' or it can't be true? I was taking you to Traxler Island because I felt like it, okay? It's a special place to me, and you're the first person I've wanted to show it to in a long time. The same way I wanted to show you the sunset from Mount Constitution. Hell, I'm a romantic. I don't have a logical explanation for everything I do. And I certainly don't have a logical explanation for why you've gotten under my skin, Annie MacPherson, but you have. It isn't the least bit logical, is it? Here you are, this brainy workaholic from the city, always having to think everything through rationally. Well I'm not like that. I do things because I feel like it. I've chosen a lifestyle that allows me the time and energy to do what I want, when I want. And I don't give a damn whether it's the least bit logical."

There was another knock on the door, and a voice called out, "Room Service."

David stood up. "I'm going. You think whatever you have to about your logical answers." He opened the door and squeezed past the young man holding the tray of coffee. Annie didn't have a chance to respond.

Annie poured herself a cup of strong black coffee. She couldn't let the turmoil she was feeling inside immobilize her. She had to keep going. She had to know one way or the other whether David was involved.

She turned back to the pile of papers and tapes, but felt like she was making no progress. The transcripts of the tapes held no discernible clues. They were all about the same length, less than two minutes long, all recordings of Marguerite's voice. The man whose muffled shout could be heard on the first tape never appeared again. Why? Annie put down the transcripts and decided to try listening to the tapes again. She started with the last tape this time, inserting it in her dictaphone and turning up the volume. The voice was quavering, fearful. It did indeed sound like someone was standing over her, coercing her to make the tapes. But it also sounded exactly like the first tape.

On this particular tape the background noise seemed to be the loudest. She could definitely hear muffled traffic noises, possibly the clanging bell of a garbage truck backing up, cars sounding their horns.

Wait. Could that be it? She rewound the tape and listened to it again. And again. Yes, she distinctly heard the blaring of automobile horns. One by one, she inserted all of the tapes into the machine. Car horns on all of them. Now she was certain. Those tapes could not have been made anywhere in the vicinity of the San Juan Islands.

Annie had spent the majority of her life in Seattle. She had learned to drive on Seattle streets. Traffic had gradually increased over the years, and she'd been stuck in more than her share of traffic jams, but one thing remained the same. Drivers in the Pacific Northwest didn't honk their horns. Not continuously, anyway, like the racket on the tapes. No more than an occasional toot if someone on the freeway tried to cut in front too close. Victoria and Vancouver drivers were even more polite.

She recalled, however, the first time she'd ridden with her

partner, Joel, a native New Yorker, soon after he had moved to the west coast. Driving through downtown he leaned on his horn constantly, yelled at pedestrians, darted in and out of lanes. They'd even joked about how he drove like a typical New Yorker. Since then, he'd been forced to tone down his driving style, and ease up on the horn.

Marc Jarrell, Marguerite Boulanger, and Nicholas Forrestor were all from New York. Annie would have bet a month's salary the tapes were made in New York City before any one of them arrived in Washington State.

She tried to put this fact together with the other evidence. Marguerite was found dead on Traxler Island, surrounded by camping gear set up for one person. There had been no evidence of a captor. If the tapes of Marguerite's voice had been made in advance, there could only be one conclusion. Marguerite Boulanger had planned her own "kidnapping."

But who was involved with her? Marc Jarrell had possession of the tapes, the chart of Traxler, and the list of camping gear. Either he had been involved in the scheme, or had discovered the evidence and was planning to blackmail Marguerite. Annie considered this possibility. It didn't sound right. It was more likely that Marc had been a co-conspirator.

What about Nicholas? They could have been in it together to defraud the insurance company. But no, the insurance was for Marguerite's *life*. She would never have participated in a scheme that included her own murder.

Annie thought about David again. He must have provided the chart and the list of gear. No one else even knew about Traxler Island. As much as she didn't want to believe it, Annie had to face the facts.

This certainly cast a whole new light on Marguerite Boulanger. Who was she really? She couldn't have been the innocent "waif" Nicholas described. Before her disappearance, Annie had seen her once or twice around the resort. She tried to think back to what she had seen.

Sunday afternoon after her kayak class Annie had gone out to the pool to relax and enjoy the sunshine. She remembered Marguerite appearing at the pool escorted by Forrestor. She had been dressed all in white, a thigh-length jersey shift, belted around her tiny hips with a silver Navaho belt. Dozens of wire-thin silver bracelets jangled musically on her wrist, and turquoise and silver earrings brushed against her pale cheeks. Dark blue sunglasses hid her eyes. Her short blonde hair was stylishly cut. She kissed her companion at the pool entrance. Forrestor left, looking distracted.

The chaise lounge next to Annie at the pool, recently vacated by an overweight matron with a romance novel, was the only one unoccupied. The diminutive blonde surveyed the scene, then had walked slowly, almost insolently, in Annie's direction and claimed the seat. She removed a St. Moritz beach towel and a copy of *Paris Match* from her shoulder bag. After languorously pulling the shift over her head, moving as if performing for an audience, Marguerite reclined on the chaise, adjusting her position like a cat. She beckoned for the waiter and ordered a Bloody Mary.

The only flaw Annie was able to notice, when the woman crossed her slender legs, was a horrible scar running across the top of her right knee and down the inner side of her leg.

If Nicholas Forrestor's story were to be believed, he had taught her the role of a sophisticate in a mere six months. Annie didn't believe it for a minute.

She reached for the portfolio of photographs. She was still troubled by the Polaroid snapshot of the young Marguerite, leaning casually on the back of a car. Something was definitely wrong about the scene.

But it was a different photo that triggered a memory. Annie picked up one of the casual shots showing Marguerite dressed in a cashmere sweater that looked several sizes too big. It was just a hunch, but it could be the connection she was looking for.

FRIDAY MORNING, JULY 27

Shortly before noon the next day, Annie found Lisa in the empty gym working out on the Nautilus equipment. She was wearing a shiny fuchsia and turquoise leotard with matching headband. Her nails were varnished a matching shade of flaming pink. She was strapped into a machine that looked to Annie's untrained eye like an instrument of medieval torture—a fitting place for an interrogation.

"Annie, are you going to join me in a little sweat? This monster will do your pectorals a world of good." Lisa's pectorals didn't look like they needed any help.

"Lisa, I don't have time for small talk. I need some straight answers from you. I need to know why you lied to me."

"Lied?" Lisa struggled to free herself from the chrome contraption. "That's preposterous. Why on earth would I make up that kind of story about Marc Jarrell if it weren't true? Do you think I'm crazy? Every word I told you was the complete and honest truth."

"*Complete*, Lisa? You know damn well you didn't tell me the complete story. You left out one rather significant fact, didn't you?" Annie was calm. Lisa clearly wasn't. "Here." Annie handed Lisa one of the photographs of Marguerite. Lisa's eyes flashed.

"I haven't the faintest idea who this is," she huffed. The brunette threw a towel around her neck and started to move towards the door. "I refuse to play your silly mind games."

"Oh, that's good." Annie applauded. "But as a trained actress you really ought to have better control of your facial expressions. If you won't talk to me, that's fine. Maybe Detective Dexter will have better luck."

"Why the hell should I talk to you? I was a fool to tell you anything."

"I told you before that I'm not out to get you, and that's still the case. All I'm interested in is your information. Detective Dexter, however, might not see it that way. Especially if I were to tell him about all the cocaine you have in your room. That really is a lovely little cloisonné box you keep it in."

"How did you? That's not legal . . . you can't . . . "

Annie walked over to the telephone on the wall. "I'm sure I've got his number in here," she said, looking through her purse. "Mmm, here it is." She began to dial the phone.

"Wait!" Lisa said tentatively. Annie glanced at Lisa over her shoulder, but continued dialing.

"Stop that." Lisa stormed over to the phone, took it from

Annie's hand and slammed it down. Annie was half-afraid Lisa might strike her.

"Would you like to talk?" Annie asked calmly. "Someplace other than the sauna this time."

Lisa's muscles tensed. "Yes."

They decided to go to Lisa's room. This time the maid had had an opportunity to remove any tell-tale champagne glasses. The bottles of nail polish were wiped off and neatly aligned in a row on the bedside table, and the ashtrays had been emptied. Lisa rushed into the bathroom to see if the cloisonné box was still on the counter. She hurriedly pushed it into a drawer.

"Make yourself comfortable," Lisa called. "I need a drink. Would you like one?" Annie declined.

Lisa returned carrying a tumbler. Her suite came equipped with a wet bar and tiny refrigerator. She plunked two ice cubes into her glass, and poured herself a generous measure of Chivas, finishing the bottle. "Are you sure you don't want some? Unless of course, drinking Scotch in one's own hotel room is a crime." They sat in the two armchairs facing the picture window.

"I've got to ask you something, first." Lisa took a sip of her drink. "Why don't you think I killed anyone?" Lisa seemed calmer now, back in her own territory. She lit one of the thin brown cigarettes and blew the smoke towards the ceiling. "I'm sure it's not because you think I'm incapable of violence."

"It's hard to explain. I was a prosecutor in Seattle for five years. The last three and a half years I did only homicides. I met enough murderers to last a lifetime. I also got to know suspects who were wrongly accused."

"Don't tell me you can tell the difference just by looking at someone." Lisa laughed, without humor.

"Not quite, but I began to sense that I could after talking to the suspects, getting to know them. I believe strongly in my gut reactions. I'm usually right."

"And your intuition tells you I'm innocent." Lisa smiled a cat-like smile.

"I didn't say 'innocent,' Lisa. I suspect that your days of innocence are far behind you. All I'm saying is that I don't think you're a murderer. Now I need to know about Marguerite Boulanger."

"Marguerite Boulanger?" Lisa chuckled, giving the name an exaggerated French pronunciation. "That's rich, it really is. Is that really what she was calling herself?" Lisa stared at the photograph. "Do you speak French?"

"Just a little."

"Do you know what *boulanger* means?" Lisa asked.

"A boulangerie is a bakery. It must mean 'baker.' "

"Right. And how about 'marguerite' ... this one's a little harder. And it has nothing to do with a salt-rimmed glass."

Annie hadn't a clue.

"It means 'daisy'—the little white flower. The name of the woman in your photograph, at least when I knew her in New York, was plain old Daisy Baker. And I thought I'd seen the last of her."

Annie had a thought. "When Marc left you. You said he left with another woman?"

Lisa got up to refill her drink, pulling another bottle of Chivas out from under the wet bar. "She's the one, the little bitch. I knew I shouldn't have mentioned anything about another woman. She was one of the first people I met in New York. We shared an apartment in Manhattan. We met in acting class, although Daisy wasn't that keen on acting. She was always more interested in modeling. You never would have believed she could model if you saw the way she looked on weekends. She always wore the same pair of ragged jeans and an old white sweatshirt, she must've had them for years.

"But the main thing I remember about Daisy is that she hated to work, plain and simple. She was always thinking up new get-rich-quick schemes. Some of her ideas were ridiculous, others were just plain illegal."

"I take it she wasn't French?" Annie asked. It was clear Nicholas had either lied about picking up the poor little gamine, or he had been conned.

"I'm shocked that she was able to pull that one off. She couldn't even speak French, but she was always trying to mimic accents. She was pretty good at that. No, little Daisy was an all-American girl."

Lisa thought for a moment. "To be truthful, I don't know where she was from. She always made a big point of telling everyone she was 'born and raised in Manhattan' but I never believed her."

"Why's that?"

"It's hard to explain, but when I met her she just didn't seem like a city person. Until I taught her a few things, her taste was atrocious, strictly Sears catalog. What else? She didn't have any family in New York as far as I could tell. And she didn't even have a trace of a New York accent. Her natural speaking voice, when she wasn't putting on airs, had a twang to it, almost midwestern."

Annie had a thought, and pushed it to the back of her mind. A certain detail she'd have to check when she got back to her room. "I'm curious about the scar on her knee," Annie said. "Did she get that while you knew her?"

"No, it was an old scar, from before I knew her. She didn't like talking about it. The only time I remember her mentioning it was one time I was dating a doctor, and she asked him about plastic surgery. He took a look at it, and said the scar would be difficult to remove. He said that it must have been quite a few years ago, before they performed arthroscopic surgery for knee injuries, and she just said 'yes, a long time ago,' and changed the subject."

"You never asked her how it happened?"

"No, but I suspect it may have been from an automobile accident. She didn't drive, and I asked her about that one time. She said she had a fear of driving because of an accident she'd been in. She didn't say any more and I didn't push it."

"How long did you share an apartment together?"

"About six months, the first time. I thought I'd seen the last of her when she managed to convince a rich sugar daddy to take her in and spend gobs of money on her."

"Nicholas Forrestor?"

"No. Before Forrestor. The first guy was an obnoxious Texan. But about a year later she showed up on my doorstep again. He'd died, but left all his money to charity, so she was back to square one."

"Then what?"

"She moved back into my apartment. She said it was just until she got her feet back on the ground. I interpreted that to mean until she found another sugar daddy. It all became clear to me afterwards that I was just a pawn in one of her schemes. She was the 'friend' who introduced me to Marc. She knew I had money, and also knew I had a taste for hunks like Marc. She'd been so successful finding wealthy old men to support her, she figured she could find a rich set-up for her boyfriend as well. She put him up to the whole marriage thing, thinking there was money in it. When the trust fund didn't work out, she came up with the alternate plan of stealing me blind and getting out of town. It was one of the reasons I never held it against Marc. The whole scheme had 'Daisy' written all over it. There was never any malice in Marc's tiny little brain."

"So you held a grudge against Marguerite, I mean Daisy?"

"How can I explain how I felt? If you've never been conned, you probably won't understand. I was angry with *myself* more than anything. I was stupid to be taken in the way I was. In a way, I had to hand it to her, that she was able to pull it off."

Lisa drained the last of her drink, and looked directly at Annie. "I'm not going to try to convince you that I didn't hate the little slut. I'm not that good an actress. All I can say is that I didn't kill her. I'm not sorry it happened, but I'm afraid I can't take the credit."

Chapter 16

FRIDAY EVENING

ELLEN O'NEILL WALKED into Annie's room and flopped down into a chair. She was attired in skimpy nylon running clothes and dripping in sweat.

"You really ought to take up running, Annie. There's such a high when you hit that fourth or fifth mile. God, it's great. If I had to choose between running and sex . . . " She thought about it for a moment, then shook her head. "What a stupid question. Let's hope I never have to choose! I came by because I have the most enormous craving for Mexican food. What do you say?"

"Sounds great," Annie said distractedly, still staring at the photographs spread out on the bed.

"That's the woman, isn't it? Mind if I take a look?"

"I really shouldn't let . . . oh, I don't know. I'm so tired at this point. Maybe a fresh viewpoint would help."

Ellen picked up one of the photographs. "She's gorgeous. Was she a model?"

Annie nodded. She filled Ellen in on the information she had gleaned from Lisa. "At least now we know that 'Marguerite Boulanger' wasn't an uneducated waif picked up off the street by Forrestor and transformed overnight into a high fashion model. According to Lisa, her name was Daisy Baker and she'd been modeling and acting for years before she met Forrestor."

"It sounds like he wasn't her first con job, either."

"She knew how to earn a living, that's for sure."

"What about before Lisa knew her? Where's she from?"

"That's what's puzzling me," Annie replied. "Lisa wasn't able to tell me much about Daisy's past. There was the auto accident that caused the scar on her knee, but Lisa said Daisy was very reluctant to talk about it. It obviously had a major psychological impact on her, to the point that years later, she still didn't drive. The only other thing we know is that Daisy always insisted she was 'born and raised in Manhattan.' "

"You said 'Daisy insisted.' You don't think it's true?"

"Lisa didn't buy it. Daisy didn't have a New York accent, or the sophistication of a native New Yorker. Lisa said she would have guessed midwest." Annie stared at the pictures again. "You're originally from the midwest, aren't you?"

"Des Moines, Iowa. Can't get much more midwestern than that. Those tapes you have, can you tell anything from the accent?"

Shaking her head, Annie walked over to the desk drawer and pulled out her portable dictaphone with one of the tapes in it. "Here, have a listen. I don't think it can help us in placing her. The problem is that on the tapes Daisy is speaking as 'Marguerite,' faking a French accent."

Ellen listened for a moment, then stopped the tape. "It's not a perfect French accent, but it's not bad. I can see why Nicholas was fooled."

"Manhattan. Manhattan." Annie was mumbling to herself. "Why would she say Manhattan, and not just New York City?"

"Annie, this could be really stupid . . . "

"Hmmm?" Annie wasn't listening. She had picked up the "before" picture of Daisy, where she was leaning against the back of a car by a highway. "I know what bothered me about this picture," she said. "When Nicholas showed it to us, he was saying she was French. But this isn't a picture of France! The car is a Chevy, it's got a U.S. license plate, and the background looks like the kind of barren highways you see driving cross-country. I'm sorry, were you saying something?"

"Annie, let me see that," Ellen said urgently. Annie handed her the photo. Ellen scrutinized it, then smiled. "We'll have to get an enlargement to be sure, but I would swear on a stack of bibles I'm right."

"What? Tell me."

"The color of the license plate on the car is right. If we enlarge it, we'll be able to read the printing, and see what state this is from. It all fits. I think Daisy was telling the truth when she said she was from Manhattan."

"What are you talking about?"

"I've probably driven this very stretch of highway. If I'm right, this picture was taken on Interstate 70, not far from Manhattan, Kansas!"

An insistent telephone stopped them as they were heading out the door. Annie picked it up and heard:

"Uh, hello?—Jason, not now. Daddy has to talk on the phone— Hello?" She could hear the drone of a children's program in the background.

"Feinstein, I've been meaning to call you. There are some things I need you to check out for me."

"MacPherson! What's going on? The last I heard was a call from the medical insurance carrier verifying coverage after they admitted you to the hospital! Then when I called the hospital you had checked out. Will you please tell me what you've been up to?"

"It's an incredibly long story, which I will tell you in complete boring detail once I get back, but . . . "

"So why were you in the hospital?"

"I got a chill."

"Why do I suspect that's a gross understatement?"

"Really, I'm fine now, but I don't have time to talk. I need a favor."

"So you think I owe you a favor, is that it?"

"We'll be even after this, I promise."

"All right. I guess I can help you out."

"Great. I need some information. Do you have a pencil? Okay, the first name is Philip Spaulding. He's heavily involved in state and local politics. I need you to find out everything you can on the candidates and causes he's worked for. From what I know so far, his candidates seem to be from the liberal side of the Democratic party, and his causes fairly left-wing."

"That should be easy enough, my brother-in-law is a Precinct Committeeperson. He'll know the right people to talk to."

"Next, I need a rundown on political contributions made by a man named Nicholas Forrestor, from New York."

"Do you think there's a connection?"

"I'm not sure. Forrestor doesn't strike me as the type who would support liberal causes, but there's some type of connection between them and I have to find out what it is. If you come up with a dead end, I'll have to go back to the drawing board."

"Is that it?"

"No, not quite. I need you to find an investigator to go to Manhattan, Kansas, to do a background check for me. The nearest major city is—Ellen, can you help me out?"

"Mmm, probably Topeka."

" . . . Topeka. I need everything they can find on a woman named Daisy Baker from Manhattan—birth certificate, any marriages, arrest record, lawsuits, anything at all. I'm particularly interested in any record of an auto accident. The accident was several years ago and may have involved a knee injury."

"Time out, MacPherson. What the hell are you talking about? Kansas?"

"Honestly, I'll tell you everything when I've got time. But right now I'm about to be beaten up by a starving marathon runner."

"This had better be good, MacPherson. Now, let me get this down. 'Daisy Baker.' That's a pretty common name. Do you have a physical description, birthdate, social security number?"

"About five feet tall, blonde, attractive. Date of birth would be approximately twenty-six years ago. Recently she lived in New York and may have worked as a model. That's all I've got."

Joel whistled into the phone. "You don't ask for much, do you? When do you need this?"

"Yesterday."

"Of course. Why not sooner?"

"I don't want to rush you."

"Right. I'll do what I can. But listen, next time a case requires a week's stay in a cushy resort, I'll go and make you stay in Seattle. I'll chain you to your desk if I have to."

"Sounds good to me, Feinstein, I could use the rest."

They settled on Bilbo's, an Eastsound restaurant famous for its margaritas and authentic Mexican cuisine, even though they knew there would be a wait on a Friday night. Twinkly white lights lit up the fence around the restaurant located in an old house. Inside, the decor glowed with desert colors, bundles of dried red chiles, and painted terra cotta dishes. The tiny waiting area was filled to capacity, with more patrons outside waiting on the patio. The hostess informed them the wait would be forty-five minutes.

"Spaulding party, your table is ready." Annie looked up as she heard the hostess mention the name. When Philip wandered in from the patio, he did a double-take.

"Oh, uh, Annie. Hello."

"Philip, meet Ellen O'Neill. Ellen, Philip Spaulding is another guest at the resort."

Philip shook hands somewhat nervously, glancing around. "A friend was supposed to meet me here, but it's been half an hour. It looks like I may have been stood up."

"That wouldn't happen to be Nicholas Forrestor, would it?" Annie asked casually.

"Uh, yes, as a matter of fact. How did you know?"

"Oh, no particular reason. It just seems like you two have been spending quite a bit of time together, so I assumed." Philip seemed at a loss for words when the hostess appeared.

"Mr. Spaulding, I have your table ready. If you're still waiting for your guest, I really should give the table to someone else."

"Uh, well. Will the table seat three? Ladies? Would you care to join me?"

It would have been awkward to refuse, and neither woman minded foregoing the long wait for a table. Annie was dying to find out the nature of the connection between Philip and Forrestor, and hoped to do a little subtle probing. Philip, however, artfully steered the conversation onto other subjects.

The dinner was excellent. Ellen said she had gotten hooked on good Mexican cooking during her college years in Tucson, and usually had a tough time in Seattle satisfying her cravings. She assured them that Bilbo's chiles rellenos lived up to her demanding standards.

Annie was trying to think of ways to bring the conversation back to Nicholas Forrestor. Before she could speak, she noticed Philip quietly humming along with the background music. "That's really lovely," Ellen commented. "What is it?"

"Oh, I didn't even know I was humming. I often do, when there's a tune running through my head. That one's quite haunting, it's been with me for days now. It's an old Irish folktune. The choral group I belong to gave a concert three Sundays ago at Meany Hall. I'm still humming all the songs."

Annie quickly looked down at her menu to hide her surprise. The date and place, as well as the tune Philip was humming, were familiar. She had attended the concert he was talking about to hear a friend sing. The fact that Philip had sung with that particular choral group got Annie thinking in a whole new direction. She wasn't quite sure what to do with this interesting piece of information. "So music is another one of your many talents?" she asked.

"Actually, no," Philip said modestly, chuckling. "I wish it were. I have to admit I'm a pretty lousy singer. Luckily I'm one of those rare creatures known as a tenor, always in demand if one can come anywhere close to holding a tune."

"Have you been singing with the group long?"

"Several years now. I got into it more for the social aspect than the singing. I've found it's an excellent way to meet people with similar interests. The singing is incidental, it's really more of a reason for a social gathering."

Philip's statement only confirmed Annie's suspicion. The thought was startling, but she realized that she could have stumbled onto the connection she was looking for between Forrestor and Philip. She decided to pursue it with Philip at another time. In private.

That evening when Annie got back to her room, the photos were still spread all over the bed. The picture of young Daisy leaning on the car was in the center, surrounded by the fashion poses. Annie began to pick them up to put them away. They still held an indescribable fascination for her, and she studied each one before sliding it back into the portfolio. The first one, the picture she had chosen for identification purposes, looked the most like the woman Annie had met with Nicholas Forrestor. Daisy Baker was dressed in a black silk suit with broad shoulders and a straight skirt, pouting as she looked at her watch. The next was playful, with Daisy dressed all in red, blowing soap bubbles and laughing. Her short hair was tousled and windblown, and she didn't look a day over sixteen. A third was a romantic pose, with soft lighting and down-cast eyes.

And then there was the picture that stood out from all the others. Nicholas Forrestor had called it the "before" picture, the young Daisy Baker in dirty Levis and a white sweatshirt, long, straight, white-blond hair pulled back haphazardly into a pony tail, no make-up. He said this was what she looked like when he found her. So many looks, it was hard to believe they were all the same woman.

Different women. Of course, why hadn't it occurred to her before? Hurriedly she gathered up the remaining photographs, forced them back into the portfolio, and dashed out of the room.

The dock was slippery and damp. Annie forced herself to slow down to keep from falling. She could see a light glowing in the cabin of the *Electra*.

"David? Are you there?"

He immediately appeared on deck. "Annie, what is it? Is something wrong?" He helped her aboard, taking the bulky black portfolio out of her hands.

"No, just the opposite," she said, slightly out of breath. "I think I may know why you couldn't remember meeting Marguerite before. Here, let me show you." She clambered down the steps into the cabin which was illuminated by the glow of a small oil lamp. David moved the book he had been reading and she spread out the portfolio on the work table.

"Look." She searched through the portfolio until she came to the photograph of Daisy wearing the black silk suit, ropes of pearls and high heels. She handed it to David. "Is this is the picture you were shown?"

He nodded. "That's the one. I swear I don't recognize her. Why, are there are other pictures?"

"There's an entire portfolio. Detective Dexter only circulated copies of this one because we thought it most closely resembled Marguerite Boulanger."

"That makes sense."

"Sure, on the surface. The other photographs in the portfolio really don't look much like the woman who was at the resort this week. But that's just the point, don't you see? Marguerite Boulanger, also known as Daisy Baker, was one of those people who had the ability to look entirely different just by changing her hair, her clothes, her makeup, even her expression. If you didn't know it, you wouldn't guess these were all the same person." She pulled several of the poses out and laid them on the table. David shook his head in amazement.

Annie continued. "You didn't recognize the picture they showed you, but you only saw one of her poses. Maybe you actually did meet her before, but her appearance was different. Maybe one of these other pictures will strike a chord."

David began to examine them one by one, and let out a slow

whistle. "I don't believe it. If you hadn't just told me, I would've sworn these were all different women. Or girls. Look, in this one she even looks like a kid." He held up the bubble-blowing picture and studied it closely.

"But she wasn't," said Annie. "Except for the snapshot, these were all taken within the last few months. According to Forrestor, she was twenty-six years old."

David carefully examined each of the pictures, but kept coming back to the one of Daisy blowing bubbles. "Something about this one," he mumbled, still staring at the childlike expression, "I don't know . . . you said there was a snapshot?"

Annie looked inside the portfolio. The small Polaroid was still inside. She pulled it out and silently handed David the photograph of the young Daisy in jeans and sweatshirt.

The color drained from his face.

"What is it, David. Do you recognize her?"

He was almost trembling. "Not *her*, Annie, *him*. A young boy! Here," he said, handing her the picture. "Stare at the face and the body. Now, instead of long straight hair, picture a boy's hair cut, sort of bedraggled, Dennis the Menace style." Annie tried to do as he said. "I remember now—but it was a teenaged boy I told all about Traxler island."

Annie could see it. Daisy had been so tiny, with no hips or bustline to speak of. Her features were not delicate, her mouth was a bit broad. Given short hair and no makeup, she could indeed pass for an adolescent boy. "When, David? Think hard."

"February . . . March? Yeah, it was the off-season, things were slow. I started working here about the first of the year, but I wasn't teaching any outdoor classes yet, just the indoor sessions on stars and marine biology. I was spending a lot of time getting the equipment in order for spring and summer. For about a week, this young kid was constantly hanging around, interested in everything I was doing, asking questions. I didn't mind, I like it when kids are curious. I can't recall everything we talked about. He kept pumping me for information the way kids do."

"Was he with anyone?"

"He said he was with his older brother who wasn't interested in the ocean or the islands. I don't recall that I ever saw him."

"I wouldn't be surprised if the 'older brother' looked a lot like Marc Jarrell."

"You're probably right."

"What about the island? What did you tell him, her, about it?"

"Okay, there was one day he was helping me paint the dock, and we were talking all afternoon. He was getting into this sort of fantasy trip, asking me about the most secluded place I knew. He was telling me that when he turned eighteen, he was going to run away and become a hermit, find an island somewhere and live like Robinson Crusoe. He wanted to know if I knew anyplace like that. It was all a pipe dream. First, I told him about some spots up in Alaska and in the Queen Charlotte Islands, a few places where I've never seen a soul. Well, that didn't appeal to him. Too remote, he wanted to be able to come back and buy food and supplies. So I told him about Traxler Island."

"The chart. Do you remember drawing him the chart?"

"I do now. He had a pen and pad of paper with him. He was writing down things I said as we talked. When we got talking about the island, he handed me his paper and had me draw a chart of it. I thought from the way he was talking that it was all a fantasy game. He told me he'd never even been in a small boat, and couldn't swim very well. I think I blanked it out because I thought we were just shooting the breeze. He was only going to be on Orcas a few days, and I was sure he'd never even come back to the San Juans. So I played along, gave him one of my Xeroxed gear lists, everything he'd need in order to camp out. The boy had never even camped out before. He left after two or three days, and I forgot all about it."

He sighed, sinking down onto the padded seat across from the chart table. "What does it all mean?"

Annie sat down next to him, the blue jean snapshot in her hands. "Can you be sure that the 'boy' you remember was Daisy Baker, the woman in these pictures?"

"No question."

"If that's the case," Annie continued, "then it was definitely Daisy Baker, herself, and not some unknown kidnapper, who found out about the island. It confirms my theory, that there never was a kidnapping. It sounds like she orchestrated the entire scheme, with Marc Jarrell as an accomplice, to extort 'ransom' money out of Forrestor."

"We've got to tell Detective Dexter. Surely he'll let me off when he hears this?"

Annie took his hand. "I'm not sure, David. Even though Daisy Baker wasn't kidnapped, she didn't murder herself. Neither did Marc. There's still a killer loose, and the only evidence the detectives have to go on connects you with Traxler Island. They might not believe your story about how you gave the information to Daisy. I'm sorry, but I know how to think from the State's point of view only too well. This additional evidence might just convince them that you actually knew Marguerite was there this week. You could have met her earlier this year, helped her devise the plan to extort money from Nicholas, then for some reason something went wrong and you decided to kill your accomplices. Or maybe someone could have paid you to do it. Do you see? You're still not off the hook till we find out who the killer is."

He looked intently into her eyes. "What about you, Annie? Now that I've got a logical explanation for the chart and list of gear, do you believe me that I didn't have anything to do with the murders?"

She returned his gaze without blinking, staring into his bright blue eyes. "Yes, David. I believe you."

He gently pulled her closer and kissed her on the forehead. "I think I can believe *you're* telling the truth this time, too." He kissed her again on the lips, running his fingers through her hair. She wrapped her arms around him and let him hold her, leaning her head on his shoulder. "I've missed you," he whispered, hardly loud enough for her to hear. She leaned back and looked at him in the yellow glow of the oil lamp, and they both smiled. "I've missed you, too."

He pulled her to him again, strongly this time. "Stay with me, Annie," he murmured, "I need you with me tonight. I want you with me." He brushed the hair away from her face. She closed her eyes and welcomed his embrace.

Annie awoke to the gentle rocking of the boat. The early morning sunshine made dancing patterns on the V-bunk, accompanied by the cries of seagulls outside and the clinking of the stays against the mast. She heard bustling noises in the galley and could smell the rich aroma of fresh-brewed coffee.

"David?" She sat up and peered out through the door into the main cabin.

"Hey, you really are a sound sleeper." David came and sat on the bunk beside Annie and gave her a gentle good-morning kiss. "I've been making all kinds of noise out here trying to wake you up."

"A futile task. I've slept through everything from earthquakes to rock concerts. Nothing but dynamite will do the trick." She reached up and put her hands behind his neck, pulling him down for a long, slow kiss. She liked the way his beard tickled. After a few moments, he reluctantly pulled away, and gave her an ultimatum. "You have to make a choice: me or a cup of coffee. It's just finished brewing."

"What kind of choice is that in the morning? Why can't I have both?"

"You can. But which first?"

"Coffee, of course."

"You're crazy." He shook his head and smiled. "Why don't you come up on deck? It's a beautiful morning."

She looked around for her clothes.

"Here, you might want this, it's a little chilly out." He pulled a bulky fisherman's sweater out of a drawer. She pulled it on and it came practically to her knees. Rolling up the sleeves, she joined David on deck, where he handed her a steaming mug of coffee. She held it in both hands for warmth. He wrapped his arm around her and held her close.

"This feels right, you know. I suspected it might."

"It's still not very logical." Annie winked at him, sipping the strong black brew.

"Not in the least. There's no rational reason for you to be sitting here, drinking my coffee, wearing my sweater, and enjoying yourself so much."

"No reason at all." Annie was silent for a moment.

"What are you thinking about?"

"Oh, past history. My endless string of bad choices. I don't know if I'm kidding myself, but this feels different. Why has it taken me so long to get here?"

"Could be because we just met," David joked.

"I'm not sure it would have made any difference if I'd met you sooner, though. I've always found myself attracted to a different type of man—fast-paced, ambitious, self-confident. 'Egotistical' would probably be more accurate. Someone who was 'going places' in a hurry. I guess I always felt I'd be pulled along for a wild ride, be able to bask in his glory."

"And it never worked out like you imagined?"

"Over and over, the part I was never prepared for was ego. A man like that doesn't want an equal partner, he wants a cheering section. No one can be allowed to eclipse his sun."

"And you don't think I'm like that?"

"Not at all." Annie shook her head, smiling. "You care where you're going, but it doesn't really matter if you get there, so long as the trip is worthwhile."

He thought about her comment. "You don't think I'm just a lazy bloke who'd rather spend his days sailing than working for a living?"

"Well, that too."

David just laughed and tousled her hair, shining coppery in the sunshine.

"You know what?" she asked, slyly.

"Hmm?"

"I've finished my coffee."

Chapter 17

SATURDAY MORNING, JULY 28

"Philip, just the person I was looking for. Can we talk for a few minutes?" Annie had just gotten off the phone with Joel and was headed for the lobby when she ran into Philip Spaulding coming down the stairs, dressed in shorts with a tennis racket in his hand. No time like the present, she told herself, trying not to think about how unpleasant this conversation might get. The truth was, she had to confront Philip with what she knew, and now was as good a time as any.

"Annie! Good to see you." He seemed a little too glad, artificially so. "Right now? Uh, sure. My court's not reserved until eleven. Would you like to grab a cup of coffee in the dining room?"

"I think we ought to go someplace private. Where we won't be overheard."

"Well, okay," he said, looking puzzled. "My room's handy, just up the stairs. Why don't we talk there?"

Entering, Annie took a quick glance around Philip's room. She was always surprised at how quickly an impersonal hotel room could take on the character of its occupant. While her room just down the hall was cluttered with lists written on yellow legal pads, scraps of discarded papers, used coffee cups and rumpled clothes, Philip's room was immaculate. His clothes were neatly hung in the closet or put away in drawers, except for a suede flight jacket carefully draped over the back of the padded desk chair. A handsome leather suitcase was tidily stowed beneath the desk, and a row of gray Clinique for Men bottles were neatly arranged in the bathroom. On the nightstand was the red Vuarnet glasses case and a stack of books, the treatise on Central America Philip had been reading before, a book on the current administration's economic policies, a biography of Benjamin Disraeli, and on top, Robert Ludlum's latest spy thriller. That morning's *Wall Street Journal* was discarded, neatly folded, in the wastebasket. Philip carefully took the flight jacket and laid it on the bed, offering Annie the desk chair. He sat opposite her on the bed and crossed his legs.

"What's on your mind, Annie?" Philip looked thoughtful and concerned. Maybe too concerned.

"Jimmy came and talked to me about how you've been disappearing for long periods during the day. He was pretty upset. He thinks you're purposefully avoiding him."

"Oh, is that all?" A look of relief crossed his face. "Nothing could be farther from the truth! I'll have to talk to him right away and set him straight. I love being around that kid. I just wish I could see him more often." She noticed that he didn't volunteer any explanation of the absences.

"That isn't all. I'm concerned as well. You know that I'm handling the financial affairs of the woman who's just inherited the resort?"

"I had heard something to that effect."

"That's left me in a position to be concerned by recent events."

"You're referring to the deaths? That man in the cottage, and Nicholas Forrestor's girlfriend?"

"Exactly."

"What does that have to do with me?" He smiled his sincere politician's smile.

"That's what I'm here to find out. When Jimmy told me about your unexplained disappearances, my first thought was that it had something to do with Nicholas Forrestor. Over the past few days I've seen the two of you together frequently."

"I don't see your point. I met Forrestor and his girlfriend in the bar the first night I was here. We struck up a conversation, and I found him to be an interesting gentleman," Philip answered, somewhat defensively. He picked up the tennis racket beside him, and began bouncing it nervously against the heel of his hand. "I simply enjoy his company, that's all."

"I don't buy that, Phil. I've met the man on several occasions. I'll be frank. He is one of the most difficult, unlikable characters I've ever encountered. He's not the type of man who would strike up a casual friendship in the bar."

"Annie, you're being very naive about this," Philip said in a patronizing tone. He set down the racket and leaned forward to speak to her. "I'm involved in politics. Networking is crucial in my job. Sure, I form friendships with people solely for the pleasure of their company, but I also cultivate individuals I feel can be useful to me. There's nothing underhanded about that. It goes on all the time. Nicholas Forrestor is a wealthy, powerful man. It makes perfect sense for me to spend time with him."

Annie shook her head. "No, Phil. It's a good excuse, which is exactly why I checked it out. In your fifteen-year involvement with the political system, you've consistently supported liberal candidates and causes. Your ethical record is unblemished. You've never solicited or accepted political contributions from an individual or special interest group whose views conflicted with your basic political ideology."

"What are you driving at?"

"I also had Forrestor's record checked. I'm sure you did the same. Despite his clout and financial status, he's stayed away from politics for the most part. His contributions have been minuscule in relation to his assets, and his contacts with established political figures have been minimal. On that basis alone, he doesn't appear to be a very likely prospect for the type of networking you describe."

"This is absurd."

"Let me finish." She rose from the chair and walked towards the window. The room seemed to have gotten smaller. She needed to place some distance between herself and Philip. "Of the contributions that Forrestor has made in the past, one hundred percent have supported extreme right-wing organizations, exactly the types of groups that you do battle with. His most recent contribution went to support military aid to the Nicaraguan Contras—a cause you violently oppose. There's absolutely no way you could have viewed Forrestor as potentially helpful to you, politically."

"I still don't understand what you're getting at. So we were friends. I fail to see how that in any way involves me in the murders that have taken place. I didn't know or care anything about Forrestor's girlfriend. I only met her once. Why would I care whether she lived or died?" Philip was trying to sound nonchalant, but his voice was strained.

"You would if you and Forrestor were more than just friends."

"What the hell are you implying?"

"I think you get my drift. You're gay, aren't you, Phil?"

"Now look here," Philip bolted up from the bed. "My friendship with Forrester is just that. He's a business acquaintance and a friend. Period. What right do you have to come in here and suggest . . . "

"You gave it away yourself, the other night when you were telling us about your choral group. When you mentioned the date and place, it rang a bell. I attended that concert. It was given by the Eastside Men's Chorale, a predominantly gay organization."

"Oh, come off it. You said it yourself, 'predominantly.' You must know that at least a third of the men are straight. Belonging to that group means nothing, Annie."

"I agree with you, not all of the members are gay. But I thought back to our conversation. You said that you weren't much of a singer, and didn't really care for music, but only belonged to the group because it was a way to meet people with 'similar interests.' If you weren't there because of a love of music, then I can only conclude that you found it to be a good way to meet gay men discreetly."

"If I still denied it, would you believe me?"

"I don't think so. Perhaps if you'd reacted differently . . . "

Philip began pacing back and forth. "Very few of my friends know. No one that I work with would even suspect, I'm sure." He laughed. "It's ironic, really, there are so few careers where it even makes a difference, anymore. I just happened to pick one where it does. The current American political climate is positively puritanical. Hell, if adultery can ruin a candidate's career, can you imagine what a disclosure of homosexuality would do?"

"So you really are interested in seeking public office yourself?"

He nodded. "It's been my only dream for as long as I can remember. I wanted to be a senator, or even President, long before I realized I was gay."

"And you've managed to keep it secret all this time?"

He nodded. "I have a few women friends who know. They help me out by attending functions, appearing with me in public situations. I even pretended to be engaged for a while. As far as I know, no one has ever suspected. The men I see know that I have to be extremely circumspect. That's one reason I belong to the chorus. It's a fairly discreet way to meet gay men, yet enough of the men are straight that I never thought it could be used against me. I could never let myself be seen in a gay bar, for instance, or join a gay rights organization." He turned and looked at Annie. "You haven't told anyone, have you?"

"No."

"Do you think you can keep it out of the media?" he asked.

"I'll do my best," she replied sincerely, then paused, trying to find the right words. "So it is Forrestor you've been seeing? That's the reason for the unexplained absences?"

Philip nodded. "I guess we do seem like an unlikely pair. But it's really very simple—it has to do with a side of me you don't know. I've always been attracted to powerful men. I've never really understood whether I'm attracted to them for who they are, or if it's because I want to be like them. Forrestor has an aura of power about him that you notice the moment he enters a room. And that aura never leaves him, Annie."

"How did you manage to connect with him?"

"I first met him in New York, several years ago, at a conference on international trade. He was alone then. There was an immediate attraction between us. It didn't take us long to realize we both wanted the same thing. We spent the entire week together."

She sensed Philip was finally being sincere with her. He continued, "We've kept in touch over the years. I go to Washington, D.C., fairly often, and sometimes he manages to be there at the same time. A couple of times I've made a detour to New York.

"A few months ago, he called me. He told me he was coming out here for a couple of weeks, and since the islands were so close to Seattle, wondered if we could get together. I'd already planned to have Jimmy stay with me, but it seemed like a perfect getaway for him, too. I knew Nicholas and I could be discreet."

"Where did Marguerite Boulanger fit into the picture?"

"As I say, I only met her once. That was here at the resort, when we met in the bar. Apparently she'd been with him for about six months, but he'd never even mentioned her to me." Annie wondered if she detected a note of hurt in Philip's voice.

"Were you surprised that he brought a woman with him?" Annie asked quietly.

"No, not really. He's had female lovers before. Forrestor considers himself bisexual. The way I understand it, he enjoys women sexually, but seems to hate them as individuals. I think he viewed Marguerite primarily as an investment. He recognized her natural talent for modeling and acting, and was determined to make her rich and famous, keeping a large amount of the profits for himself. He didn't need the money, but he's always been obsessed by the desire to control other people. Unlike Pygmalion, however, he would *never* fall in love with his creation." Philip made the last statement with conviction, but Annie wondered. If Nicholas had fallen in love with Marguerite, how would Philip have reacted?

"I think it was because of his basic inability to have a complete relationship with a woman," Philip continued, "that he turned to male lovers. With men, he could experience not only sex, but trust and emotional sharing. Nicholas simply isn't capable of loving a woman."

"Does he love you?"

"In a way," Philip replied. "We have something very transitory, but deep nevertheless. I'm not sure we'll even see each other after this week, but what we've had has been very special."

"Phil, let me ask you something. You probably knew Forrestor better than anyone here. Do you think he is a violent person?"

"You're asking me whether I think he could have killed Marguerite?" Philip paused. "Annie, I'm going to tell you the truth. This is what I believe, and I don't care if you pass it along to the detectives." He placed his fingertips together, trying to think of the best way to put it. "The simple answer is, yes, I believe he can be violent, although I've never seen it. He's an extremely stubborn and powerful man, accustomed to having his own way. Nicholas is quick to anger if someone tries to prevent him from wielding his authority. If someone were to cross him, over the wrong issue, then I think he could easily, out of frustration and anger, resort to violence."

"You said 'the simple answer.' " Annie looked puzzled. "I take it there's more to it than that?"

"Absolutely. What you're trying to get at is whether Nicholas, in a fit of rage, could have killed Marguerite."

"And you don't think so?"

"I'm convinced he had nothing to do with her death, " Phil stated resolutely.

"Why?"

"Because," Philip answered calmly, "she simply wasn't that important to him."

Annie was stunned. "So you don't think the loss of Marguerite meant anything to Nicholas?" She asked.

"No, I really don't. At least, no more than the loss of any piece of property. If he was tired of her, he would have tossed her aside. You have to understand Nicholas's view of women. He ignores women. He doesn't take them seriously. They're playthings, that's all."

Annie watched Philip closely. "You weren't aware of the insurance, then?"

"What insurance?"

"Forrestor had Marguerite's life insured for half a million dollars in the event of accidental death."

Philip stared straight ahead, without replying.

Back in her room, Annie noticed the red message light blinking on her phone. She dialed the front desk.

"Nathan? Hi, this is Annie. Do you have a message for me?"

He read her the unfamiliar name and number and said that the man who called had indicated she would probably want to call him right away. She was confused for a second, and then realized that area code 913 was the one for Topeka, Kansas.

"Lincoln and Associates, Investigative Services."

"Yes, I'm calling for Mr. Walter Lincoln. My name is Annie MacPherson."

"Speaking. How are you, Ms. MacPherson? I reported to Mr. Feinstein this morning, and he said I should call you directly with the information I found on one Daisy Baker, from Manhattan, Kansas."

"You found something, then?" Annie asked excitedly.

"Absolutely. Mr. Feinstein said you were specifically looking for an auto accident. I'm sure this is what you're after. It's from ten years ago. Driver, Daisy Ann Baker, age seventeen, involved in a one-car accident in Manhattan, Kansas. Two other girls were riding in the car, one of them was killed. A lawsuit was filed against Baker by the parents of the deceased girl. I've gone over the court file and police reports, and I've talked to the local reporter who did a series of articles on the case. He attended the entire trial and interviewed all of the family members at the time, and was able to bring me up to speed in a hurry."

Where did Joel find this guy? Annie wondered. This was fantastic. Annie was sure that once she knew more about Daisy Baker's past, everything would start falling into place.

"I can send you a complete written report, ma'am, but Mr. Feinstein said you were in a hurry for the information. I thought I'd call and see if I could give you a basic rundown over the phone. Where do you want me to start?"

"Start at the beginning. I've got plenty of time."

Annie must have spent a good two hours on the phone with Walter Lincoln. The charge for the phone bill was going to be horrendous, but that was the last thing on her mind. Finally Daisy Baker was coming alive for her as a genuine person. Somewhere in the history of Daisy's past, Annie knew she'd find the key.

The story was not a unique one—similar tragedies occur every day across the country. As elsewhere, one of the favorite Friday night pastimes for high school students in Manhattan, Kansas, was 'cruising.' The kids would borrow the family car and simply drive around, meeting up with friends at various predetermined spots. Liquor was frequently involved.

Daisy Baker and a girl named Dee Paransky weren't particularly close friends at Manhattan High School, but they had friends in common. Like most of the kids their age, they enjoyed cruising. Daisy had learned to drive the year before, but didn't have a car of her own. Her father, a Methodist minister, was extremely strict, and never let Daisy take the family car. As a result, Friday nights spent with friends were always in someone else's car.

On the Friday after Christmas of her senior year in high school, Daisy Baker decided to go cruising with two other girls. One was a friend named Stephanie Miller, and the other was Dee Paransky. They were using Dee's car, a fire engine red Mustang convertible with vanity plates that read 'PARTY.'

The girls bought cokes at a nearby McDonald's to which they added cheap rum. There were rumors that Dee's twenty-one year old brother, Bud, home from college on Christmas break, had supplied the alcohol. The roads that night were extremely icy. At about 12:15 A.M., a clerk in an all-night convenience store on the main street of town heard a screeching of tires and a loud crash. The clerk looked out and saw the red convertible wrapped around a cement utility pole. Apparently no other cars had been involved. He quickly called an ambulance and rushed out to the car.

The medics arrived almost immediately. Stephanie was screaming hysterically from the back seat. Daisy was pulled from the driver's seat unconscious. Blood from a gash on her forehead covered her face and had stained her white sweatshirt. Her long white-blonde hair was matted with blood. Daisy's injuries were severe. She was strapped to a gurney and loaded into the waiting aid car. The medics noted on their chart the strong smell of alcohol and observed a broken fifth of rum and a couple of empty beer bottles in the back seat of the car. But an oversight occurred. For some unknown reason Daisy's blood alcohol level that night was never tested.

Daisy spent the next eighteen hours in the critical care unit of Manhattan General Hospital. Her injuries included a shattered left knee, several broken ribs and a severe concussion. She said she was never able to remember the period of time two days preceding the accident or a week following. Her first memories after the incident began in the hospital.

Stephanie, who had been riding in the back seat was badly bruised, but not critically injured. Her memory, however, was just as poor as Daisy's. Stephanie's blood alcohol level one hour after the accident was .18, well over the legal definition of intoxication. She thought she recalled vomiting in the back seat. But she remembered almost nothing of the accident, except being pulled from the car.

Later, Stephanie recalled a few details. She said that Daisy had been driving because she'd been the most sober of the three. Stephanie had no idea how much any of them had had to drink, except she knew that she herself had had too much. She also knew that Dee Paransky had been very drunk, and may even have passed out in the passenger seat before the accident. She was unable to say whether or not Daisy had been drinking. Stephanie also remembered something about an animal in the road. There may have been something that darted in front of the car, causing Daisy to swerve.

Dee had not been able to add any details. She was dead when the medics arrived on the scene. The tests showed that she had been severely intoxicated, even more than Stephanie.

The little red car with the 'PARTY' vanity plates, crumpled like a tin can, had to be pried loose from the cement pole.

"The reporter gave me some photographs that were taken near the time of the accident," Walter Lincoln reported. "The picture of Daisy shows she was a very petite young woman, long straight blonde hair worn pulled back in a pony tail. In all of the pictures she is wearing faded Levis and a white sweatshirt." Annie thought of the Polaroid snapshot.

"What about Dee Paransky? What did she look like?" Annie asked.

"Taller than Daisy. Wavy brown hair, green eyes. Very pretty."

"Go on, you said there was a lawsuit?"

Lincoln continued his account. Even though the car belonged to Dee, she had no insurance. It had been canceled after Dee was cited for drunk driving six months before. Despite the fact that his own son might have provided the alcohol, Dee Paransky's father filed a lawsuit against Daisy Baker.

The case went to trial, and Daisy's attorney did a masterful job. He pointed out that there was no evidence Daisy had been drinking, nor that she had been driving recklessly. He argued that she probably swerved to avoid hitting an animal, hit a patch of ice and went out of control.

The failure to test Daisy's blood had been a clear error on the part of the hospital, but the jury was told they were not allowed to speculate as to what that test *might* have shown.

The jury may have believed Stephanie's story about swerving to avoid hitting an animal, and that the accident was caused by the icy conditions of the road. But what probably happened was that the jury was swayed by sympathy. Small, blonde, doe-eyed Daisy had hobbled to the witness stand on crutches. Her original casts had long since been removed, but she'd recently undergone further corrective surgery on her knee. It was her third operation attempting to alleviate the permanent damage she had suffered in the crash. She testified that she would never be able to run again, and was in constant pain. Her pretty face was shadowed by her obvious suffering. Her parents, the minister and his wife, testified that Daisy was a straight-A student who never drank and had never been in trouble at school or with the police. "A true angel," said Daisy's mother, with tears in her eyes. The jury returned a verdict for Daisy, clearing her of all responsibility for the accident.

Annie held the telephone to her ear with her shoulder and was rapidly scribbling notes. The accident explained the scar on Daisy's knee, and why she didn't drive. The death of a friend and the subsequent lawsuit had undoubtedly had a major impact on her. But Annie felt she was no closer to learning who Daisy's killer might have been.

"Did you learn anything else about the father, Robert Paransky?" Annie asked Lincoln. If anyone harbored ill-feeling towards Daisy, it was Paransky.

"The reporter got to know him quite well during the trial. Apparently he was a very bitter, angry man." It seemed that Paransky's lawyer had urged him to accept the settlement offered by Daisy's insurance company, but Paransky was adamant. To him, the case was clear. His daughter had been innocent, and Daisy had to be "punished" for Dee's death. He was unable to see the other side of the story. Taking the money from the insurance company and settling the case, he said, would be like letting Daisy off scot-free.

Annie wondered if Paransky could possibly have figured in Daisy's death? Had this man carried his desire for retribution with him for ten years?

"Mr. Lincoln, by any chance did you try to locate Robert Paransky? Is he still living in Manhattan?"

"I checked it out, ma'am. And the answer is no."

"Where is he?"

"He died last December."

"What about other family members?"

"The wife died several years ago. Neighbors said the son, Bud, left town shortly after the trial, and hasn't been heard from since."

Detective Dexter was just starting to look for another cigarette when Annie rushed into the music room, carrying a legal pad filled with notes. First, she quickly ran through her revealing conversation with Philip Spaulding about his connection to Forrestor, and then excitedly told Dexter what she had learned from the investigator in Kansas.

"Ridiculous! That accident happened when the girl was seventeen years old! That Paransky character sounds like an angry old bastard, but he's dead. I say you file that report away under 'Past History' and we concentrate on the here and now. The connection between Forrestor and Spaulding—now that's significant! I want to talk to each of them again. Forrestor could have killed her for the money, or Spaulding could have killed her out of jealousy. Both are good, strong motives. Or they could even have done it together. Good work, Annie."

"I'm not ready to drop this yet, Dex. Something about that story is haunting me. I still think it's important."

"But the father's dead, and besides, I've never known anyone to harbor a grudge for ten years. I think we can just file that away. What about that stuff you got on Lisa Hargraves?" Dexter asked. "She's the only one with a connection to Marc Jarrell. And we've established that it was her cigarette lighter found in his room."

"I don't know. She doesn't deny she was there, but somehow, I don't see her as a killer," Annie argued. "I got the impression she was genuinely fond of Jarrell. I don't think she wanted to see him come to harm. Lisa's more the type that would lie, cheat, or manipulate to get what she wanted, but I don't think she'd use violence. The way I see it, Marc Jarrell was the link to get to Daisy Baker."

"Why do you say that?" Dexter remembered that he'd been looking for a cigarette. He found one and lit it.

"That notepad that was found in his room. It was found by the phone, wasn't it? My guess is he was talking on the phone to someone about Daisy. He was planning to meet someone."

"And the reference to the fifty thousand dollars?"

"A payoff, maybe? In exchange for his information on her

whereabouts. What if he told the killer where Daisy was, then got killed himself? The timing is right. Marc would have met with the killer early Monday afternoon, then Daisy was killed that same night on Traxler Island."

"It fits." Dexter coughed a harsh, hacking cough. "It's pretty wild speculation, but I have to agree that it does all fit. If you're right, it would mean that we should be looking for someone who premeditated the murder of Daisy Baker."

Chapter 18

SATURDAY AFTERNOON, JULY 28

UP IN HER ROOM that afternoon, Annie put her notes in order, trying to reconcile what she had just learned about Daisy Baker's past with what she knew about the con artist, "Marguerite Boulanger." In front of her as she wrote her lists, she kept two of the photographs, the young Daisy leaning on the car, and the black-suited sophisticated Marguerite. It seemed like she had enough facts, too many in fact, but they weren't fitting together to give her any answers. She jumped at the sound of the phone.

"Miss MacPherson? This is Renalda Ruiz, I talk to you on Tuesday about the man in the cottage, do you remember me?"

"Of course, Renalda. What is it?" The girl sounded terribly afraid.

"I have a very big favor to ask. I am afraid to ask Mr. Perkins, because he will think I am being silly. I don't know anyone else with a car, so is why I am asking you. My friend Sue, you remember her? The other maid you talk to? She is not come to work today like she is supposed. I don't know why she didn't telephone, because she needs this job very badly, and would not want to be fired. I clean all her rooms today, but I am worried and I telephone her house, but no one answers. I am scared with all these killings. Would you drive me to her house so I can see is she all right?"

"Of course, Renalda. We'll go right now. Meet me down at the front steps."

"Thank you so much, Miss. I meet you at the steps."

Annie shoved her notes and the photographs into a manila envelope and headed for the lobby.

"When was the last time you saw Sue?" Annie asked the frightened girl as they stood waiting for the valet to fetch Annie's red Fiat.

"Let me see. Yesterday was Friday, yes, she was at work yesterday. She was not sick and when we got off work, she say 'See you tomorrow.' That was why I am so surprise she is not at work. If something happen, she would have telephone Consuela. I don't understand why she did not telephone." Renalda had not taken the time to change out of her navy blue and white uniform. She was clutching at the handle of her shoulder bag so tightly Annie thought she would break it.

"What time did she leave yesterday?"

"She gets off work at four o'clock, the same as I do. She lives in a little trailer near Eastsound. She has a little motorbike that she uses to come to work, but it was not running this week."

"How was she getting to work, then?"

Renalda looked down at her feet, and said quietly, "She was hitchhiking. I told her it was not a good thing. That is why I am worry about her."

The parking valet screeched around the curved driveway, jumped out, and held open the Fiat's door. The engine coughed spastically before slowing down to an uneven idle.

Annie was worried as well. Hitchhiking, even under the best of circumstances, was risky. But with a murderer on the loose? She prayed there was a simple explanation for Sue not showing up at work.

"What was she wearing?" Annie asked as they drove off. She remembered seeing Sue working in the blue and white uniform. "A uniform like yours?"

"Oh, no. She hated being seen in this. She always changed before she went home." Renalda closed her eyes to concentrate. "Yesterday, I think she was wearing jeans. Yes, levis. She always wore white tennis shoes. And a white cotton sweatshirt." A wave of *déjà vu* passed over Annie as she listened to the description. Levis and a white sweatshirt. A tiny young woman with long, white-blonde hair. An eerie coincidence.

"Renalda, there's a manila envelope in my purse. Can you reach it?" Renalda pulled it out. "Yes, that's it," Annie continued. "There's a snapshot inside, take a look. . . . " Annie heard Renalda gasp as she looked at the photo.

"Miss MacPherson, this looks like . . . no, it is a different woman, but it looks so much like Sue. The same clothes, the hair. I don't understand."

"I don't either, Renalda. I don't either."

There was only one road leading from the Windsor Resort to Eastsound. Annie drove slowly, scanning the sides of the winding road for any indication that Sue had been there. The lush green undergrowth held no answers. She tried to picture the tiny young woman ambling along the narrow shoulder, turning around to hold out her thumb for passing vehicles. Had one of them picked her up?

Annie pulled over when she heard Renalda shout "Alto!" She, herself, would have missed the patch of white in the grass beyond the left-hand shoulder. Renalda was out of the car before the engine was even stopped. "Stop, Renalda, don't . . . " Annie was afraid of what she'd find, and wanted to save the girl the shock.

But it was too late. Getting out of the car, Annie was able to see the crumpled heap in the grass. Renalda was crying uncontrollably, whimpering "no, no," afraid to touch the body, yet unable to turn her eyes away from her friend.

Annie reached down to touch Sue's neck. It was stone cold, no hint of a pulse. The young hotel maid was dead. Her face was covered with blood, apparently from a gash on her forehead. She must have been thrown into the air when the car hit her. Her neck lay in a contorted, entirely unnatural position. It probably broke when she fell, killing her instantly.

Annie took Renalda by the shoulders and led her away from the sight. Back on the right hand side of the road, she held the girl through harsh, body-shaking sobs. In a few minutes, the sobs stopped coming. Annie grabbed a box of Kleenex from the Fiat's glove compartment and Renalda wiped her eyes.

Annie debated about what to do next. She didn't want to leave

either Renalda, or the body, alone. But a passing motorist could too
easily move the body. It was crucial that Detective Dexter view the
evidence undisturbed.

"Do you think you can stay here, Renalda? Only for a few
minutes while I go back to the resort to call the sheriff? It's very
important that no one touch the body. Do you understand?"

A look of fear passed through Renalda's eyes, then she nodded.
"Yes. I will be all right. But hurry. Please."

"Yes, I will. Stay over here on this side of the road. If anyone
comes, just tell them to keep moving, that the Sheriff's Department
has been notified. Don't let anyone go near Sue, all right? I'll be
back before you know it."

Annie got back in the car, pulled a tight U-turn and screeched off
in the direction of the resort. In her rear-view mirror she could see
Renalda standing stiffly by the side of the road, bravely clutching
the box of Kleenex, and trying not to look at the bloody scene.

For the third time that week, Detective Dexter placed a call to the
coroner in Friday Harbor. For the third time that week, he had a
close-up view of death.

The road was cordoned off as well as possible. Since it was the
only road connecting Eastsound and Westsound, the few cars that
passed had to be allowed through, one at a time, the drivers
gawking to see what the commotion was all about. The Sheriff's
Department photographer was busy snapping pictures of the
crumpled body in the grass.

"This is exactly how you found her?"

Renalda, her eyes bloodshot and wet, nodded. Annie was proud
of her. She was holding up well, answering all of the detective's
questions. After telephoning Detective Dexter, Annie had located
Consuela and brought her to the scene to be with Renalda. The
large woman had a strong protective arm around the girl's
shoulders.

The homicide detective looked down at the small, broken body.
Sue had been thrown completely off the roadway by a powerful
impact, coming to rest face up in the weeds. It was surprising
Renalda had spotted her, since the bright green undergrowth was at

least two feet deep. Sue's tiny feet, in white sneakers, barely reached the gravel shoulder. Her head and back were abraded from the fall. Fine strands of pale blonde hair, loosened now from the straggly pony tail, lay limply across the bruised and bloody face. Her once white sweatshirt was sticky with a combination of blood and grime. The detectives were finally finished questioning Renalda, and Consuela helped her over to the Deputy's van for a ride home.

Annie walked over to where Detective Dexter was standing, staring down at the pitiful body. "Can you tell what happened, Dex?" she asked.

"Not completely. The angle of the fall doesn't make sense. Miss Ruiz said she was walking home, going north towards Eastsound, which would mean she was facing traffic coming south. We know she was hit face-on, because shards of glass from a headlight are imbedded in her thighs and stomach. She landed off the road, next to the southbound lane, but with her feet on the gravel and her head angled to the north. A southbound car couldn't have done that. I'd be willing to swear she was hit face on by a car going north towards Eastsound."

"Did Renalda tell you Sue was hitchhiking?"

"No, but let me think about that."

"The road's narrow, and the shoulder over here on the right is muddy. Let's assume for the moment she was walking on the other side of the road facing oncoming traffic, where the shoulder is gravel instead of mud. Then when she heard a car approaching from behind, she turned around to face it and stick out her thumb."

"And then a northbound car struck her face on. Yeah," Dex looked north and south, trying to visualize the accident, "that makes more sense given the angle of the body. But how did she manage to get herself hit? Surely she wouldn't have crossed over to stand in the path of an oncoming car. The way Renalda describes her, she doesn't sound that aggressive. And look at the pavement. There are no skid marks. You'd think the car must have crossed over into the left hand lane to hit her standing on the shoulder. That driver must have been blind."

"It's hard to believe it could have been an accident," said Annie. "This happened in broad daylight. There's no curve in the road, and yesterday was clear and sunny. The driver of the car had to have seen her, plain as day."

Dex stared at Annie. "Are you trying to say the driver *intentionally* swerved into the opposite lane of traffic to hit her? Why?"

"Dex," Annie lowered her voice so the prying spectators wouldn't hear, "it's hard to tell now the way the body's mangled, but I think this is a look-alike murder." She got out the photo of Daisy and showed it to him. "Renalda Ruiz looked at this and said that was exactly what Sue looked like when she left work yesterday."

"Jesus," he exclaimed. "What the hell have we gotten ourselves into?"

Annie scanned the faces in the crowded bar, but David wasn't there yet. They'd arranged to meet for drinks and dinner, and for once, Annie was early. At a small table in the corner, Lisa was making elaborate gestures telling a story to Roger, the clothing store king, who was hanging on every word. Nathan, off-duty, was sharing a table with the two University of Washington students. Marcie, the bubbly cheerleader, was sulking over her piña colada while her friend, Claire, was engaged in an animated discussion with Nathan. Annie went over to their table and saw Nathan and Claire drawing bizarre pictures of molecules on bar napkins.

"Annie, have a seat." Nathan pointed to an empty chair. "Claire's telling me all about her thesis on genetics."

"It's a fascinating conversation," Marcie added sarcastically.

"I was looking for David Courtney. Have you seen him?"

"Not yet. Have a seat while you wait for him."

"Sure." Annie sat down absentmindedly. She was dead tired. She was looking forward to spending the evening with David, but wasn't sure she had the energy to hold up her end of the conversation.

"Can I get you something?" The cocktail waitress took the order for another round, but all Annie wanted was coffee. One glass of wine and she'd be under the table. Marcie continued to search the room for available young men while Nathan and Claire excitedly swapped scientific terms. Annie propped her feet up on an empty chair and closed her eyes.

"Well, what do you think?" she heard, as the chair was pulled out from under her feet. Annie opened her eyes to see Ellen O'Neill sitting in it.

"Huh? What? Oh, Ellen, hi. What do I think of what?"

"Oh, no! You mean I just spent sixty dollars and an entire afternoon of my life for nothing? This, dummy," she took both hands and tousled her shoulder length hair. "I'm supposed to have more fun now." Ellen's formerly mousy brown hair now was now a light frosted blonde.

"Well, I think it looks great," Marcie the cheerleader contributed. "I've been telling Claire for ages that she ought to do something like that to her hair. See, Claire, doesn't it look good?"

"It really does, Ellen," said Annie. "I like it. I'm sorry, I'm a little tired this evening. Did you just do it this afternoon?"

"Uh huh. Spent all afternoon sniffing foul chemicals while a terribly sweet man pulled strands of my hair through a plastic skull cap with a crochet hook. What women won't do in the name of vanity. But I think it was worth it, I like being blonde for a change." Annie started to close her eyes again. "You look beat," said Ellen. "I was going to ask you if you wanted to go into Eastsound for Chinese food, but I think the answer is no, right?"

"I would, but I'm waiting for David. We planned to have dinner together."

"Sounds great. In that case, um, I hate to ask, but I'm still desperately craving Szechuan. Do you think I could borrow your car for a bit to get take-out? Those little cartons are awfully awkward on a bike."

"Sure, no problem." Annie fished in her purse for the keys, then remembered. "The valet's got the keys. Just tell him I said it was okay for you to take it. You can drive a stick?"

"With my eyes closed." She saw Annie's look of apprehension. "But I'll keep them open, I promise."

"Are you going dressed like that?" Ellen was wearing jeans and a short-sleeved silk blouse. "You'll freeze if you don't put the top up."

"A sporty little red convertible with the top up? That's sacrilege."

"Do you want to borrow my sweatshirt?" Claire offered.

"Oh, that would be great, thanks." Ellen pulled the white cotton sweatshirt on over her head. She noticed the small sorority emblem and said, "Hey, this is great, do I look twenty years younger? Annie, do you have anything I can use to keep my hair out of my eyes?" Annie searched through her purse until she found a rubber band.

"Super. This will keep my newly golden tresses under control." She reached up and pulled her hair back into a pony tail, and started to leave.

"What?" Annie asked, laughing. "Is that it? You don't need money, too?"

"You've got a full tank of gas, don't you?"

"Get out of here!"

"I'm gone!"

It all came together just a moment too late.

Annie dashed out of the bar. All afternoon she had been pondering over the bizarre turn that events had taken, the apparent look-alike murder of a young woman exactly matching the young Daisy Baker's description. She had been concentrating on the people who knew Daisy when she habitually wore jeans and a white sweatshirt—Lisa, Nicholas, or perhaps someone from further back in Daisy's past.

But Annie's mind had been so taken up with theories that she almost missed what was right in front of her eyes. Muddled with exhaustion, Annie watched Ellen leave the bar. A tiny woman with a blonde pony tail, blue jeans, white sweatshirt. Annie was suddenly alert. If Sue had been killed merely because of her striking resemblance to a young Daisy Baker, Ellen was in terrible danger.

Annie reached the curved front driveway just in time to see the tail lights of the Fiat heading up the road. Ellen would be safe if the killer hadn't seen her. But if he had . . . ?

The parking valet had just pulled up in a long black sedan. He exited the car, tossing the key in his hand.

"Hey, she said it was all right to borrow your car. She wasn't stealing it, was she?" he asked.

"No, I loaned it to her." Annie's voice shook. "I just forgot to tell her something. Does the resort have any rental cars, or anything I could borrow? It's very important that I catch her." Annie was starting to feel a tight knot of fear in her stomach.

"Well, I don't think so. The resort van's in the shop with a broken headlight. . . . "

Just then Russ appeared, hurrying slightly down the front steps. He reached out to take the key of the sedan from the valet.

"Oh, Russ, I'm so glad to see you. Are you driving into town? Listen, it's really important that I catch up with Ellen, she borrowed my car. Could you give me a lift?" Her voice was pleading, almost frantic.

"Into Eastsound? Sure, I guess so. What's so important?"

"It's really hard to explain. Maybe nothing. I hope it's nothing. But I have to catch her first."

"Hop in."

They drove in silence down the winding, tree covered road. Russ was driving fast. He must have sensed the urgency in Annie's voice. The darkness enveloped them.

Annie saw the glimmer of tail lights up ahead.

"That might be her. It looks like a convertible. See if you can catch up."

Russ stepped on the accelerator. Taking a curve too fast, the car seemed to lift up on two wheels. Annie held back a gasp, and grabbed tightly onto the door.

"Russ, I'm sorry I asked you to hurry, I don't want us to get killed."

He didn't answer, but just kept staring into the darkness. The headlights of the sedan illuminated the road, but made it difficult to see the color of the small car ahead. The distance between the two cars lessened.

"I think it's her. Russ, slow down, it's okay. We'll just follow her into town."

"I knew it was her. She's back." Russ said in a strange voice, as he continued to accelerate.

"For God's sake, Russ, slow down!"

"You know, Annie. I have no idea what I did wrong." Russ continued to stare intently ahead. "Everything was working just fine. She arrived at the resort just like she was supposed to. I watched her. I followed her, but I blew it somehow." Russ's voice sounded numb. "This time I won't fail. She'll really die this time. I don't know what went wrong. I was so sure I killed her, but she kept coming back. She kept coming. She won't come back again."

"Oh, my God. Russ. Russ! Stop the car." She tried to speak slowly, calmly, despite the panic that was gripping her. "That's not Daisy Baker. Daisy is dead. Stop the car now." The sedan spun around another turn. Ellen, thinking the sedan was tailgating, accelerated the red convertible. Annie prayed the Fiat was up to it.

"I was sorry about the man in the cottage. I didn't want to kill him. But he wouldn't tell me where she was. I had to find out, didn't I? I was sorry I had to kill him."

Annie was scared out of her wits. She didn't know what to say to make Russ stop.

"She's not dead, Annie. I don't understand it, but she's not. I thought I killed her on the island. It was so simple. I shot her right through the heart. You'd think that would have killed her, wouldn't you? I swear she looked dead." Russ sounded like he was talking in his sleep, slurring his words. His voice was strained. "I saw her fall, there was lots of blood. I don't know what I did wrong."

"Why, Russ, why?"

"But there she was again, walking along the side of the road. She appeared from nowhere. That long, blonde hair. I remembered that long, blonde hair." He chuckled. "She wanted a ride. Imagine, asking me for a ride. I really gave her one, didn't I?" He laughed at his own morbid little joke. "I gave her a ride." He still had his eyes fixed firmly on the car ahead. Annie was sure that with each turn they would go spinning out of control. Escape was out of the question. She had to stay with him, or Ellen would never survive. She tried to think of a plan.

"I thought it worked that time, too. I could hear the body breaking when I hit her, the bones being crushed. I heard her screaming, and I heard when she stopped screaming. How could she come back?"

Annie's mind was racing. She didn't know what to do.

"But there she was leaving the bar tonight. I saw her walk right past my office and I couldn't believe it. Why won't she die?"

"Russ, you have to listen to me, that's not Daisy Baker. That's Ellen O'Neill, your old classmate. You just think she looks like Daisy."

"Don't be silly. Of course, that's her. See, she's driving Cordelia's red convertible. Once we get closer, you'll see the license plates."

Suddenly Annie understood. Russ's sister Cordelia. Dee. Dee Paransky, the girl Daisy killed in an auto accident. She had an older brother named Bud. Now it all made sense.

"Bud Paransky, stop this car. This won't bring your sister back. That was a long time ago, Bud."

He started at the sound of his name. "No one calls me that anymore," he said angrily. "I've come this far. I can't stop now. I won't."

"You have to, Bud. Stop the car. Now! Why are you doing this?"

"For Dad, of course. He would have wanted me to do this. He loved Cordelia so much. This is the only thing I can do to make it up to him for what I did."

"Make up for what, Bud?"

"The liquor. Buying the liquor. He never knew for sure, but I think he suspected. Everyone suspected. That's why he hated me after that. That's why he never spoke to me again. But killing Daisy, that will make it up to him. As soon as I can do it right."

A flat stretch of road appeared. The red convertible was pulling over towards the shoulder. Ellen must think the speeding sedan wanted to pass. No, Ellen, keep going! Annie thought. Keep going!

It was too late. Russ was aiming straight for the red car in a collision course. He stepped on the gas.

Annie lunged. In a single motion she threw herself into Russ, slamming his head against the window and pushing the wheel hard to the left. The black sedan went into a spin and skidded off the left side of the road towards a huge cedar. She braced for the impact.

At first Annie wasn't sure what had happened. Deep mud off the road had slowed the speed of the sedan. She wasn't hurt. Russ was unconscious, having hit his head on the window. Ellen came running over from where she had parked the Fiat. Annie got out of the car and fell to the ground.

Fear had turned her muscles to quivering jelly.

Chapter 19

SUNDAY AFTERNOON, JULY 29

"Okay, Annie, we're ready to come about. Grab the jib sheet and be ready to haul 'er in."

"Ready."

David slowly turned the wheel, bringing the *Electra*'s bow into the brisk afternoon wind. The huge jib started to luff. Annie waited until the wind catching the forward sail started to push the bow around, then she deftly released the starboard sheet and hauled in the sail on the port side. David handled the mainsail.

"Beautifully done. Bring her in just a little bit more," he directed her, "use the winch if you have to. That's it, perfect. What a team." He smiled broadly at her. The graceful sailboat heeled over onto the port tack, and Annie settled herself in the sunshine on the high side, taking a moment to apply some more sunscreen to her freckled nose.

"So go on with what you were saying," David said. "A psychiatrist spent all morning examining Russ? Has he been charged with all three murders?"

"Yes. And attempted murder for the attack on Ellen. There'll be a full hearing to determine if he's competent to stand trial, but the psychiatrist who talked to him this morning said he's pretty far gone. In the meantime he'll be admitted to Western State Hospital for intensive therapy. It was bizarre. He was able to recall what he'd done, but couldn't comprehend the consequences of his acts. He actually believed he was killing Daisy each time, but that somehow she kept coming back to haunt him. His ability to distinguish fantasy from reality is gone."

"I thought I knew the man," David said sadly. "He seemed so sane. How can the shrinks explain that?"

"It's complicated, but from what I understand, Russ had been living with some very powerful guilt feelings ever since his sister's death ten years ago. He was the older brother who bought the girls the liquor that night, and he felt responsible for Dee's death. But instead of dealing with those feelings at the time, he repressed them."

"Why did Russ change his name to Perkins?"

"It was partly his father's doing, actually. At the trial, Stephanie Miller testified that she thought Russ had supplied the rum, but that she wasn't sure. Russ's father, Robert Paransky, was furious. Even though Russ denied it, he knew his father suspected the truth. As a result, Robert Paransky disowned his son, refused even to speak to him after that. Paransky wrote Russ a letter saying that he was ashamed that Russ carried the family name, and that after what he'd done to Cordelia, he had no right to call himself a Paransky."

"Pretty heavy stuff."

"It was, and Russ took it to heart, and changed his name. He was willing to do anything to try to appease his father."

"But why did all of this happen ten years later?"

"Russ went through a long period of denial. He had no contact with his father and had taught himself to avoid thinking about his sister's death. Then, in December, he learned that his father was dying. He made one last attempt at reconciliation."

"And did it work?"

"No, it was a terrible mistake. The timing made things worse— it was the same week as the tenth anniversary of Cordelia's death. The father was furious that Russ had come, refused to acknowledge him as his son, and cursed him from his death bed."

"That was what pushed Russ over the edge?" David asked, trimming the sail slightly to adjust their course to clear the point up ahead. The boat heeled at a steeper angle, and Annie had to brace herself to keep from sliding.

"Apparently so. From then on he began dwelling on his sister's accident, becoming more and more obsessed. He took on his father's opinion that it was really Daisy who had killed his sister, and that if he could kill Daisy, his father would finally forgive him."

"You know, now that I think about it, I remember when he got back from his dad's funeral last Christmas. He did seem different after that, more withdrawn. I guess I just assumed it was natural grief."

"Not natural at all."

"But do they think Daisy's murder was premeditated? That he plotted to bring her out to the resort?"

Annie nodded. "He was absurdly proud of how he accomplished it, and told the psychiatrist the whole story. Soon after his father died, he started to look for her, going first to their old home town, Manhattan, Kansas. A local newspaper there had printed a story saying that Daisy Baker had gone to New York to seek fame and fortune as a model. He first found an old address for her in New York, which turned out to be the apartment Lisa and Daisy had shared. Lisa was still living there, and received a call from Russ."

"I was wondering how Lisa was connected to all this."

"Lisa first told him she didn't know Daisy's whereabouts, and that he should try the modeling agencies in New York that Daisy used to work for. She suggested sending a picture, since she thought Daisy had changed her name. Russ didn't believe her, and kept pushing. He said Daisy had won a free week's stay at the Windsor Resort, and he had to know where to send her gift certificate. Lisa, never one to pass up a bargain, told him to send it to her—she'd forward it to Daisy. Russ did, on the off chance that it might work. Because of Lisa's comment about Daisy changing her name, he left it blank. But the dates were filled in. It had to be used in a certain week this July." Annie shifted position to keep the sun out of her eyes. "Are you getting thirsty, Captain?"

"I was just starting to think about a cold beer."

Annie went below and came back with two Henry Weinhards from the ice box, handing one to David.

David chuckled. "That's really rich. Lisa used the gift certificate for herself. A personal invitation to attend a murder."

"Right. She had no idea that Russ would find Daisy and get her here the same week some other way. He really didn't think the gift certificate idea would work, so he kept trying the modeling agencies—saying he wanted to hire this particular model for a publicity brochure. Once he got her address, he was able to find out she was living with Forrestor. That's when he got the idea of getting Forrestor interested in buying the resort. He sent brochures and got Forrestor to agree to come out and see the place."

"So what about all this kidnapping business?"

"We can only guess about that. I think that Daisy and her lover, Marc Jarrell, had been planning their fake kidnapping for some time, but didn't know where or when to pull it off. Nicholas had too many connections in New York, and could have stopped them before they ever got out of the country."

"But why the San Juan Islands?" David asked.

"We'll never really know, but if you think about it, it makes sense. Daisy knew they'd be coming out in July. The brochures described the islands as secluded and sparsely populated, yet not very far from major cities. Marc and Daisy's primary goal was to collect the money from Nicholas, and get out of the country—fast. The San Juans could provide them with a sheltered hiding place to wait while the ransom money was obtained, then once they were ready to clear out, Vancouver, B.C., is only about fifty miles away, and has an international airport with flights all over the world. The U.S.-Canadian border is one of the least patrolled borders in the world. Americans aren't even required to show passports, and thousands of tourists cross the border every day, especially in the peak summer months. Within hours of collecting their money they could have been on a flight to Mexico or South America."

"So that's why Marc and Daisy came out to check the place over this spring, when Daisy disguised herself as a boy."

"Exactly. I'm sure she knew about her ability to change her appearance, and capitalized on it. She knew that she and Nicholas would be coming for a week in July. In March, she could have made some excuse to Nicholas about having to go away for a week, maybe she had to visit a sick friend, then she and Marc came out to Washington on a reconnaissance mission. Marc's role, both in March and July, was to stay out of sight as much as possible."

"But wouldn't Russ have seen Daisy when she and Marc were here in the spring?"

"I was curious about that, too, and checked his calendar. Russ was at a week-long seminar in March, which coincided exactly with Daisy's first visit."

"Lucky coincidence for her."

"It's hard to say Daisy was lucky."

"I guess you're right, there."

"And the hiding place. That's why she was asking me so many questions. She really had me fooled, with her pretended 'adolescent curiosity.' "

"Don't give yourself a hard time. Daisy was an excellent actress and con artist. Remember, she had Nicholas totally fooled, and he lived with her for six months."

It was time to come about again. Annie took her position at the jib sheet and waited for the graceful boat to swing into position. The brisk wind carried the *Electra* along at a playful pace.

Traxler Island came into view as they rounded the point.

"Your special place," Annie said quietly. "Can it ever be the same for you?"

David shook his head. "I wish I'd been able to show it to you before all of this happened. That day we were headed there—was it Russ in the ski boat?"

"I'm afraid so. Right after the accident, Ellen told me she'd seen a metallic blue ski boat at the resort. I was all set to check it out, but in all the confusion over your arrest and the body being found on Traxler Island, it slipped my mind."

"And?"

"It was registered to Russ. If I'd remembered to check, I would have learned that he was the only one with access to the key."

"But how did he know we were going to Traxler Island?"

"I remember before we left, I went up to the resort to tell Detective Dexter where I was going. I couldn't find Dex, so I asked Russ to tell him where I had gone, and I mentioned Traxler Island. The psychiatrist said he was acting almost entirely on instinct at that point. For the most part, he was able to carry on the function of running the resort as if nothing were the matter. But deep down, he was obsessed with his goal of destroying Daisy. Whenever that goal was threatened, he reacted without thinking. The doctor didn't think he was intending to kill me when I dumped in the water, only to stop me from going to the island."

They were both silent for a moment. It was still hard to comprehend the seriousness of Russ's illness. "It was the same when he killed Marc," Annie said. "He wasn't intending to, his only goal was to find out where Daisy was. As soon as she arrived at the resort, he started watching her, almost twenty-four hours a day. He was watching and waiting for the perfect moment to kill her, but it was difficult because she was almost always with Forrestor. Then, on Sunday night, he saw her leave in a boat with Marc Jarrell. He didn't have time to follow them, so he stayed up all night, waiting for the boat to return. When it returned carrying only Marc, he had to think of a way to get Marc to tell him where Daisy was."

"The message that was found on Marc's notepad? Was that from Russ?"

"It was. Early Monday morning Russ called Marc, and offered him fifty thousand dollars to tell him where Daisy was. But it was only a bluff. He didn't have that kind of money to give Marc. When Marc found out there wasn't going to be a payoff, Russ had to kill him. He was the man Renalda saw leaving Marc's cottage."

"So that night, after learning where Daisy was, he went to the island to kill her in cold blood," David surmised, shuddering at the thought. "You know, I was the one who taught Russ about boating. I even taught him scuba diving. He probably anchored off shore beyond the kelp bed and swam ashore, the same as you'd do if you were diving."

Annie closed her eyes and sighed. "After the murders of Marc and Daisy, Russ actually felt proud of himself. He felt like he'd accomplished his goal. But the effect on his mind when he saw Sue, walking along the side of the road wearing jeans and a white sweatshirt, looking exactly like Daisy Baker the way she looked in high school, was devastating. He went berserk, thinking Daisy had somehow survived. Again acting on instinct, he ran her off the road. The same thing happened when he saw Ellen, with a blonde pony tail, similarly dressed, walking past his office. The vision of her in a red convertible only made matters more intense."

"So what about the resort—is it still going to be sold?"

"Yes, but not to Nicholas Forrestor. The lawyer who's administering the estate called. There's a syndicate of Seattle dentists who are interested in the place as a tax shelter. I'm pretty sure we'll be able to work out a deal. If I'm lucky, when all the attorneys' fees and taxes are paid, Mrs. Lymon should have a nice little sum left over."

They both looked as the sailboat passed the tiny island that had been at the center of the tragedy.

"It's over now," David said quietly, "but it will never be the same." He paused, and then added, "I'm going to miss it."

Neither one said anything for several minutes. Even though there wasn't a cloud in the sky, Annie felt her mood growing dark.

"You're really going, then?" she said softly.

He nodded. "I can't stay here. The resort won't be the same under new management. Besides, I want to make it to the south Pacific before the monsoons come. I'll have to leave soon if I'm going to do it."

Annie fought to hold back her tears. "You won't be frightened, sailing by yourself?"

"No, I'm looking forward to a bit of solitude. And I'll only be alone as far as Hawaii. That's an easy crossing this time of year. I'm sure I'll be able to pick up a crew member in Honolulu. And believe me, this boat is a seaworthy old gal. She'll take good care of me." He saw Annie turn her face away from him. "Hey, now. None of that. Come over here."

She moved over to sit next to him, putting her arm around his broad back and laying her head on his shoulder. "Damn it, I'm going to miss you, that's all," she said.

David stroked her hair and kissed her lightly on the forehead. "Are you sure you won't change your mind and come with me?"

"I wish I could."

"You can. Just drop everything and come."

"You don't understand, it's not that easy for me. I can't just drop everything and run away. I've got a job, responsibilities."

"And also ambition, drive, and excess amounts of manic energy?"

"You make it sound so dreadful, but it's the way I am. You don't know how tempting it is for me to imagine a quiet life on a sailboat with the most gentle and caring man I've ever met . . . "

"Who's madly in love with you by the way."

"You're making this awfully difficult."

"I know."

"I . . . I just don't know. I've been pushing myself all my life, and for the most part, I enjoy what I do. Sailing around the world, with no pressures, no schedules, it sounds idyllic, but I'm not sure I could do it. What if I went crazy in a week? You'd hate me."

"We could always try it and find out." David's blue eyes twinkled.

"Goddamn it," Annie sniffed. "You're not allowed to make me cry." He held her tightly as she buried her face on his shoulder, but she couldn't keep the tears from coming.

Epilogue

"VAL! HAVE YOU got the pleadings section of the *Downtown Development Coalition* file? I've got to be down at the courthouse for the motion calendar at nine-thirty."

Annie quickly downed the rest of her coffee and slipped on her wool coat in anticipation of the wet November wind that awaited her outside in downtown Seattle. It was only four blocks to the King County Courthouse, but far enough to get chilled to the bone in this weather.

"Calm down, honey. It's right here on the corner of your desk." Val shook her head at the stacks of letters, phone messages and documents completely covering the large oak desk. "It's an absolute miracle you never lose anything in there."

"Never have yet," Annie replied. "But I keep trying."

The secretary handed Annie her briefcase. "I stuck your mail inside. Have you got your umbrella?"

Annie looked around.

"Over there," Val pointed. "Under the *McWilliams* file. How anyone can work in this mess . . . now get going while you've still got a chance to be on time. And good luck!"

The harsh November rain was being driven sideways through the ever-present construction on Third Avenue. Annie's flimsy folding umbrella was promptly rendered useless by the bitter wind. The sky was the color of a dirty dishrag. She drew her coat closer, cursing as she stepped off the curb into a four-inch puddle, feeling the water seeping in through the sides of her leather pumps.

On the corner across the street from the courthouse a drunk huddling in a doorway asked her for a quarter. She gave him her umbrella instead.

She rushed across the marbled foyer of the courthouse just in time to see the crammed elevator close its doors. She glanced at her watch. Water clouded the crystal, but she could discern that it read 9:40. So much for being on time.

She entered the crowded courtroom and hung her coat on the overburdened rack which exuded the smell of damp wool. Signing in with the bailiff, she saw that her case, *Citizens for Non-Growth vs. Downtown Development Coalition* had been bumped to the end of the calendar. As punishment for her tardiness, Annie would have to sit and wait while eleven other summary judgment motions were argued.

With a sinking feeling, Annie collapsed into a seat at the back of the courtroom and opened her briefcase. The last thing she needed was to have to sit in the courthouse all morning waiting for her case to be heard. She had too many things to do. The office had been deluged with new files lately. Impossible deadlines to meet, letters to answer, hostile opposing counsel to contend with, bills to collect. It never seemed to end. And it often didn't seem worth it. Take today, for example. Could she really feel good about fighting a battle to allow a developer to build yet another downtown sky-scraper? What was the point? Reluctantly she opened her brief case and reached for her stack of mail.

Underneath the stack of business correspondence was a postcard showing the white sandy beach and blue sky of Tahiti. She smiled at the all too familiar slanted scrawl.

> —TAHITI—*October 5*
> *It's spring now south of the equator, getting warmer*
> *every day. It's hard to make curry for one. I'll be in*
> *New Zealand through Christmas. Please come, I miss*
> *you more than ever. Send a telegram to the American*
> *Express office in Auckland and I'll meet your plane.*
> *—Love always,*
> D
> *P.S. You know how terrible I am at handling rejection.*

Annie left the courtroom having won the battle for more downtown office space. As she peered out the glass doors to Third Avenue and saw the rain coming down harder than ever, she tried to figure out the closest place to buy another umbrella. She had to be quick because there were a million things she had to get done before the hearing she had scheduled at 1:30.

Abruptly she turned around and strode back through the courthouse foyer to the public phone. She picked up the yellow pages and flipped to the section she wanted. Just as Annie thought, there was a Western Union office in Pioneer Square, not far from the courthouse. She headed out into the rain without worrying about an umbrella, rehearsing in her mind how she would phrase the telegram. So what if she got a little wet on the way?

About the Author

Although born and raised in southern California, Janet L. Smith has applied for naturalization as a northwest native. She has lived in Seattle for the past ten years. After graduating from law school at the University of Washington, she practiced law for five years as a trial attorney with a large regional law firm, and now works as an administrative law judge for the state of Washington. She enjoys watching whales from her kayak.

About the Publisher

Perseverance Press publishes a new line of old-fashioned mysteries. Emphasis is on the classic whodunit, with no excessive gore, exploitative sex, or gratuitous violence.

#1 *Death Spiral, Murder at the Winter Olympics* $8.95
by Meredith Phillips (1984)

It's a cold war on ice as love and defection breed murder at the Winter Olympics. Who killed world champion skater Dima Kuznetsov, the "playboy of the Eastern world": old or new lovers, hockey right-wingers, jealous rivals, the KGB? Will skating sleuth Lesley Grey discover the murderer before she herself is hunted down?

Reviews said: "fair-play without being easy to solve" *(Drood Review)*, "timely and topical" (Allen Hubin), "surprises, suspense, and a truly unusual murder method" (Marvin Lachman), "Olympic buffs and skating fans will appreciate the frequent chats about sports-lore and Squaw Valley history" *(Kirkus Reviews)*.
Not recommended for under 14 years of age.

#2 *To Prove a Villain* $8.95
by Guy M. Townsend (1985)

No one has solved this mystery in five centuries: was King Richard III responsible for the smothering of his nephews, the Little Princes, in the Tower of London?

Now, a modern-day murderer stalks a quiet college town, claiming victims in the same way. When the beautiful chairman of the English department dies, John Forest, a young history professor beset by personal and romantic problems, must grapple with both mysteries. Then he learns he may be next on the killer's list . . .

Reviews said: "a mystery set in academe that's wonderfully free from pedantry or stuffiness" *(ALA Booklist)*, "a tight, fast-paced tale" *(Louisville Courier-Journal)*, "nicely constructed and unfailingly interesting" (Jon L. Breen), "entertaining and illuminating" (Allen Hubin).

#3 *Play Melancholy Baby* $8.95
by John Daniel (1986)

Murder most Californian: murder *in* the hot tub, murder *with* the wine bottle, murder *by* . . . ?

When the obnoxious piano player is discovered floating face down with a fractured skull, no one has a Clue whodunit. Casey has his hands full already, what with his job (playing old songs in a new world) and new and old loves, not to mention thugs of various nationalities who keep popping up.

But the past won't stay dead. When he finds himself in hot water as prime suspect and/or next victim, he realizes it's time to play Sam Spade and dig up some clues. And all he knows for sure is that it wasn't Col. Mustard.

Reviews said: "readers will thoroughly enjoy the engaging first-person narrative, snappy dialogue, and references to popular music" *(ALA Booklist)*, "a mellow mystery with freshly drawn characters—more Woody Allen than Clint Eastwood" (Ralph B. Sipper), "well-written and invigorating" *(The Armchair Detective)*, "I suggest that you 'linger awhile' with this one, for 'this is a lovely way to spend an evening' "*(Santa Barbara Magazine)*.

Not recommended for under 14 years of age.

#4 *Chinese Restaurants Never Serve Breakfast* $8.95
by Roy Gilligan (1986)

The Monterey Peninsula art world is the background for private investigator Patrick Riordan's brush with death, as he stumbles across the nude, blood-covered body of a promising young painter in her Carmel cottage. On an easel nearby stands an oil painting which exactly depicts the murder scene—and which the artist has neglected to sign.

Riordan and his feisty sidekick Reiko chase clues from the galleries and boutiques of Carmel to bohemian studios in Big Sur to the moneyed world of Pebble Beach. The solution? An immutable condition, an inevitable conclusion: Chinese restaurants never serve breakfast.

Reviews said: ". . . characters are vivid and sharp . . . the narrator has an engaging, naïve charm. Gilligan also conveys the locale effectively" *(Publishers Weekly)*, "a likable sleuth and writing of assured irony" (Howard Lachtman), "fast-paced, detailed and skillful—worthy of a long series" *(Monterey Herald)*, "a likable work, notable for its well-realized Carmel setting, appealing characters, and unpretentiousness" *(The Armchair Detective)*.

#5 *Rattlesnakes and Roses* $8.95
by Joan Oppenheimer (1987)

When Kate Regal inherits a fabulous San Diego estate, family resentment turns to murder. She must learn that being tied to the past is as futile as trying to escape from it. The bonds of love, as well as hate and jealousy, are too strong to break—a lesson which puts Kate's life in jeopardy.

Reviews said: "well-turned-out romantic suspense" (Allen Hubin), "an appealing heroine, a good story, and the perfect book for a quiet Sunday" *(Union Jack)*, "unexpected plot turnings and rich, concise characterization . . . Oppenheimer's natural dialogue and spare, vivid imagery make this an enjoyable, fast-moving story" *(Southwest Book Review)*, "well-written, cleverly constructed, and entertaining; recommended" *(Small Press)*.

#6 *Revolting Development* $8.95
by Lora Smith (1988)

The condo developer wasn't known for her community spirit, but that was no reason to push her out of a third-story window, or to dispose of her in a dumpster. Housewife/writer Bridget Montrose, who discovers the body, reluctantly pursues clues through Palo Alto from behind a stroller. She uncovers suburban goings-on that really belong in the dumpster, as the mystery spreads to involve friends, neighbors, and some surprisingly simpatico cops. By the time she finally tracks down the truth, the murderer's right behind her . . .in a really revolting development.

Reviews said: "a solid whodunit" *(Ellery Queen Mystery Magazine)*, "Bridget Montrose is an appealing . . . central character, and

Lora Smith is a promising newcomer on the crime scene" (Jane Bakerman, *Belles Lettres,*) ". . . intelligent, believable characters and a strong plot" *(Mystery News),* ". . . an American cozy, where the plot keeps you turning the pages and the characters make you smile. Wickedly apt" *(Peninsula Times-Tribune.)*

#7 *Murder Once Done* $8.95
by Mary Lou Bennett (1988)
Edgar nominee: Best First Novel

They came to the north Oregon coast to live out their lives in serenity, three women who'd been friends for decades. Alison's remodeled house in the quaint village of Windom was a haven for Plum and Jane. They thought they'd spend their quiet days in a little needlework, a bit of gardening, and leisurely strolls along the beach. They thought they could forget the secret of murder once done.

But Tommy Weed, a street smart young punk, follows them. He knows all about the murder and plans to work out his own retirement plan through blackmail. Overpowering three vulnerable old biddies ought to be a piece of cake. Age and experience are surely no match for youth and strength—or are they?

Reviews said: "Bennett knows how to turn up the suspense, and her deft blend of comedy and terror is worthy of Hitchcock in one of his chilling domestic moods" *(San Francisco Chronicle),* "the action is well staged, the characters beautifully developed" *(Ellery Queen Mystery Magazine),* ". . . delightfully refreshing, written with warmth and a perfect mix of humor and suspense" *(Mystery News),* "well-drawn characters, a credible plot, and fine writing" (William Deeck, *The Criminal Record.)*

#8 *The Last Page* $8.95
by Bob Fenster (1989)

A mystery editor is found slumped across her desk, with a rejection note stapled to her sleeve and a bullet hole through her heart—for the second time. Does the murder have a personal motive, or is it just a frustrated writer who can't deal with rejection? The New York City police captain vetoes an investigation of thousands of suspects, so Detective Brian Skiles and editor Anne Baker must set a deadly trap to catch the killer, and to prove the pen is mightier than the sword.

Reviews said: "a sharp and witty satirical mystery" (Scotland Yard Books *Monthly Mysteries*), "what fun! A rare treat for those who appreciate a scintillating, literate mystery" *(Kliatt Paperback Guide),* "one of the funniest books I've ever read. Read it and laugh!" (Sue Feder, *Mystery Tour*), "wickedly funny . . . a very readable and offbeat mystery. Recommended especially for those who aspire to write mysteries and those in the business of publishing them" *(ALA Booklist).*

#9 *Sea of Troubles* $8.95
     by Janet L. Smith (1990)

TO ORDER: Add $1.05 to retail price to cover shipping for each of these quality paperbacks, and send your check for $10.00 to:

Perseverance Press
P.O. Box 384
Menlo Park, CA 94026

California residents please add 7.25% sales tax (65¢ per book).